SHORT
SHARP
SHOCKS

SHORT
SHARP
SHOCKS

Julian Lloyd Webber's
Masterclass of the Macabre

Weidenfeld and Nicolson

London

Introduction and selection
© Julian Lloyd Webber, 1990

Published in Great Britain by
George Weidenfeld & Nicolson
Limited
91 Clapham High Street
London SW4 7TA

ISBN 0 297 81147 9

Typeset by Deltatype Ltd,
Ellesmere Port
Printed in Great Britain by
Butler & Tanner Ltd, Frome and
London

To Ron, June, Wally, Minnie and Ngomo

CONTENTS

CONTENTS

ACKNOWLEDGMENTS

Thanks are due to the following for permission to use copyright material:

Sydney J. Bounds for *A Complete Collection*; Leonard Carpenter for *Dead Week*; R. C. Cook for *Green Fingers*; R. A. Hall for *The Other Woman*; A. M. Heath & Company Limited and Francis King for *The Doll*; David Higham Associates Limited for *The Tower* by Marghanita Laski, first printed in *The Third Ghost Book*, published by James Barrie; Conrad Hill for *The Bushmaster* and *The Grief Condition*; John Johnson Limited for *Miss Smith* by William Trevor, first printed in *The Day We Got Drunk on Cake*, published by The Bodley Head, 1967; James Kisner for *The Litter*; Henry Morrison Inc. for *But at My Back I Always Hear* by David Morrell; William F. Nolan for *Dead Call*, first printed in *Frights 2*, 1976, copyright © 1976 by Kirby McCauley – reprinted by permission of the author, William F. Nolan; the Peters Fraser & Dunlop Group Ltd for *De Mortuis* by John Collier, *She'll Be Company For You* by Andrea Newman © Andrea Newman 1969; Janet Pollock for *The Bright Boy* by Arthur Machen; Bernard Taylor for *Pat-a-cake, Pat-a-cake*; J. Yen for *A Weird Day for Agro*.

INTRODUCTION

The fault for this nasty little volume lies entirely with Mr Conrad Hill of Cornwall. Indeed it is doubtful whether anyone *but* the possessor of such an extraordinary sense of the macabre could have suggested so grotesque an idea to Messrs Weidenfeld in the first place. Please allow me to explain . . .

It may seem a trifle strange that someone who spends so much of his life feeling 'scared to death' awaiting his fate on the concert platform should choose for his reading matter stories which are primarily designed to achieve an identical effect. Yet from about the age of eleven – around the time, in fact, that I began to support Leyton Orient – I have been a fan of horror stories. And, as horror aficionados will know, the genre is strangely addictive. During the intervening years I must have read many hundreds of stories, taking in all the anthologies I could lay my hands on. As aficionados will also know, a lot of these stories were pretty bad. Yet amidst the dross lay a handful of gems – stories that immediately stood out from the sea of mediocrity which all too often masquerades as horror. Hence the idea of this volume. At a rough estimate I would say that from every fifty stories I read just *one* has been chosen for this book. This does not necessarily mean that forty-nine out of fifty were bad – there were quite a few 'near misses' and several others that might have been included but were in the end omitted either for reasons of balance or through lack of space.

Obviously, as in any anthology, the choice is personal. I did not want to re-tread old ground yet again so there are no Bram Stoker's and Edgar Allan Poe's here. With one exception (Arthur Machen) the stories are relatively contemporary, and the famous names have arrived purely because they happen to have written a story which resolutely refuses to leave me in peace. There is little 'splatter' – too much blood and gore quickly palls for me. Nor are there too many monsters – for what can be more monstrous than *human* behaviour itself when that thin dividing line (which we think we know so well) wavers ever-so-slightly? And, although the writing is a crucial factor, there are no irritating 'pretentious' stories where the author seems more concerned with style than content. You *will* find plenty of the least desirable attributes of human nature – there are tales of obsession (*But at My Back I Always Hear*), guilt (*She'll be Company for You*), revenge (*Pat-a-cake, Pat-a-cake*), jealousy (*De Mortuis*), hatred (*Miss Smith*), depravity (*The Bright Boy*) and lots of cold, naked fear. You will also find humour – of the black variety.

When it comes to the short story, there seems to be a marked lack of the grotesque – stories that revolt, in both senses of the word, against the worst excesses of today's world. This brings me back to the dastardly Mr Hill and the origination of this virulent collection. During the mid-seventies a number of masterful excursions into the macabre by one Conrad Hill suddenly began to appear in various anthologies. Supreme amongst these was *The Bushmaster* – the terrifying tale of Minnie the housewife's all-consuming battle with the household chores. In all I managed to trace six of his stories by which time I had become a hardened Hill freak! Then, just as suddenly, the stories stopped. Avidly I would scour each new horror collection in the hope of another outrageous dosage of Hill – but to no avail. Any attempts to elicit further information on the mystery writer from his publishers were met with a wall of silence; I even contacted the royalty department to see if *they* could shed any light on his whereabouts. But they couldn't (or wouldn't) and that seemed to be the end of the matter. Yet Minnie and Wally and the rest of his deranged characters continued to prey on my mind and fourteen years later I found myself discussing this sad state of affairs with the literary editor of one of our national newspapers. We both decided that Conrad Hill was probably some eminently respected author who had thought it better to hide his disturbing proclivity behind the mask of a pseudonym. Perhaps, the literary editor suggested, I might write a piece for his newspaper outlining the whole sorry saga? More in hope than expectation I duly obliged. Publication day arrived; the headline *'Where are you Conrad Hill?'* screamed across the nation – and, the next day, a Mrs Hill from Cornwall was in touch with the paper! Yes, Conrad did exist and yes he *had* written those shocking tales. No, he would not travel to London to meet the literary editor and no he would not be photographed for next week's newspaper. I also received a cryptic message from 'the decomposing desk of Conrad Hill.' Now contact was finally established I became determined to try and coax further monstrosities from his long-dormant pen. A bizarre exchange of letters followed during which time Hill wrote – unbeknown to me – to one of his previous publishers, Messrs Weidenfeld, asking whether they might be interested in my editing a collection of horror stories. They were. My newly acquired literary agent then announced that if I were to agree to the project he would write a new story for the collection. After several moments' hesitation (after all, whoever heard of 'The Casals Book of Horror Stories'?) I succumbed to the blackmail and I am very glad I did – for *The Grief Condition* is a gruesome yet strangely poignant masterpiece of the macabre.

I have yet to meet Mr Hill of Cornwall. I mean to tell him he has a lot to answer for. In the meantime, should you meet him first perhaps you might mention it.

Julian Lloyd Webber, May 1990

PAT-A-CAKE, PAT-A-CAKE

Bernard Taylor

I like it here in this place. It's warm and cosy. And the people around me are nice. The face on the dark-haired lady who leans over my cot is especially nice. She has the softest brown eyes. I kept stealing little glances at her as she tucked me in with this beautiful new Rupert Bear eiderdown. I never had anything like this before. It's really nice. Not that I could *tell* them, of course – the man or the woman. Well, I *could* tell them, but they just wouldn't understand, and I've learned now that it's quite useless to try, no matter how clear I make myself. I think it must be something they learn – an ability they develop as we grow older and bigger. I hope so. I hope they will learn. There's so much I want to tell them.

I think this place is going to be my new home. Just now the woman leaned over me and said: 'You're going to stay here with your Daddy and me for ever and ever.' Oh, I felt so glad. It's exactly what I wanted. I would have hugged her except that my arms aren't long enough. So I sort of clapped my hands instead. Just think, these two people are going to be my New Mummy and Daddy. They must be.

I had a Mummy before. But the new one is much nicer. I never had a Daddy before, though. I must say I like it. This one's got a faint tobacco-y smell about him. I can recognize it. But it's not unpleasant, and his voice is very kind and gentle. I wonder if all Daddies are like him . . .

I'm going to stay here. I shall. I don't think I'll ever move on again. It's so nice.

I just clapped my hands together again, and the lady – I must always try to think of her as *Mummy* – went all smiley and happy. She said to me: 'That's it! Clever boy! That's it – *Pat-a-cake, pat-a-cake, baker's man . . .* Go on . . . *Pat-a-cake, pat-a-cake, baker's man . . .*' So I clapped my hands together even harder – as well as I could – and gave her a big grin. She laughed then, and said again:

Pat-a-cake, pat-a-cake, baker's man,
Bake me a cake as fast as you can.
Pat it and prick it and mark it with B,
And put it in the oven for baby and me!

I think that's how it went. Mind you, I'm not absolutely sure what this pat-a-cake thing is. I think it must be this clapping thing I do – waving my arms around – things like that. Though I'm not all that good at it yet – the clapping, pat-a-cake thing, I mean. It's not always easy to make your hands actually *meet* – hit together, you understand. The New Mummy seems to know this, and she took my hands and held them and gently clapped them together. And all the time she sang about pat-a-cake. I suppose I shall get the hang of it all sooner or later. I hope so. Some people do seem to set such store by these funny things, and I would so like to please her. And Daddy. I wonder what a *baker's man* is . . . I expect I'll find that out some time as well. That must have been what I did with my First Mummy – the pat-a-cake, I mean. Well, something like it.

My First Mummy. She was my *real* Mummy.

I didn't like her.

I'm not proud of it. Because she *was* my real Mummy, after all. But she was quite horrid. I've no idea where a Daddy was – if there was one. There was just her. And me. Well, sometimes there were other men around – strangers who'd stay for an odd night or so in her bed – but no one I ever got to like. Oh, I'm so glad I'm not with her any more.

This lady now, this New Mummy, calls me nice names like – like Baby, and – Sweetheart, and Darling, and other things, and the way she says them they sound *nice*. I can tell she's smiling even when I can't see her face. You see, her smile is in her voice. But the other Mummy – the real one – *she* didn't call me nice things. She used to call me things like Bloody Kid, and Bastard, and Snivelling Little Sod. And they didn't sound nice. Not at all. Not the way she said them.

My nose is always clean now. It wasn't before. Before I often had a runny nose. That Mother never bothered at all. Once I got up all my courage and said to her: 'How would you like it if *your* nose was never wiped. . . ?' But she just said: 'I'll bloody well goo-goo-goo-goo *you* in a minute!' Oh, it's best to forget her. I must try.

My New Mummy and Daddy are both near me now. *He* just looked down at me. His smile is so wide. He put a hand to my face. And I flinched. I didn't mean to. But his hand turned out to be the softest, gentlest touch you ever felt. So I put my hand up and held on to his thumb. He looked so pleased that I held on even harder. He likes that a lot. It's funny: it's very easy to make some people happy. The New Mummy said:

'Look, Dave. Look at the little love . . .'

She never talked like that – the First one.

But I won't think about her. I said I wouldn't. I shall just think about these two. They love me. You can tell; it's easy. They're nice. I think these are the two I would have chosen if I'd had any choice, any say in the matter. I think it's a great pity that babies have to put up with what they get in the way of parents. I mean, without any thought or consideration at all I just got dumped with that awful woman who swore all the time, who had nicotine-stained fingers and bad teeth. And her breath was really terrible. Not that she ever kissed me or anything, I'm glad to say. Most of the time she just left me sitting there in this terrible battered old pram she got from somewhere. And I could be really *filthy*, honestly, and she wouldn't bother in the least. She used to go out to the pub and play darts most evenings, sometimes with one or other of the men who came to the door. Or else she'd go to Bingo. It didn't make much difference to me. Wherever she went, I'd be left. For ages and ages and ages. Sometimes with a woman who lived next door and sometimes – mostly – on my own. Yes, I think it's really unfair that we can't choose our own Mummy and Daddy.

I remember thinking that first of all when I was sitting outside the supermarket one day – in my pram. And I was looking at some of the other babies around me. They were so clean and smelt so lovely. And you should have seen some of the Mummies and Daddies – *beautiful*. Absolutely. And I thought then – how unfair it all was. I felt really ashamed. There I was, covered with this disgusting old blanket (not like my Rupert Bear eiderdown!), and feeling very uncomfortable because I hadn't been changed for ages and I decided, then and there, that I had to do something about it. It couldn't go on. I mean, it just couldn't, could it?

My New Daddy just said to my New Mummy:

'That scar on his arm. Poor little chap. Really must have hurt him. Fancy burning a kid like that – accident or no accident. Still, the doctor says it'll fade in time . . .'

They mean that mark where she spilt boiling milk over me from the saucepan. Honest, I just wasn't safe. I *had* to get out.

Anyway, as I said, I'd made up my mind. Now I just had to wait for the right chance. And the right time. And I had to think of a good way. And there weren't that many ways open to me, still being on the little side as people go. But I was sure there'd be something.

All this, of course, was still outside the supermarket. I didn't have much chance to think on the problem then, as she came out loaded down with groceries. The next second I was almost smothered under a whole heap of instant mashed potatoes, tinned beans and tinned spaghetti and sliced bread. I said, before I could stop myself:

'For goodness' sake have a bit of consideration, will you? I mean, I'm not made of *rubber*!'

And she said, crossly:

'Don't you start bleedin' cryin'. If you've got the wind it's your own bloody fault. I wish to Christ I'd never 'ad you.'

You can see what I was up against. One felt totally impotent. It was just so hard to get anything across to anyone. I remember once when I was in my pram outside an off-licence one lunchtime. A policeman came by and stopped and crouched down by me. He said: 'Hello, young fellow. Waiting for your mother, are you? She won't be long.'

I thought, now's my chance. I said to him:

'Look at the state I'm in. You wouldn't believe it. I've had this nappy on since last night. Last night! And she doesn't care. Not a bit. Do you suppose you could report the matter to the proper authorities when you get an opportunity. . . ? Do you think you could help to get me moved to someone else. . . ? Another

8

Mummy? As you can see, things are just not working out as they are . . . *Please. . . ?*'

I didn't have a chance to say any more as *she* came out of the shop carrying the bottles. The policeman stood up as she approached and smiled at her.

'I think he's getting impatient for you,' he said. He turned back to me and put his face close up to mine. 'Go on,' he said, 'say it. Mum-mum-mum-mum-mum-mum-mum-mum. You'll be talking next, won't you. Mum-mum-mum-mum . . .'

I dribbled and made a rude noise.

That night we went to the pub. It was her darts night. She wheeled me into the shadow of the wall that I knew so well, grabbed her darts and her handbag and went off inside. I was left alone. Just like that.

It's a good job it was summer. Honestly, I could have frozen to death, otherwise, for all the notice she took of me. I was there for ages, and she never once even looked out to see that I was all right. One time some strange woman with breath that smelt of beer and onions came out and stuck her face close to mine. She turned and yelled back through the open pub door:

'Yeh, 'e's all right, love . . .'

All right. . . ? I tell you. There I was, hungry, thirsty, miserable and dirty. I hadn't been changed *still.* The least she could have done was given me a clean nappy. I mean, supposing I'd got knocked down . . .

God, it was boring out there. I had a bit of a chat with a dog for a few minutes, a collie crossed with a spaniel; not the most communicative breed at the best of times, but at least it broke the monotony for a while. Later on, the beery-oniony woman came out again and looked at me. I said to her, as plainly as I could:

'Would you ask her if we can go home, please? Tell her I'm tired and bored, will you? And I'm so *wet.* I want to be *changed.* Please . . .'

A look of real concern flashed across the woman's face for a second, and I thought: at last I've got through to somebody. Then she said:

'That's right, darlin'. You cough it up.' And then patted me on the back. What can you do. . . ?

Anyway, at least *she* came out. She flung her stuff on the pram by me and started to wheel me up the street. Looking out I saw this man there. Not nice though. Not like *this Daddy*. And they were talking and talking. We stopped outside the fish and chip shop where the light was very bright and got in my eyes. She braked the pram and joined the end of the queue leading to the counter; the man was with her. They didn't take any notice of me at all, and didn't even look to see what I was up to. Of course, by this time I was really awake. What with all that noise in my ears and that light in my eyes I couldn't very well be *expected* to sleep, could I? Actually it's a good job I didn't. Otherwise I might still be with her today.

I thought she'd never come back to the pram. It seemed ages before I felt her shadow over me and smelt the smell of her – chips, fish and vinegar all mixed up with the beer. I had my eyes closed now and I heard her say:

'Oh, bloody 'ell. Look what the little bastard's gone and done.' Her voice got nearer and louder, and angrier, and all the time I kept my face turned away. 'He's emptied every bleedin' thing out of my 'andbag,' she said. 'Look at that bleedin' mess.'

And then she leaned down, right low, over the pram. And that's when I did the pat-a-cake. But I did it against her neck and as hard as I could. It wasn't easy to aim properly – I'm not that good, as you probably know – but this time I got it *just right*. And the next thing she was straightening up, and clasping her hands to her throat, and I got a sudden glimpse of the red coming out between her fingers. She half shouted, half spoke:

'Oh, my God, what's that little sod done to me? Jesus Christ, I'm *bleedin'*, for God's sake!'

The man went up next to her then and I could see him putting up his hands, trying to stop the blood coming out of her neck. But he couldn't. Of course he couldn't. No one could. And all the time her cries were getting louder and more frightened. Lots of people were gathering around us – I think it must be the blood that does it – and you should have seen and heard the panic going on.

'Quick!' somebody was shouting, ' – it's the jugular vein. She's bleeding to death!'

And then more voices:

'Get a tourniquet! That's what she needs.'

'What for?'

'To stop the bleeding – !'

' – A tourniquet? Round her neck?'

'Yes! It'll stop the bleeding.'

'Yeh! – stop her breathin' as well . . .'

You should have been there, seen them all running around. I was the only calm one there and for a good few minutes nobody took any notice of me . . . and all the time I still had the darts in my hand. Then this strange woman came over and took them away from me; she did it anxiously but quite gently.

'Let's have these before you do any *more* damage,' she said. 'We don't want *you* hurt as well.' Her face was close as she bent down to me. She looked very sad. She murmured softly: 'Poor little devil . . .'

'Listen,' I said, looking up into her eyes, 'I had to do it. I *had* to. I mean, what kind of a future did I have with her. . . ?'

The woman shook her head. 'Listen to him chortling away. Poor little bugger. He thinks it's all a huge joke. Thank God he's too young to understand what he's done . . .'

And that's when I *really* started to laugh. I mean, you've *got* to.

THE BUSHMASTER

Conrad Hill

Minerva Cannington was distraught. She could *feel* the house spawning dirt as she sat there. Each passing second allowed a further million particles to gather unseen and unheard.

The tide of battle was turning in favour of the house and Minerva imagined it sniggering as it contemplated final victory. The ultimate degradation. Her face burned with shame at the prospect of friends and relatives, garbed in protective overalls and wellington boots, wading through a knee-high layer of dust and filth, smirking behind their gas masks at her misfortune.

Problem; Minerva's principal strategic weapon was temporarily out of front-line service; the VibraGlide, fully automatic, remote-controlled vacuum hover-cleaner had broken down. Although only five months old, this brain child of domestic warfare technology was at present lying on a repairer's workbench, its powerful motor silent and exhausted, casualty of too many hard-fought campaigns.

True, Minerva possessed a variety of secondary armaments which she used to supplement the VibraGlide. These included brooms, dustpan and brushes, a hand-operated Ewbank cleaner, chamois leathers, dusters, and an array of solvents and polishes. But all these were small-arms to be deployed in conjuction with, not as a substitute for, the VibraGlide. They could vanquish the superficial dirt, the type that massed on window ledges, floors, and carpets, but they hadn't the power to cope with the *deep down* dirt cunningly secreted by the house from its putrid glands. However much she swept, dusted, and polished, she knew that without the VibraGlide the war was being lost.

Since the VibraGlide had gone AWOL, Minerva's nerves, tautly tuned at the best of times, were developing frayed edges. She found herself unable to concentrate on anything for more than a few minutes at a time. Thus she might begin to scrub the kitchen floor when into her mind would flash a picture of the bathroom windowsill passively allowing itself to be defiled – raped by huge ejaculations of dust. Immediately she would fly to the bathroom brandishing brush and cloth and polish, there to commence a ferocious assault upon the befouled area. Halfway through, she would remember the three bedrooms standing uncleaned for at least two hours . . . Bursting breathlessly into the first bedroom to deal with carpets, covers, curtains, she would be mentally catapulted back to the unfinished kitchen floor and conjure up visions of the cat (staunch ally of the house) strolling in from the garden, leering as he contemplated the muddy paw-prints on the gleaming, still damp tiles . . .

The whole process was debilitating and self-defeating. There were too many holes in the dike and Minerva hadn't enough fingers to plug them all. Physically exhausted and on the brink of nervous disintegration, she would collapse into an armchair, gulping sedatives, stimulants, and a hastily made cup of tea, invariably the colour and consistency of thin acorn soup.

But even sitting quietly, gratefully accepting the restorative action of the pills, she was unable to rid herself of a feeling of doom, a certain knowledge that, without the VibraGlide, the insidious dirt was likely to engulf the house. Nevertheless, her resolve was strong. She would never surrender; she was determined to die fighting rather than be driven ignominiously from her own home.

She and Roger *must* have an emergency conference tonight when he returned from the office. They would plan the rear-guard action to be fought until the VibraGlide was returned. Roger would know what to do. He was a pillar of strength, a fount of wisdom. In short, he was Commander-in-Chief, Combined Forces.

Roger Cannington wasn't enjoying his lunchtime beer and sandwich because Minnie was on his mind. Or rather, Minnie's mind was on his mind. There seemed little doubt that her unhealthy preoccupation with the house had become an obsession, particularly since the vacuum cleaner had broken down.

He had consulted his GP some six months ago who had then

seen Minnie without finding anything seriously wrong: 'Onset of the menopause – affects different women in different ways,' he had explained glibly.

'Try riding with it, old man, things are bound to improve.'

Menopause? At thirty-six?

The doctor backed his diagnosis with a barrage of tablets, which had given the first-aid cupboard in the bathroom the appearance of a chemist's dispensary. Shortly after, Roger bought the VibraGlide for Minnie. Three hundred and ten pounds worth of electronic wizardry. Just to clean the bloody house. But, upon reflection, it had perhaps been worth it.

During the act of purchase, the rapturous look on Minnie's face had transported Roger back to their honeymoon days. For a time, speculation was intense and exciting, but alas those far-off libidinous weeks were not to be recaptured, at least not by him. Minnie, though, had seemed to gain a lot of satisfaction from having the VibraGlide in the bedroom and fondling it well into the small hours . . .

As a vacuum cleaner, the VibraGlide was efficient. It provided Minnie with a peace of mind not seen by Roger for many a month. Although still mumbling about the 'legions of dirt' in the house, her condition, whilst not improving, had at least stabilized. That is, until now. A new motor within five months didn't augur well for his wallet once the guarantee expired.

He left the pub and strolled through the comparatively quiet streets off Shaftesbury Avenue, heading for his favourite shop. Ngomo's fascinated him, plucked him from his own mundane world to one of mystery and menace, charm and cheerfulness. It was packed with fine examples of contemporary African craft-work as varied as the continent itself. Gorgeous headdresses and exquisitely carved figurines were displayed beside earthenware pots and combs fashioned from bone. Occasionally he would purchase some small article which took his fancy, knowing only too well that he would be braving Minnie's scathing disapproval, the little *objet d'art* being indiscriminately labelled 'dust trap' and consigned immediately to Roger's garden workshop.

Minnie intruding, trespassing on his thoughts again. He quickened his step.

That she, with her qualifications, should choose to rot away in the house day after day was nothing short of criminal negligence. Why the hell didn't she get a job or an outside interest? He had suggested it once and recalled her reaction as bordering on the physically violent. Likewise his suggestion that they take a holiday: 'Do you know,' she had said, aghast, 'have you *any* idea what would happen in this house if I left it for any length of time? Well, have you?'

No, Roger had replied. Could she enlighten him?

'This house would be so full of dirt that you wouldn't be able to get in the front door!' She spoke the words with a sense of triumphant relief, as though revealing a terrifying secret which previously only she had been privy to.

Roger hadn't dared to laugh, although the impulse to do so had been overpowering.

He had tried to discuss selling the house with her, but she would have none of it. She said she wasn't going to be defeated that easily, and anyway who in their *right mind* (he giggled at that, but she hadn't noticed fortunately) would buy it? Besides, she said, the same problem would face them wherever they moved. Look at sister Lucy, look at the battle she was fighting – and she lived in a *brand new* house. Sister Lucy, Roger had reflected at the time, was not the best person to hold up as an example, for the psychosis, or whatever it was, seemed to run in the family. Brother-in-law Barry was having a hard time of it too . . . However, Roger hadn't said anything, just listened, nodded or shook his head in the appropriate places . . . He was 'riding with it', to quote the doctor.

Ngomo's was a lonely corner shop, an oasis of simple culture amidst streamlined, complex office-blocks and anonymous, crumbling warehouses.

Roger allowed his eyes to adjust to the interior gloom of the shop lest he stumble over and damage anything valuable.

Minnie pondered the possibilities of survival. Three days! Three days before the VibraGlide came back and could be hurled once more into the front line. In the meantime, Roger would help, she could rely on him. He must take time off from work. She longed to hear the heady whine of the VibraGlide's big motor and see the quivering, aesthetically pleasing machine move into action at her command.

She started as her gaze fell upon the television in the corner of the immaculate room. *The television!* Gasping, she rushed to it and swung it round on its little table until the screen was facing the wall. She cupped her hands to the sides of her head and peered through the ventilation louvres cut in the fibreboard back.

No need to pull the fibreboard past its retaining clips – she could see the fluff and dirt caking the chassis. The condition in there emphasized the deteriorating overall situation. Only last week had she removed the back of the television and, using the VibraGlide's sophisticated TV Interior Cleaning Module, every speck of dirt inside the cabinet had been sucked out under her close and critical supervision.

She lifted the television, her arms trembling with the strain, and staggered into the kitchen with the intention of depositing the disgusting thing in the garden for Roger to deal with when he came home. She rested one corner of the set on a convenient formica work-top, enabling her to open the door to the garden with one hand. As she manoeuvred herself through the opening, she tripped over the incoming cat (remember? staunch ally of the house). She yelped and the cathode-ray tube exploded as television and Minnie hit the concrete patio simultaneously.

In the brilliant afternoon sunshine little puffs of dust rose from the shattered set. For a few moments they hung together in the still air before settling at random on the prostrate, weeping form of Minnie.

Roger was peacefully browsing when he saw it, coiled unobtrusively in a secluded corner. He moved it gently into the slightly better light that filtered through the myriad objects piled in the window.

It resembled a large snake, but unlike that creature the dark green triangular head was out of proportion to the rest of the body. Made of a firm yet pliable substance beautifully moulded to simulate the features of a snake, it was approximately seven inches across at its widest point, twelve inches in length, and some four inches deep. The mouth gaped, giving the 'jaws' a seventy-degree angle of join. The head tapered sharply to connect with a muddy-coloured body perhaps four inches in diameter. The nondescript base colour of the body was randomly adorned with brilliant red and yellow designs.

Ngomo was an ancient but remarkably stealthy African gentleman. He approached Roger on silent soles to explain, in his most un-African BBC accent, that the 'Bushmaster', as he called it, wasn't merely an object of admiration: 'You will be interested to know, sir, that this,' he stooped to pat the coiled body, 'is a West African tribal equivalent of the vacuum cleaner. In the region where it is made each village owns at least one, to be shared communally for hut cleaning and suchlike.'

During the discourse the old man's eyes contained no tell-tale twinkle of humour. In fact when Roger intimated that he might be having his leg pulled, be became quite prickly and insisted upon giving a demonstration.

At the far end of the shop were several cane baskets brimming with what appeared to be rubbish. Ngomo deliberately tipped the contents of one of them on to the floor.

Roger sensed a movement beneath his immediate range of vision. He lowered his eyes quickly to the thing near his feet. The head was twitching, then it jerked twice and slid off the top of the coil to the floor. Behind it, the body began to unwind smoothly like oiled nylon rope.

Mesmerized, he watched the Bushmaster glide with a noiseless, undulating movement to the pile of rubbish. Empty cartons, balls of paper, matchsticks and cigarette ends disappeared at high speed into the open mouth. Within seconds the floor was clean and the thing now lay motionless in an elongated S-shape. He estimated its length at ten feet or so and also noticed that the tail, like the oversized head, was different to that of a conventional snake. It hadn't the tautness of the rest of the body, and it fanned out to give the impression of a flat, crinkled paper bag. Roger broke the ensuing silence to say pointlessly: 'Electricity?'

'I see no wires,' Ngomo responded smugly.

Roger bent to prod the inert Bushmaster. 'How the hell does it work then?'

Ngomo hesitated, obviously shaping a careful reply: 'Our craftsmen have acquired their skills over many thousands of years, and yet they cannot manufacture nuclear weapons, computers – or even motor cars and washing machines. Why? Because we, the people, have no need of them. They make only what we need. And those needs are simple.'

He pointed a bony black finger at the Bushmaster. 'That is simple. So simple – and I mean no disrespect when I say this – that a mind like yours, confused and muddled by unnecessary complexities, could never understand how it works.'

'Magic?' Roger suggested whimsically.

Ngomo shrugged his puny shoulders and smiled indulgently. 'When I was a very young man and first saw an aeroplane roaring above the tree tops, I said, "Magic." And to me it *was* magic . . . No. Let us say that our technology – *ingenuity* is possibly a better word – has taken a different path to yours in the so-called civilized societies.'

Now there, thought Roger, was a fine piece of homespun defensive African philosophy. In an earlier age Ngomo would doubtless have been a precinct witch-doctor. Certainly it was easy to imagine him leaping and chanting around a cauldron containing a couple of lightly cooked missionaries . . .

He demanded, and was given, more demonstrations during which the Bushmaster unerringly devoured the contents of three more wastepaper baskets. Try as he might, Roger could see no power source or gadgetry of any kind.

'Please. Do not be too overawed,' Ngomo purred. 'This device has its limitations.'

'I'm glad to hear it.'

'Yes. Once it is full, the Bushmaster will cease to function for a time.'

'What d'you mean?'

'It needs time to . . . digest. The larger and denser the input, the longer the delay before it starts to work for you again. Nothing is perfect. It is functioning quite efficiently at the moment due to a light diet of easily assimilated material.'

From what he had seen, Roger was almost convinced of the Bushmaster's authenticity. Nevertheless he was unable to suppress entirely the notion that he might be the butt for some gentle, esoteric African humour.

'Is it guaranteed?' he inquired wryly.

Ngomo stared at Roger, his expression serious. 'If you treat your Bushmaster with care and consideration,' he intoned solemnly, 'it will still be with you when you die.'

'Yes, but if it didn't work at home, could I bring it back?'

'If you are not completely satisfied, yes, you can return it for a full refund.' Ngomo wagged a warning finger at the ceiling. 'But bear in mind the prime responsibility of the Bushmaster owner: he must never allow it to go without . . . food. It must always have dirt and rubbish to eat when it wants. If not, it tends to become . . . agitated and I as vendor cannot be held liable for this.

'Look carefully at the inside of my shop – see how wonderfully clean it is. When the Bushmaster first arrived from Africa, it cleaned the premises thoroughly, finding enough dirt here at first to fulfil its requirements. Although it still cleans for me regularly, and *because* it still cleans for me regularly, it no longer finds enough dirt to keep it content. Therefore it is necessary to have those baskets filled with my neighbour's excellent rubbish. Very occasionally the dustmen, against union regulations, kindly reverse their lorry to the door and tip in a few morsels. Naturally, being ignorant of the true motive behind my request, they look upon me as just another immigrant with dirty habits.'

Roger listened, hysterical disbelief combining with an almost overpowering sense of elation. *If only it wasn't a joke!* In the context of Minnie's pathetic little war, the Bushmaster would be her nuclear device. Even now he saw her, eyes gleaming manically, marching behind it as it slithered about the house consuming both real and *imagined* dirt.

'How much d'you want for it?' His question was compulsive.

'Forty pounds.'

For forty pounds Minnie would be receiving Harley Street therapy at a Woolworth's price. 'If this is on the level, Mr Ngomo, then it could solve a big problem.'

'Dirt, rubbish, trash, garbage, refuse – call it what you will . . . This is the only problem the Bushmaster will solve. Please do not expect miracles in any other sphere.'

Roger asked Ngomo about the bag-like appendage at the tail end of the Bushmaster. The old man squatted on his haunches.

'Like any other vacuum cleaner, the bag must be emptied from time to time,' he said.

He deftly removed the bag and handed it to Roger. It was made of a thin but strong skin-like material reinforced at the circular end where it joined the body of the Bushmaster. A third of the way up the inside was a black glutinous substance which gave off an odour of . . . swamps?

Ngomo reacted to Roger's quizzical glance by dipping a finger into the substance, then holding the damp digit aloft for inspection.

'A useful by-product,' he said. 'For each hundredweight of rubbish the Bushmaster devours, one bag full of this – an excellent manure – is produced. Our villagers use it on their crops, and when other people's fail through drought or disease ours grow tall and strong with unfailing regularity. I suggest you spread some on your English roses and see them bloom as they have never bloomed before.'

It occurred to Roger that if Ngomo wasn't a humourist – and he certainly didn't seem that way inclinded – then he was probably quietly insane. He should meet Minnie . . . a couple of nuts together. Like her, Ngomo required careful handling.

Endeavouring, without much success, to keep incredulity from his voice he said: 'D'you mean to say that this thing actually cr– . . . defecates?'

For the second time Ngomo smiled. 'Almost the reverse,' he said. 'It converts unsightly, useless waste into a rich humus to be used to man's advantage. You say the dog is man's best friend: we say the Bushmaster is man's best friend.'

To smother his laughter, Roger stooped to pick up the end of the Bushmaster. Apart from its size and unusual colouring, it looked like any other vacuum-cleaner pipe. Ngomo took it from him and refitted the bag, making an O-shape with his finger and thumb around the joint. 'Self-sealing,' he explained.

He must have detected Roger's extreme scepticism for he said, 'You yourself have actually *witnessed* the Bushmaster's cleaning capabilities, but if you now doubt my word regarding the contents of the bag, please speak to Mr Essenberg next door. He is a respectable businessman, an importer of precious stones. We have a barter arrangement: for every five baskets of rubbish he delivers, I furnish him with a one-pound tin of Bushmaster manure. Consequently his garden is the envy of Muswell Hill and he begs me to supply him with bulk loads.'

'Well, why not sell him the Bushmaster?' Roger asked.

The smile again, this time tinged with sadness.

'He would want them by the gross and our craftsmen do not have mass-production facilities. Besides, Mr Essenberg does not *need* the Bushmaster; he would ill-treat it, use it only for profit . . . No, he has his diamonds, he should be content with the profit from those.'

Roger was puzzled. That Ngomo was trying to sell him the Bushmaster was obvious, hence the demonstration and explanations. Yet on his previous visits to the shop, the old man never put in an appearance until Roger had chosen the item he wished to buy and wanted to pay for it. And far from being the loquacious individual of today, Roger had regarded him as taciturn, if not downright secretive.

'What makes you think *I* need the Bushmaster?' he asked.

'My intuition is rarely wrong in these matters. You have the air of a harassed man, a man with a garbage disposal problem on his mind. Please correct me if I am mistaken, but I think the Bushmaster will restore the lustre to your life.'

The air of a harassed man? The words disturbed Roger. He knew Minnie's behaviour was playing hell with his ulcer, but he hadn't been aware that his worry hung externally on him like a rusted halo. He resented the bitch for that. *Anything* was worth a try which might cure her bloody nonsense . . . If this Bushmaster device turned out to be a pig-in-a-poke he could always stop the cheque, then hit old Sunshine here under the Trade Description Act.

'I'll buy it,' he said decisively.

Ngomo became positively effusive. 'My dear sir, you are the owner of the first Bushmaster in the United Kingdom. Furthermore, you have taken a step nearer to that priceless commodity, Peace of Mind . . . "A Spotless House *and* a Beautiful Garden" . . . Can Electrolux boast a slogan like that?' He coiled the Bushmaster and began wrapping it in brown paper.

Thinking of the VibraGlide, Roger asked, 'If it breaks down can you repair it?'

Ngomo paused, gripping a roll of Sellotape. Then he actually laughed, displaying a fine set of yellow teeth which appeared almost white against the blackness of his face.

'Breakdown?' he said at length. 'An emotive word in your modern pressurized society. You must have little faith in either yourselves or your products to be continually concerned with breakdowns. If it is of any comfort to you, sir, there is no recorded instance of a Bushmaster breakdown, merely petty malfunctions due to mistreatment by the malicious and the ignorant.

'The internal components are self-renewing up to a certain age. After that the appliance eventually expires. We have no parts-renewal policy or reconditioned exchange service. Both are neither necessary nor possible.'

'Fine,' Roger said. 'But how do I know I haven't bought an old one?'

With studied, good-humoured patience, Ngomo unwrapped the parcel he was about to seal. He lifted the sinister-looking head and pointed to the brightly marked flexible hose.

'The Bushmaster is old at fifty years when these colours fade. Simultaneously, the body becomes slack and sponge-like. At this point there are five years of serviceable life remaining and the thoughtful owner should assign the appliance to light dust-collecting duties only and give consideration to the purchase of a successor. As I said earlier, this one will outlive you, sir, if we base the assumption on current longevity averages for the male Caucasian . . .'

Was the man insane? Or was the thing he held in his crinkled black hand an ad-man's dream come true?

'. . . I can assure you that this is a young, ah, new model designed specifically for export. By comparison, our domestic models are crude indeed.'

Ngomo may well have been a star Bushmaster salesman, but he was the world's worst parcel-wrapper. The result of his labours was a misshapen pile of brown paper held together with twenty feet of Sellotape.

Roger made out a cheque with some misgivings, then waited, watching Ngomo write rapidly, filling several sheets of paper bearing the heading 'West African Enterprises'. When he had finished he handed Roger the sheets in exchange for the cheque.

'A few operating hints,' he said. 'Some of them I have already covered orally, but I think it is best if you have the important ones available for reference. Please study them carefully. Oh yes, one other thing . . .'

He slid, eel-like, through a beaded curtain at the rear of the shop to reappear clutching something membraneous. '. . . A spare collection bag for use when the other is being washed.'

Roger pocketed the bag and the notes. Ngomo presented him with the badly wrapped Bushmaster and accompanied him to the door.

Slightly dazed and a little rueful, Roger said, 'I'll probably want my money back, you know.'

'Most unlikely,' Ngomo replied with the assurance of superior wisdom.

As occasionally happened, Roger had no meeting to attend that afternoon or paperwork unable to wait until the morrow. Usually he took advantage of such a situation to call his lissome honey-blonde secretary into his office on the pretext of 'dictation'. Miss Hornby would perch opposite his desk upon the swivel chair (thoughtfully wound to its maximum height by Roger before-hand) dutifully recording in shorthand nonsensical letters to fictitious clients. By slumping low in his chair, playing the overburdened young executive, he was able to get a leisurely and detailed view of Miss Hornby's anatomy above and way beyond the hems of her demure dresses. He often wondered why she didn't realize what was going on, for she must have spent a good few hours typing those phoney letters before leaving them in his 'in' tray for perusal and signature. Yet they never came out of his office, not even the copies, because Roger ripped them up and consigned them to the wastepaper bin.

Either Miss Hornby was lacking in job interest or she was well aware of what went on and actually enjoyed flashing her shapely thighs at him. He couldn't quite summon enough courage to find out which.

He picked his way furtively through her small outer office, ignoring her inquiring glance at the bulky parcel. In his inner sanctum he placed the Bushmaster in a corner and hung up his jacket. Instead of making preparations for the clandestine ogling of Miss Hornby as his instincts dictated, he settled comfortably in his chair to read Ngomo's 'operating hints'. The bold, powerful handwriting seemed oddly at variance with the Negro's diminutive stature.

The Bushmaster: another fine product brought to you by West African Enterprises

Operating:
Ensure that an adequate supply of refuse is always on hand for your Bushmaster.

The Digestion/Conversion Delay time (hereafter referred to as DCD) must be taken into account before tackling any job with your Bushmaster.

The DCD is the period of total inactivity required by the appliance to digest its last intake of material and begin converting it to a rich, manageable fertilizer. The DCD is variable and depends upon the density and quantity of the input: i.e. ten wastepaper baskets full of light assorted rubbish ingested by the Bushmaster in one operation results in a DCD of three hours, during which period the input-limiter mechanism built into your Bushmaster will cause it to disregard even the most succulent garbage proffered.

However, an infinite number of baskets will be accepted provided they are proffered one at a time at thirty-minute intervals. By staggering the input in this manner the limiter mechanism is not activated and DCD is avoided. This is a sensible and balanced method of operating your Bushmaster: by maintaining a steady flow of material through the appliance, it receives sufficient sustenance to allow it to be stored conveniently out of the way between feeds. At the same time, it is ready to tackle any detritus arising from a domestic emergency, i.e. a collapsed ceiling. (In this case, the nature of the resultant debris to be cleared would give rise to a very lengthy DCD – a small price to pay for such a task.)

With reference to the ratio of input quantity to DCD time, it must be emphasized that the mention above of wastepaper baskets is for example only – quoted because your particular demonstration involved their use. The constituents of garbage are many and varied; therefore the new owner must proceed by trial and error to discover how best his own brand and quantity of garbage can be dealt with by the Bushmaster.

Warning:
The Bushmaster reaches peak efficiency when empty (hungry). The appliance becomes dificult to control in this condition, developing a tendency to seek out the nearest dirt or rubbish regardless of fixtures and fittings standing in its way. Therefore, unless a large quantity of difficult waste material is to be disposed of or an experienced operative is on hand, the domestic user is advised to observe the golden rule of 'little and often'.

Routine Attention:
When the collection bag at the rear of the appliance expands to the shape and size of a South African rugby football, it must be detached (using yesterday's newspaper to catch any overspill of contents) and a replacement bag fitted. Superior design ensures that both operations are the work of a few moments only. Failure to remove the collection bag when full results in erratic and sluggish performance.

The Bushmaster requires an intake of 1 cwt (50·8 kg) of raw material to eventually fill the collection bag with 4lb (1·8 kg) of excellent fertilizer. This can be distributed over ground containing decorative or edible plants without fear of toxic chemical side-effects. The soiled collection bag must then be washed in warm, soapy water (no detergents), rinsed and left to dry naturally.

Care and Maintenance:
None required other than the common respect which any owner should retain for his personal property.

A soft, damp cloth used occasionally on the Bushmaster will enhance its appearance.

Like most manufacturers' instructions, they had to be read several times before some sense could be made of them. Afterwards Roger sat for five minutes, gazing at the untidy parcel in the corner of the office, while he mulled over the essential message contained in Ngomo's written words.

In effect, the Bushmaster had to be fed at regular intervals.

So it would appear that Minnie was getting a bloody pet as well as a new vacuum cleaner. He imagined trying to explain to dear, unstable, unreasonable Minerva that she had to feed her vacuum cleaner in the same way she fed the cat. He would demonstrate, put their dishes side by side – saucer of milk for the cat, a plate of garbage for the Bushmaster . . . Observe her reaction to such undiluted madness . . . Watch whatever sanity she still possessed disintegrate as the few screws remaining in her head worked loose and dropped out . . .

He shook with silent laughter. Tears ran down his face to splat on the leather-edged blotter on his desk.

'Roger,' he burbled, 'you're nasty.' Then he sobered as the perpetual crushing responsibility he felt for her welfare came trickling back into his mind like liquid lead, causing heavy mental indigestion.

Surely even *she* would see that the benefit to be derived from the Bushmaster (if the damned thing worked) far outweighed its drawbacks? Perhaps not. In which case it seemed a good idea not to mention any drawbacks until she saw for herself what a boon the appliance could be to her.

Anyway, he thought maliciously, Ngomo's instructions presumably applied to *normal* operating conditions and few things Minnie ever did could be construed as normal – least of all her operating conditions. If, as she claimed, the house was spawning dirt at such a prodigious rate, then the Bushmaster need never be empty and the question of regulated amounts of rubbish need never arise . . .

Cynical reasoning perhaps, but somehow it was shot through with a compulsion to let her get the hell on with it without complicating things unnecessarily. If the Bushmaster brought about a psychological crisis so much the better: an immediate cure or a total breakdown followed by prolonged compulsory therapy in hospital. Either way the prognosis was positive . . .

The parcel started to move, tiny shivers and ripples rattled the brown paper. Alarmed, Roger frantically consulted the hand-written pages in front of him until he found what he was looking for: *ten wastepaper baskets full of light assorted rubbish ingested by the Bushmaster results in a DCD of three hours . . .*

He looked at his watch. An hour and a half had elapsed since it polished off *four* basketfuls during Ngomo's demonstration. So – Christ, it needed feeding again!

The parcel was now perceptibly rocking from side to side. Roger watched it, seized with the paralysis of panic. The paper ripped and the Bushmaster broke out. The first three feet of it protruded, erect and swaying, from the top of the parcel. Its appearance was that of some monstrous swan. Roger could swear it was looking at him, trying to skewer him with those dead/alive eyes.

He dived for the wastepaper bin bext to his desk: four miserable balls of screwed-up quarto and an empty tube of butane lighter fuel. He rifled the drawers in his desk: half a box of paper clips, an obsolete £.s.d. pocket calculator, and a framed photograph of Minnie. He threw them all into the bin together with a few cigarette ends from his ashtray and tipped it out on to the floor in front of the Bushmaster. The evil triangular head dropped to deal with the little pile of rubbish.

Roger remembered the filing cabinets. From the top drawer of one, he selected the fattest file. A cursory examination of the papers in it showed them to be a comprehensive history of the two-million-pound Economax account, including the records of the delicate negotiations leading up to award of contract. Without compunction, Roger tore the file in half and fed it to the thing on the floor. The Economax contract vanished into the ever-open mouth.

To be spread later on the garden . . .

He grinned sweatily at the irony of it. What else was the Economax contract but a load of crap anyway?

Apparently satisfied for the moment, the Bushmaster lay inert. Roger gingerly held the head with one hand, using the other to thread the exposed part of the body back through the tear in the parcel.

He suddenly realized that he had to get the Bushmaster home. On the train. Rush-hour train. Supposing it started misbehaving in a crowded carriage? The prospect propelled him briskly into Miss Hornby's office cradling his wastepaper bin. It had to be fed. Enough to keep it quiet on the train, but not too much, otherwise it wouldn't work when he gave a demonstration for Minnie.

'Janice, could we exchange bins?' he asked in a businesslike manner.

He bent down next to her and noticed, apart from her legs and the perfume she wore, that her bin was nearly full. Excellent.

'But Mr Cannington – ' she protested, not so much at the removal of her bin as at the substitution of his own in its place: a flagrant violation of the pecking order, for hers was a plain dark green one whereas his was a junior-executive model sporting a stainless-steel rim and sprayed to match his tan nylon carpet.

'I'm fed up with mine,' he said, scurrying into his own office before she could reply.

He tipped out Miss Hornby's bin, noticing a chocolate-bar wrapper peeping ostentatiously through the used carbon paper. He wished he could admonish her. She shouldn't be spoiling a figure like that by eating chocolate. But thinking of her heavenly lips caressing the rich brown squares, he could forgive her anything . . .

The pleasant conjecture evaporated rapidly as the Bushmaster popped its head out of the parcel to deal with the fresh provender.

Roger got down on all fours, his face close to the mouth. The rubbish seemed to be *attracted* into it, rather like iron filings winging to a magnet. There was no sound inside to indicate a vacuum mechanism, so quite what the intake principle was he couldn't say. He watched a hefty piece of cardboard jam awkwardly across the mouth. This would be interesting . . . He caught a glimpse of the innermost edge of the cardboard rapidly turning into a soft, dark mush before the whole piece disappeared into the black void. He remembered when constructing radio sets as a boy how he used to feed the solder on to a hot iron and see its comparatively sturdy composition become instantly fluid.

Heat? He gripped the Bushmaster's head for confirmation. No. Chemicals? Possibly. But how did an African tribesman obtain a chemical sophisticated enough to dissolve a wide variety of garbage without damaging the Bushmaster itself?

The thing would have to be dissected.

Meanwhile, two immediate problems nagged at him as he replaced the quiescent Bushmaster once more into the parcel: keeping it in order on the train; and ensuring that it performed immediately Minnie saw it. He closed his eyes, kneading the lids savagely, trying not to think of the scene when he spread a load of rubbish around the lounge only to discover that the Bushmaster was ignoring its cue due to a Digestion/Conversion Delay, or whatever it was called.

He sighed. It required careful calculation. He rummaged around in the files to find a sheet of blank paper and took it back to his desk.

10 wastepaper baskets = DCD of 3 hours; therefore:

$$1 \text{ wastepaper basket} = \frac{3 \times 60}{10} = 18 \text{ minutes.}$$

So: eighteen minutes for one. Eighteen minutes? He referred again to Ngomo's instructions: *However, an infinite number of baskets will be accepted provided they are proffered one at a time at thirty-minute intervals* . . . His eyes moved to the paragraph above: *ten wastepaper baskets . . . light assorted . . . in one operation . . .*

The three-hour DCD was only applicable if the ten baskets were consumed in one operation, which made nonsense of any calculations designed to find a DCD for one basket. Full stop. Not quite – it could be done by estimating the volume of the contents of ten baskets, taking into account the fact that one basket fed at thirty-minute intervals created no DCD, then gauging how long the Bushmaster had been in his possession, and remembering exactly how much rubbish he had given it during that time. From here he might be able to estimate the further amounts of rubbish needed to keep it quiet on the train, yet active for Minnie . . . Oh, God!

For the next hour Roger grappled with complicated equations based tenuously on Ngomo's already tenuous figures. During this time he paused only once, when the Bushmaster came out again for food. Swaying. Menacing.

How easy, he thought, to change fear into farce by having a boot-polished, olive-oiled Miss Hornby, clad only in a turban, play some Far Eastern strangled-chicken music on a blow-pipe for the Bushmaster to dance to.

He fed it the Powertrain Inc file instead.

Finally he gave up. He screwed the tightly packed page of

algebra into a small damp ball, nearly threw it into the waste-paper bin, checked himself, then rolled it along the carpet for the Bushmaster.

Ngomo had summed it all up in his instruction manual: *the new owner must proceed by trial and error . . .*

Yes, he would have to be content with that.

For the remainder of the afternoon Roger detailed a bewildered Miss Hornby to collect full secretarial wastepaper bins from other offices, which he assiduously fed to the Bushmaster at half-hourly intervals. He knew she was bursting with curiosity but he frustrated her attempts to gain entry to his office by conducting the exchange of full bins for empty ones in a series of tight little rituals through a barely open door.

He might perhaps have been interested, if not quite flattered, had he been able to eavesdrop on some of Miss Hornby's conversations with her fellow secretaries:

Miss Dennison (fanning herself with a copy of *Cosmopolitan*) 'Hi, Janice. Hot, isn't it?'
Miss Hornby 'Hello, Midge. Is your wastepaper bin full?'
Miss Dennison 'Uh?'
Miss Hornby 'It's Randy Rodge, he's playing silly buggers again. This time he wants all the full bins I can get for him.'
Miss Dennison (laughing) 'Is it another pet project or something?'
Miss Hornby (shrugging) 'No idea. Might be the heat. He's acting very strangely.'
Miss Dennison 'Somebody said his wife was a bit screwy. Perhaps it's contagious. (Grinning) I think you should lay him, Jan, bring him back to his senses. He's pretty dishy so why don't you give him a service?'
Miss Hornby (ruefully) 'Opportunity would be a fine thing . . . If only he wasn't such a . . .' (taps temple significantly with beautifully manicured forefinger)

Just before he left the office, Roger gave the Bushmaster the last three binfuls of rubbish all at once. Then he filched some sticky-tape from Miss Hornby's desk and sealed the split in the parcel.

The 17.40 train from Liverpool Street was predictably crowded and extremely hot. Roger, unable to grab a seat or fit his unwieldy parcel into a luggage rack, was faced with fifty minutes of tedious discomfort, crammed into the carriage like a factory-farmed animal. With the parcel crushed against his chest as it was, he had serious misgivings regarding the efficacy of his hasty repair.

On the approach to Stratford station the train came to one of those interminable halts, pioneered by Southern but newly adopted by Eastern Region, to break the monotony of a smooth journey home. A thick, self-conscious silence, disturbed only by the polite rustle of newspapers, descended on the carriage. Directly in front of Roger was a very attractive head of hair – masses of smooth copper, highlighted in gold by the dusty rays of the sun. Usually he viewed other passengers merely as items that filled a railway carriage to a high level of inconvenience, but the owner of hair like that *must* be worth a little attention. He moved and she turned her head fractionally to reveal a perfect profile. At the points where he gripped the parcel, he was suddenly aware of the backs of his hands gently pressing her shoulder blades through layers of hair and flimsy clothing.

Roger silently cursed the Bushmaster in his arms, for had he not got it, another two people could have jammed into the carriage, pushing him forward until his crotch was snuggled against her buttocks and his face lost in that marvellous hair.

A perfect finale to a hard day at the office.

Abruptly, wondrously, the object of his admiration turned her head right round to address him. As he had expected, the face was flawless, the angry eyes the colour of lush spring lawns.

The flaw was the voice; a strident, truculent East End voice; a querulous squeal, like badly maintained automobile brakes.

'D'you mind keeping your hands to yourself,' it said.

Like discreet applause at a pornographic film show, the newspapers all rustled in unison as commuters sought refuge behind the headlines.

Stunned, Roger said, 'I beg your pardon?'

'You're playing with my drawers,' she brayed to the world at large.

He watched the muscles flexing around her mouth, moment-arily destroying the symmetry of her lips, causing them to twist into a snarl.

'Am I?' he asked. The idea of playing with her drawers appealed to him and for a few seconds he allowed an inane grin to hang on his face. Then the blood came rushing to his cheeks. He felt his features pulsing, burning, prickling as the blush took hold.

'Look, dear,' he found himself gabbling, 'how can I be doing a thing like that when my hands are up there?' He used his head to indicate the position of his hands on the parcel. The girl's eyes swooped downward as she attempted to survey her back. They met his again, the anger in them supplanted by perplexity.

'Well, if it's not your hands, it must be . . .' She hesitated, then those big green eyes flared brighter than before. 'You *dirty* sod!' she shouted, struggling to push herself away from him.

The applause from a multitude of *Evening Standard*s grew deafening; the ostriches buried their heads in newsprint.

Roger didn't know whether to laugh it off or pretend to lose his temper, put on a display of indignation. His face felt thoroughly cooked. He was conscious of everyone in the carriage waiting for his next move. They probably hoped he would hurl himself through a window and on to the track and make his escape through adjoining gardens, snatching underwear from clothes-lines on his way in the time-honoured manner of the fugitive sex-maniac.

He felt it. Something moving, twisting, curling round his ankles. He shifted one hand to the bottom of the parcel . . .

The Bushmaster was out.

His ulcer jerked into action, tearing at his insides, the agony sending perspiration rolling down his face. His executive training saved him from total confusion and collapse.

'Not guilty,' he said. 'It's my vacuum cleaner pipe.' Despite the turmoil within, he smiled at her disarmingly.

'Yeah? That's a new name for it.'

'No, honestly. Look!' In the limited space available, Roger caught a section of the Bushmaster's body, praying that the head was well below, out of sight. In his hot hand the body felt cool but not lifeless. It twitched, in fact the whole parcel was moving against his chest. He gave the girl just a fraction of a second to peek at the 'vacuum cleaner pipe' before letting go his hold. His relief was marginal; at least the head hadn't reared up in full view of the carriage. If it had, there would have been pandemonium.

Although thankful for small mercies, Roger realized the situation was still desperate.

The girl seemed somewhat mollified; nevertheless she elbowed her way to the other side of the carriage.

'Lucky for you I'm liberated, else I'd have the police on you!' she grumbled loudly.

A distinguished-looking middle-aged man had snapped into the girl's recently vacated place in front of Roger. He turned to glance apprehensively at the suspected sex offender before returning to his share prices.

The train jolted into motion. Roger mouthed a silent thanksgiving to the British Rail gods responsible. By the time it pulled into Stratford, the Bushmaster was positively thrashing about his legs. He noticed the scrawny sinews in the neck of the man in front were rigid. If the Bushmaster was assaulting him, he was too much of a gentleman to say so.

At last the doors slid open to disgorge Roger on to the platform. An observer, not preoccupied with the miserable business of getting home, would have seen in the crowds a youngish, attractive man with dishevelled hair wearing a rumpled ninety-guinea suit. The main point of interest would have been the convulsive nature of the brown paper parcel in his arms, not to mention the nasty thing hanging from it.

Roger battled with the mass of people waiting for the underground connection, impatiently thrusting bodies aside in his search for salvation.

He found it.

As litter bins go, it was of moderate size only, but it contained treasures to set the heart soaring: two banana skins, several apple cores, a newspaper and – most spectacular of all – someone's discarded jam sandwiches.

Roger slipped the head and front part of the body into the bin and then laid the parcel, still containing some seven feet of coiled Bushmaster, across the top.

And nobody noticed. Rush hour, someone letting what appeared to be a king cobra loose into a British Rail litter bin . . . and nobody noticed. Light-headed and silly with relief, Roger wondered if he would be noticed cartwheeling naked through the ticket barrier.

Having dined, the Bushmaster allowed itself to be pushed back into the sorry-looking parcel. Roger collapsed on to a seat to wait for the next Southend train. On top of everything else, he was going to be late now and be subjected to Minnie's martyr-like moaning.

The journey passed without further incident, but not until the Bushmaster was safely stowed in the front of the car did Roger fully regain his composure. As he drove out of the station car-park he began to brood over the events of the day. What exactly had he got himself into with this Bushmaster thing? He felt physically and emotionally drained; his routine had been disrupted and, more important, his pride had taken a beating. He couldn't recollect the last time he had lost control of a situation, human or otherwise. But that afternoon had seen him cringing abjectly in his office and an hour ago charging along a station platform like a schoolgirl with a bladder problem. Not to mention the undignified scene in the train. He glanced at the parcel beside him. The Bushmaster was impossible, ridiculous, farcical, a sick practical joke. Yes, the emancipated black man's novel method of revenge for centuries of oppression and exploitation. Definitely the new White Man's Burden. After years spent pandering to Minnie's obsession, he himself was developing an obsession about her obsession. Why else, he reasoned, should he pay forty pounds for a 'West African tribal vacuum cleaner'? Absurd. Tomorrow Ngomo could have it back. As for Minnie, if her trouble got any worse she would have to be committed – forcibly if necessary.

Funny its going up that girl's skirt though . . . almost as though the thing had a dirty mind of its own.

He drove the car into the wide driveway separating two bulky pre-war semis. The one on the left was his and he was forced to admit that it looked very neat, very substantial, indeed almost pretty in the mellow sunshine of early evening. It excluded an air of security and solidity – a no-nonsense atmosphere precisely matched to his present mood. The house was perhaps the only sane foundation remaining to an insane marriage.

He parked in front of his garage doors, gathering up the parcelled Bushmaster and entered the rear gate to the garden.

His eyes rested on three hundred pounds' worth of colour TV. Smashed. On the patio.

Roger lost his temper.

'What have you done now, you stupid bitch?' he roared at the white pebble-dashed wall and glinting windows. He stormed through the open kitchen door, seeing the cool *empty* cooker. No food ready. *What again?*

Into the hall, then first left. She was sitting at the dining room table staring blankly at the wall. She had been crying. Her eye make-up was smudged which made her look like a panda; the tears had cut canals through her face powder. She didn't acknowledge him.

He dumped the Bushmaster into an easy chair by the French windows.

'What the hell have you done to the television, Minerva?' he demanded loudly. 'Just what d'you think you're playing at?'

No reply. No change of expression. He noticed a nasty graze on her left kneecap and her tights were holed and laddered. She might have fallen over. He calmed down, a little ashamed of his outburst of wrath. 'What happened? How did you hurt your leg?'

'The house did it.' Her reply was delivered without moving any part of her body except her lips – and their movement was minimal. The voice was pitched lower than usual and had no cadence whatsoever.

She's catatonic or something, he thought. Maybe she's been at the pill cabinet.

'Quite, darling, but *how* did it do it?' he persisted with as much patience as he could muster.

She ignored the question. Instead she began to drone, 'Roger, we're doomed. You realize we're doomed, don't you? Prisoners of the house. Condemned to death. And do you know how we're going to die? No, of course you wouldn't know that, you wouldn't *want* to know that – you the unbeliever. Well, I'll tell you. By suffocation. We are going to suffocate in filth.'

Roger sighed, gazing round the room at the spotless paintwork, the burnished furniture, windows that positively scintillated. 'Yes, dear,' he said.

Further declarations apparently not forthcoming from those lunatic lips, Roger made a decision. The big one.

He went into the garden, averting his eyes from the wrecked

television set. He returned twice to the dining room, each time with a dustbin.

'Now listen, Minnie,' he said slowly and clearly to her back. 'I've brought you home a present. It's a vacuum cleaner and a good one. Very special, much better than the VibraGlide. This one can't be beaten by dirt, by dust, or anything else. D'you understand, Min?'

She showed no sign of interest, of having heard even. Roger bent until his mouth was a few inches from her ear. If the Bushmaster failed now, he would impale Ngomo on it . . .

'To demonstrate it, I'm going to empty the dustbins on the floor. Do you hear? *I'm-going-to-empty-the-dustbins-in-here. Think-of-it: a-great-stinking-sticky-heap-of-rubbish-on-the-carpet!*'

Her head whipped round. 'What?' she said.

Certain now of her attention, he acted quickly. He ran to the Bushmaster, unceremoniously tore off the brown paper wrapping, then tipped both dustbins upside down in the centre of the room. A rotten-sweet smell arose from the piled garbage to waft gently to his nostrils.

Minnie leapt to her feet, screaming and sobbing alternately, beating at him with determined but ineffectual fists. 'You bastard!' she shrieked. 'You dirty sneaking rat! What have you done to my beautiful room! You – '

She hesitated. Roger took the opportunity to dart to the other side of the big heap of rubbish. From there he saw her eyes narrow suspiciously. Then her face became one huge cunning leer. With her sooty eye-sockets and her hunched posture she was every psychiatrist's ideal case: Instantly and Undoubtedly Certifiable.

'Bastard!' she spat. 'You and the house together; both of you want to drive me out, kill me, don't you, bastard?'

Roger held out his arms with the palms of his hands turned towards her in a placating gesture. He was worried, frightened too if he cared to admit it. 'Now, now, take it easy, Minnie. Nobody's trying to kill you or drive – '

He sensed it before he saw it. 'Look!' He pointed eagerly at the Bushmaster heading silently for the rubbish, its body blending nicely with the thick Wilton. 'There's your present, darling . . . Watch!'

36

Minnie whimpered. She stumbled to the fireplace, snatched up a heavy antique brass poker, advanced on the Bushmaster. 'Snake!' she yelled, spraying saliva behind her like an aircraft contrail. 'The rat bought a snake!'

'Give it a chance, Minnie!' Roger shouted despairingly.

'The rat, the snake, and the house. Planning to murder poor Minnie the mouse . . .' She mouthed the impromptu rhyme over and over again, keeping the beat by savagely hitting the Bushmaster with the heavy poker. Impervious to the rain of blows, it deviated not an inch from its course. It stopped at the base of the heap and began sucking garbage.

Definitely a quality product, Roger thought deliriously. Try bashing a hoover like that and see what happened . . .

The sight and the sound and the smell of the horrifying little scenario being enacted before him brought on a curiously detached and disgusted amusement: *Is this my life? Does it only add up to this . . . this nauseating mess?*

How would he feel if that grinning Irish fellow – what was his name? Amos Andrews? – walked in now with a camera crew? Amos wearing ear plugs, a handkerchief over his nose, merry shamrock eyes averted . . . handing Roger the big book and mumbling: 'Roger Cannington. *This* is *your* life!'

Ashamed.

A sharp pain in his collar bone brought him quickly back to reality. Minnie had turned her murderous attention from the Bushmaster to him. He staggered backwards as she raised the poker for the *coup de grâce*. It narrowly missed him and splatted harmlessly into damp newspaper-wrapped potato peelings on top of the pile. By the time she had retrieved the situation and was ready for another strike, Roger was safely on the opposite side of the pile. To reach him, she would have to skirt the edge, only this time he wouldn't be caught napping. He formulated a plan to let her chase him round and round the heap until she tired sufficiently to see reason. He hoped she wouldn't take a short cut over the top, for that would involve defending himself and disarming her. The prospect dismayed him; Kung Fu jungle antics were not his forte.

She came over the top.

Her face contained no vestige of its former prettiness, it being now a dripping, twisted mask of hate. With the poker held high above her head like a double-handed sword, she resembled some demoniac avenger. To avoid an untimely end, Roger prepared to hurl himself through the french windows. Then her left foot sank into the summit of the stinking trash, throwing her off balance. The poker flew from her grasp as she fell face down into the muck. She lay there unmoving and wailing.

Inches from her head the Bushmaster was feeding voraciously.

Roger's sense of relief was so strong that he laughed, although the sound which reached his ears was that of an ailing bullfrog. Minnie's banshee wail suddenly dropped a few octaves to become a gurgle and finally petered out altogether. The reason was plain to see, although he didn't believe it.

Her head had gone.

All he could see on top of Minnie's shoulders, apart from some tufts of blonde hair, was a short stump of neck. And that was slowly disappearing into the Bushmaster's mouth.

His own scream triggered him into action. He grabbed her ankles and pulled, gritting his teeth with the effort. He . . . had . . . to get her . . . head out of . . . its . . . *mouth*! Minnie came free, slipping easily through the refuse.

Minus her head.

Roger dropped the ankles and puked, making his own small contribution to the unholy mess in the room. Seconds later he found enough self-control to examine . . . Ugh! Inconsequential observations somehow insulated him against shock.

No blood. No gore. Thankful for that anyway. In fact she looks quite normal really. Well, almost. And she isn't kicking up that awful racket any more. There were worse ways to go. Under a train for instance.

A ragged gushing hole in the centre of the shoulders is the type of wound consistent with the indiscriminate removal of the head. Not so in this case. The only evidence to suggest that Minnie ever had a head was a neat dark circular patch on the top of her torso. It looked like Bostik.

The Bushmaster was behaving strangely, as well it might. The front part of it was vertical, assuming the swan's-neck shape that Roger had seen at the office. Only now it was quivering, not swaying as it had done earlier. The imitation eyes fixed him with a beady, soulless stare. He couldn't remember reading anything in the instruction manual about a situation like this, but he nevertheless felt he was getting to know the Bushmaster a little better. Right now he suspected that it was aggrieved – probably annoyed at having the succulent Minnie removed so precipitately from its mouth.

But how . . . (Slowly, so slowly Roger's legs reversed him in the general direction of the door) . . . could such a proposition be feasible? The Bushmaster only dealt with rubbish . . .

A soothing, amplified voice within him said: Well, let's face it, Roger, Minnie *is* dead you know, and a body is only another piece of detritus to be cleared by Nature one way or another.

Behind the big voice was another – small, screaming, muffled, as though locked in a trunk: *She wasn't dead! She was still alive when it got her!*

The hard edge of the door frame gouged his back. He flung himself through the doorway and fled.

Before the sound of the wildly revving car faded, the Bushmaster was tunnelling through the rank hillock in the dining room.

Roger purged the taste of vomit from his mouth and throat by means of three high-speed double whiskies. After two more, his hands stopped trembling, and his face, reflected in the mirror behind the bar, regained some of its colour.

One thing was painfully obvious . . . He had to go back, whether now or later. But had he? Why not call the police? Were they not equipped to deal with the kind of horror that was back there? Of course they were! Although there was no mention of it in the recruitment advertisements, Roger was willing to wager that the mandatory handling of headless corpses was written into the policeman's contract of employment these days. Yes, it would be easy to take advantage of their admirable facilities. Superficially. But what then of the Bushmaster and all its crazy ramifications? Could the Police Mind, welded shut as it was by inflexible rule and procedure, cope with something as incomprehensible as the Bushmaster? He doubted it, for the phlegmatic Essex Constabulary would put this most amazing of phenomena into its departmental mincer, thereby reducing it to a simple workaday murder investigation. With Roger as suspect number one.

Right sir, we'll go over this again, shall we? You say your wife attacked you for no apparent reason? . . . Accuse you, sir? Good Lord, no! Mr Cannington's jumping to conclusions, isn't he, Sergeant? But to be on the safe side, sir, perhaps I'd better warn you that anything you may say will be . . .

Suspicion, surveillance, interrogation, photographs, interviews, reports, statements, analyses, post mortem, inquest, innuendo, publicity. Trial.

No. No police.

Alternatives? One came to mind. Dispose of the body, dispose of the Bushmaster. Carry on normally, discreetly informing anyone interested that Minnie, after months of threatening, had finally left him. For the immediate family, a little more creative embellishment was required; something mildly scandalous for Minnie's repressed relatives to get their teeth into: Minnie stealing away in the dead of night, catching the inter-city sleeper to hasten her into the rampant arms of her secret lover – a pools-winning postman from Halifax or somewhere.

Roger drained his glass, lighted a cigarette, and began to feel better. He bought a refill, stood propped against the bar swirling the liquid. He attempted to muster some emotion befitting Minnie's early demise. None came. Admittedly he felt distressed, not so much because of her departure from life, but rather the deplorable manner of her going. Undoubtedly he would miss her as one misses a perpetual pain in the neck, but he could adjust to that, given time. No question though of ever obliterating the image of her, up to her neck in the Bushmaster's mouth.

He wished her well in her new environment, hoping that she had been admitted into the Kingdom of Heaven *prior* to making a fuss about tarnished gates and grubby wings . . . If the Good Lord couldn't find her a cleaning job up there, they wouldn't get much Eternal Peace.

Roger was just sober enough to recognize whisky-ravings. He crushed them and suppressed the smile on his face. His problem, his immediate and gruesome problem confronted him.

He was surprised to walk out of the pub into darkness. Had he really been such a long time in there? One consolation to be derived from this unpleasant business; he was now able to go anywhere for as long as he liked without any more of those reproachful silences and the old dewy-eyed gaze from you-*knew*-who. He pointed the car in the general direction of home, his resolve stiffened by a good charge of alcohol and tempered with four ham rolls. Fear momentarily stabbed him in the stomach as he passed a police car lurking in a lay-by. He kept an apprehensive watch on his mirror but it didn't pursue him. He relaxed. So stupid to be afraid of a drunk-driving charge when something rather more terrifying awaited him in the dining room.

Was the Bushmaster lethal, or had it made a mistake? How did it differentiate between rubbish and anything else – living human flesh for instance? Perhaps it couldn't. Perhaps it ate whatever was in its way when it was hungry. True, he had actually seen the thing eat only rubbish (apart from Minnie's . . . head), but had Ngomo stated categorically that it would eat nothing *but* rubbish? Roger couldn't remember. If he hadn't, then the Bushmaster was highly dangerous in the wrong hands, for whatever it ate was entirely dependent upon the operator's definition of the word 'rubbish'. Adapt the old but sound adage 'One man's meat is another man's poison' and you had a formula for trouble.

On the other hand, Minnie *had* shamefully abused the Bushmaster with the poker, so maybe its subsequent behaviour was a reaction – a 'petty malfunction due to mistreatment by the malicious and ignorant' as Ngomo had put it. But if the 'malfunction' constituted a revenge killing, there was nothing petty about it and it also implied that the Bushmaster had the ability to reason. However limited that ability and rudimentary the reasoning, it nevertheless placed the Bushmaster in a category above that of a mere exotic domestic appliance. Whilst Roger agreed with Ngomo that Electrolux were unable to claim for their products 'A Spotless House *and* a Beautiful Garden', he also realized that they had no need to conceal the derivative slogan: 'If You Kick It, It Will Kill You'.

Something would have to be done about the Bushmaster.

The headlights slashed a path along the driveway, illuminating the black windows of the house with brief reflected tracers of brilliance. Roger switched off the ignition and lights, sitting in the car for a few moments to allow his eyes to adjust to the night. An opulent wall-lit glow oozed through chinks in his neighbour's fence accompanied by the muted strains of quadraphonic Sibelius. A discreet but distant welcome back to the middle-class fold. Very comforting, very reassuring . . . except that he was not about to enter the snug after-supper home of his neighbour, but his own bleak, lightless house of horror.

He got out of the car, walked through the fence gate into the garden. He turned right, away from the house, towards the distant outline of his workshop at the end of the garden. Despite his recently imbibed determination, he felt the pincer movement of suspense on his ulcer. He fumbled, cursing in the dark shed, then remembered his lighter. The flaccid flame barely provided enough light to find the long-handled axe which leant against the wall between the spade and the hoe. Once in his hands, the axe bolstered his confidence; he was able now to face the Bushmaster on equal terms. But the smooth wood was damp where he gripped it too hard.

A balmy, starlit Essex sky above his head, a well-tended green baize lawn beneath his feet. On either side, well-lit, solid, suburban houses casting comfort across spacious gardens.

In front? An open kitchen door, the yawning black entrance to Minnie's tomb. The Bushmaster's playground. The unbelievable stuff of madness.

The stench of decay was floating in the kitchen. Roger stood still in the gloom. Listening. Not daring to walk to the light switch on the far wall. His resolve was peeling off him in layers, like skin from an onion. Beneath, he knew, was raw fear. Could it hear him? Could it smell the whisky bile on his breath, the stinking, streaming sweat filling his body creases? Could it sense his presence, anticipate the action he was about to take?

Something snaked around his ankles. *It was in the kitchen!*

He kicked wildly with both feet, caught a blurred, dim movement of something skidding on the tiles. Terror super-charged his reflexes. He brought the axe down so forcefully that it split the object into two smaller objects, then buried itself in the floor. 'Got you!' he breathed exultantly. He released the quivering axe handle to cross to the light switch, screwing up his eyes against the fierce fluorescence.

'Jeee-zus!' he sobbed.

The cat. He had axed the cat . . . in two pieces. The front half still twitched, glazing, censorious eyes turned up at him. His head reeled, the brain within rotating until the centrifugal force threatened to fracture the skull. He slumped against the washing-machine desperately wanting to make amends, do penance for his appalling deed. Minnie, he could find justification for her death. The cat, none at all, particularly as he himself had struck the death-blow. He wanted to hold the cat, comfort it, try to explain that it wasn't his fault. But he knew if he tried he would definitely regurgitate the rapidly rising ham rolls.

With a supreme effort of will, he pulled the axe out of the mangled lino tiles. There was still a job to be done. He faced the open doorway to the hall, braced himself, then strode purposefully into the dining room and turned the light on.

Everything was as he had left it except for one small item. Minnie wasn't there. The Bushmaster lay quietly on the carpet, its tail-end buried in the pile of rubbish. From its mouth protruded something thick. Guessing he had nothing to fear from the Bushmaster at the moment, and inured now to any further horror, Roger glided nearer to look. What he saw explained Minnie's absence from the room. Suddenly he felt remarkably placid. His physical discomforts receded, he was floating in an underwater world where he could hear nothing, smell nothing, feel nothing. Only his eyes informed him of reality – and even that was filtered kindly through anaesthetized lenses.

The thick object in the mouth was a pair of swollen legs from the knees downward. Two unshapely wedges of Danish blue cheese. Minnie's legs – he recognized the varicose veins, never much of a problem to her before, but now accentuated under pressure beneath the tattered tights.

The Bushmaster was obviously in the middle of a Digestion/Conversion Delay. Everything waited for a DCD so Minnie was stuck. Roger laughed, destroying his pleasant disembodied state.

The silly cow was enough to stick in anyone's craw.

He was grateful to the present slippery thinking which allowed him to step so deftly over the boundary between horror and humour. A fleeting impulse came and went – an impulse to chop the Bushmaster into pieces while he had the opportunity. Harmless it might well be during its DCD, but soon (twinge: how soon?) it would become reactivated, swallow Minnie's trotters and start misbehaving again. But, he reasoned, once already this evening the premature and panic-stricken use of the axe had given him cause for regret. Essentially he was not a cruel or ill-natured man and the accidental killing of puss had upset him greatly; in fact he made a note to grieve for her properly when the time was appropriate. After all was said and done, the Bushmaster could not be faulted. It had functioned as Ngomo said it would function. Indeed, if he considered Minnie's death the most successful and enduring treatment she was likely to receive for her illness, then the Bushmaster's performance had been admirable. So, little would be gained by the churlish destruction of such a benefactor purely because he had no further use for it. If anything, the Bushmaster should be rewarded . . .

There presented itself an idea. An idea perfectly tailored to both his and the Bushmaster's requirements.

Gingerly holding the back of the head at arm's length to ensure that Minnie's legs were as far away from him as possible, Roger dragged the Bushmaster to the car. He bundled it into the boot and drove cautiously to the main road, turning left in the direction of the railway. He was acutely aware of the likelihood of a late-night vehicle check. The effects of the alcohol had long since worn off, but if the police examined the boot his explanation of the contents would have to be the ultimate in plausibility.

Two miles on, he turned right at the railway bridge into a narrow lane running parallel with the tracks, ignoring a 'No Through Road' sign on the corner. Soon the tarmacadam surface was replaced by ruts and potholes, forcing him to reduce speed. Beyond the headlamp beams lay a ten-acre wilderness. Ten acres of barren land in the midst of house-hungry suburbia which even the council's favourite speculators were reluctant to build upon. True, some of the land was currently being worked by the council itself but much of it, particularly to the eastward, had been returned to a semblance of its natural state and was ripe for profit. Roger's nostrils wrinkled, involuntarily reacting to the odour seeping into the car. Ethics didn't come into it, he decided. Only the zero sales potential due to the stink prevented them from building here. And the stink of a million maturing dustbins was a powerful dissuader.

The car passed through sagging high wire gates into the heart of the council rubbish tip. Forbidding mountains of refuse reached obscenely for the stars like lepers for the starched white hem of a passing doctor's coat. In front of him at the end of a canyon, Roger could see the most recent workings – distinguished by a cluster of stained, silent bulldozers and diggers. He parked nearby, taking tiny breaths as he got out of the car to minimize the suffocating stench of freshly turned, sun-warmed waste. No salary, he thought grimly, could be too high for the men who had to work here. Was it feasible that they were a species of super-man, immune from the smell and the disease-bearing germs? Improbable, for as far as he knew, any super-men working for the council sat behind desks plotting misery for thousands and were immune only from reality.

The pattering claws and squeaks of outrage of the tip's scurrying residents hastened Roger to the boot of the car. He removed the Bushmaster, noticing as he did so the distended tail section in the sullen glow of the rear lights. The collection bag was full to bursting point. He knelt down on to hard-packed, rubbish and detached the bag as Ngomo had demonstrated, splattering some of the slime inside over his hands and clothes in the process. Immediately the Bushmaster began twitching. Minnie's legs, mauve and hideous in the red light, slid smoothly into the mouth.

Not a DCD at all, Roger reflected, a little wiser. The reason for the Bushmaster's lethargy had been acute constipation.

He waved farewell to the disappearing soles of Minnie's feet, then jumped back as the head reared into the familiar menacing attitude. It twisted slowly, first one way then the other, as if confused by the thousands of tons of surrounding rubbish and trying to get its bearings. Roger tensed, ready to run for his life, but the head sank to the ground. The Bushmaster moved off. Roger watched the dark elongated shape of it slither alongside the car, then into the headlamp beams, gathering momentum; beautiful yet loathsome; ten feet of enigma melting into the night.

In his hand he still held the collection bag and was suddenly aware of what it contained (mostly mucilaginous Minnie). He flung it from him and heard it plop somewhere in the unconsecrated foothills of the nearest mountain. Distant thunder rebuked him for his disrespectful scattering of Minnie's remains. The rumbling grew to a roar, bombarding his ears, shaking the ground underfoot . . .

Behind the towering peaks the last train to Liverpool Street sped past on the embankment, providing a valediction apposite to Minnie's low-profile funeral ceremony.

Upon his return, Roger cleared up the mess in the house. The two dustbins were refilled and placed on the patio next to the scrap television set. He reverently shovelled the cat into a polythene bag, digging a hole for it in the vegetable plot behind the garage. A transplanted cabbage served as a temporary headstone. Using bucketfuls of hot soapy water and disinfectant, he scrubbed the dining room carpet. The kitchen was easier by reason of its smooth surfaces and washable wallpaper. When he had finished, only the mutilated tiles remained to tell of the small tragedy enacted there.

By 2.30 am he was feeling like the floor cloth he had wrung out so many times. Weary yes, but jubilant too. It was all over, bar the explanations; a bit of care and attention to detail here would ensure that Minnie's departure caused little more than a few raised eyebrows. The close relatives who knew her for the clinging nutcase she was would be dealt with first. By portraying the incensed, deserted husband and hitting them over the head with his injured pride, he was assured of a sympathetic, if mystified reception. Yipee! And to think he could have actually *murdered* her and got away with it!

Roger took a shower, surprised to find himself bursting into song in the booth. When he stepped out on to his sticky, blemished suit, the tune became merely a soundless whistle. He donned his pyjamas, then stood indecisively in the bedroom, *their* bedroom.

He took two blankets and a pillow and slept in the car.

Janice Hornby had a shock when her boss walked in at a quarter to ten. He looked awful, like death warmed up. The trendy suit he was wearing (which she hadn't seen before) didn't seem to fit him either. That wasn't like Rodge at all – he was usually a swishy dresser. On second thoughts, maybe it wasn't the suit . . . It was him. He didn't fit the suit. All of a sudden he was out of shape.

Add that fact to the black gutters under his eyes and the grey, caved-in jowls and the answer was: a heavy night. He'd been looking peaky for a long time now, but nowhere near as bad as this.

'Coffee. Black,' he snapped. 'And send out for some sandwiches.'

'Yes, Mr – ' Before she could finish, he was through to his office and had slammed the door.

Rodge had a bit on the side.

Apart from the effects of a sleepless night in the car, Roger felt good. For the first time in months (or was it years?) he had total command of an integrated self. He sat at his desk, hands out-spread on its top, marvelling at the transformation, the billowing confidence, the positive feeling of control. This, he declared to himself, is Roger Resurrected, Roger freshly hatched from his shell of introversion. The office was no longer a place of escape where he could brood over Minnie, wallow in self-pity or fantasize on Miss Hornby's sexual capabilities. Good God! What an apathetic, snivelling worm he used to be. How many times had he unknowingly forfeited a seat on the Board because of it? Well here was the new Action Age!

He jabbed at the intercom switch. 'Janice?'

Her voice crackled brightly back at him. 'Won't be long, Mr Cannington. I'm waiting for the kettle – '

'Never mind that. Get your pretty little arse in here, will you?'

Janice couldn't believe her ears. She rushed in, not knowing quite what to expect. He was standing sternly by the window trying to snarl up the traffic below with the aid of mind-power. He somehow didn't look so bad now – the suit was beginning to fit him.

'I'm taking a holiday,' he announced briskly. 'Three, possibly four weeks.'

'Yes, Mr Cannington?' I was right, she thought bitterly. He's found himself a bird. No more views of the undergrowth for you, Sonny Jim. Have a fabulous time, Casanova . . . I hope it drops off.

'Would you like to come?' He smiled as he said it.

Janice was thunderstruck. Malice cooled to pity. Poor guy, he's flipped his lid at last. 'But Mr Cannington . . .'

'Roger's my name. Use it.'

'But, but . . . What about your wife?'

'Kinky, eh?' he joked. 'I suppose you want a threesome. Don't bother your gorgeous head about her. She's, ah, left me.'

Hope lived in Miss Hornby's shapely breast. 'I've had my holiday how can I get away they won't be able to manage here,' she said all in one breath.

Roger sat on his desk grinning. 'I'm going to see the Chairman in a moment, to see if I can persuade him to make it a working holiday – check up on the European offices, that sort of thing. If he agrees, I'll *need* a secretary, will I not?' He patted the space on the desk next to him. She joined him, felt his arm creep round her waist.

'If he vetoes the idea . . .' He shrugged. 'Then we'll go under our own steam. One thing this outfit can't begrudge me is a vacation. You can go sick or be called to your dying American aunt's bedside. Don't look so serious.'

'I was thinking about the cost.'

'Forget it. Money absolutely no object as far as you're concerned. This will be five years' holidays rolled into one. Uhmm . . .' He rolled his lower lip between finger and thumb, casting her a sidelong, mischievous glance. 'First stop Rome . . . Coming?'

Janice pivoted into his arms, thrusting greedily at him with her lips. 'Yes, Roger,' she breathed. 'Whenever you like.'

The Chairman was affable and amenable, especially when, in response to a routine question regarding Minnie's health, Roger broached the news of her decampment.

'My dear boy,' he boomed. 'Congratulations! D'you know, I was about your age when my own dear bugger upped and left me for some machine-tool rep. I never looked back – had a seat on the Board in no time and dollies galore. And the whipper-snapper salesman wound up with one second-hand machine-tool he could never sell! Bloody hilarious!'

Roger waited for the laughter to subside before disclosing his detailed proposals and projected intinerary. The Chairman seemed to be totally involved with his cigar, chomping and choking on it with gusto. In fact, he was listening carefully to Roger's plans and was surprised by the change in young

Cannington. Here was an example of a woman preventing a man from realizing his full potential. Now his wife had left him, there was only one way Cannington could go. Up. His idea to shake up the European marketing operations was near to brilliant. If the truth be known, the Chairman had a soft spot for dynamic, clean-cut junior executives. They were tomorrow's Captains of Commerce. And dammit, he was one once – a regular eager beaver . . .

He gave his blessing to Roger's project – with a jovial warning to watch the expenses.

Roger and Janice spent the morning making frenzied arrangements for a night flight to Rome. At lunchtime they parted reluctantly, each confessing that they were barely able to wait until they met again at the airport.

Roger entered the house accompanied by a vague feeling of trepidation, as though he expected to discover some enormous oversight, some catastrophic retrospective hitch to last night's propitious disposal of Minnie. In the train that morning a similar feeling had squeezed his bowels as the rubbish tip came into view, but no policemen, or animated zoologists were swarming over the giant heaps. Thankfully the area had appeared dismally normal.

Other than a faint fragrance of dustbin and disinfectant throughout the house, and the gouged kitchen floor, nothing suggested that astounding and horrendous events had taken place the previous evening. The heavy hygienic hand of Minnie still lay over the spotless, impeccably arranged rooms, and would probably continue to do so in spite of any efforts by him to create a comfy pig-sty.

It only remained then to put this mausoleum on the market as soon as he returned from his European capers. And after that? For Roger, a cosy mews flat in London. Later perhaps a seat on the Board and a Dino Ferrari – not to mention hordes of eager young ladies flocking so forcefully as to be unavoidably impaled . . .

Freedom. Owed solely to the Bushmaster. Ngomo's voice rang in his ears: *You have the air of a harassed man, a man with a garbage disposal problem on his mind . . . I think the Bushmaster will restore the lustre to your life.*

Buster, how right you were. Minnie was the problem.

During the afternoon, Roger packed his suitcases. Surplus items, instead of being returned to drawers and wardrobe, were scattered about the bedroom. A cigarette was stubbed out on the cream carpet. He was hesitantly baiting Minnie's ghost, daring her to materialize and admonish him. Emboldened by lack of response, he tried goading her into paroxysms of helpless fury by playing hoopla with his underpants, managing to drape several pairs over the baluster post at the top of the stairs – no mean feat considering the distance from their point of launch in the bedroom doorway. That he could indulge in such behaviour without reproof was a sure sign of Minnie's spiritual absence. She must have been busy elsewhere; doubtless some ethereal unfortunate was having his sceptre and baubles polished at that very moment!

In the bathroom, Roger's jocular mood fled upon sight of yesterday's suit screwed into a stiff filthy bundle next to the shower booth. He almost felt the squirting goo from the Bushmaster's collection bag. Dry-cleaning might well erase the physical evidence, but to wear it again meant enduring intolerable images and sensations. No, the suit would take its place alongside other Minnie memorabilia destined for the Oxfam shop.

As the afternoon wore on, Roger slipped steadily into depression. Something to do with the house. Looked at through renascent eyes, the place was a dull and anonymous prison. Hardly surprising that Minnie should have lost her sanity trapped in it day after monotonous day. Perhaps children (those two children which were flushed from her delicate body disguised as formless bloody lumps) would have helped; brightened her up, enlivened the house, and in turn given *him* an incentive to enjoy life. Perhaps. Perhaps not. If, as he suspected, Minnie was a latent lunatic from birth, then there would have been a couple of kids for him to cope with in addition to everything else. As it was, things had worked out nicely now – if a little later than he would have liked.

The house, though. How could he have held for so long the cherished belief that this dreary, nondescript edifice represented the sum total of his aspirations? Truly appalling, for the belief naturally implied that he himself was dreary and nondescript, and would probably have remained so. But for the grace of God and the Bushmaster. The future prior to yesterday was today easy to envisage . . . Roots irretrievably embedded in sterile suburban soil . . . Life's autumn within a few years . . . Roger Cannington, paunchy, balding, impotent stereotype commuting his way to retirement.

Whilst waiting for the taxi to take him to the station, his thoughts turned to the tops of Janice's legs. He cheered up no end.

Rome, Vienna, Geneva, Paris, Madrid. For Janice and Roger it was a case of love at first touch and then four licentious weeks working hard and playing harder. Once or twice Roger found himself unable to rise to the occasion's demand due to a sudden stark, almost photographic recall of Minnie's ghastly blue-veined legs in the mouth of the Bushmaster. At such times Janice was Sweet Understanding itself ('As you get older, darling, you're bound to . . .'). In fact, she was so infuriatingly smug and serene in her presumptuous wisdom that he was tempted to tell her of the Bushmaster and the true circumstances of Minnie's desertion. But on the whole, their relationship took the path which many true lovers had trodden before them, and by the time their plane touched down at Heathrow on a dying, dull August evening, both were hale, hearty and – dare they admit it? – just a teeny weeny bit bored.

The taxi deposited Janice near her flat en route for Liverpool Street station. Claiming fatigue, Roger declined her half-hearted plea to stay and romp for the rest of the weekend. Waving gaily to her through the window, he wondered now whether his decision to proposition her had been a trifle hasty. All sorts of complications could arise out of an office romance – the fouling-your-own-nest syndrome. Still, he could always sack her as a last resort.

The grey, squalid station with its grimy waiting trains brought the prosaic, familiar facts of life creeping back. Saturday night on Liverpool Street station is a sobering experience for the most ardent dreamer. A small consolation for Roger was the absence of rush-hour crowds. At Stratford (scene of minor crisis, how long ago – a month?) his stomach began to knot. What awaited him at home? Policemen with warrants? The Bushmaster returned to roost? Minnie? . . . Was she really *dead*? He spent the remainder of the journey trying to rid himself of unwarranted fears, succeeding to a certain extent by scoffing at them. Deep down, however, he knew he wouldn't be satisfied until he saw for himself that everything was in order. That done, only the quest for his bachelor pad and the logistics of actually moving house need detain him for a few weeks further.

At last he felt the driver shut off power to the motors as the train began the long gentle descent to the station. He peered out of the streaky window into the darkness beyond. Not far below was the rubbish tip, but he could see nothing save his own gaunt reflection and the distant yellow aura of town-centre sodium lamps with its twinkling suburban periphery.

A long white Ford bearing the illuminted red legend 'Shirley's Taxis' squatted on the station forecourt. The driver was a hard-looking blonde sporting a late-fifties hair style. Roger ascertained that she was for hire, put his cases on the rear seat and slid into the front beside her. He gave her the address, covertly noting details: thirty-fivish; a pair of rib-crusher thighs bursting the trousers of her lilac pants-suit; the jacket bulging with mammary magnificence.

The type attracted him. Even prior to his marriage to the wilting, insipid Minnie, he had harboured a secret but unfulfilled desire to dally with the ladies of social groups 4 and 5. He used to see them in pubs at weekends; vulgar, uninhibited creatures in shiny, clinging dresses performing 'Knees Up Mother Brown' after two gin and tonics. Somehow he had never been able to summon the courage to walk through to the public bar and pick one of them up for a slumming session in the back of his car. My, he thought. How things have changed since then. No qualms about charming the lilac pants off this Amazon . . .

God! From Roger Reticent to Roger Rampant in four short weeks. Remarkable.

She handled the big car with flair and expertise. Roger presumed, with a delicious tremor, that a gentleman friend would be handled likewise. Regardless of size.

'Nice tan you've got on you, love,' she said breezily. 'Been to Spain then?'

Roger smiled, hamming up the visuals (dazzling ruler-straight teeth in a handsome brown face), projecting hopefully an image of himself as rakish adventurer; peripatetic, virile quarter-millionaire. 'Water sports in Acapulco actually,' he said, extending his recent travels a little.

If impressed, she had a strange way of showing it. 'Oh, you're one of them queer beach boys, are you?' she asked, her face a study in mock concern.

Roger had no other choice but to laugh it off. Oh no, he groaned inwardly. Please not a male ego deflation expert, not a conscientious soldier of the Women's Liberation Army . . . Maybe she was only a conscript doing her mandatory National Service . . .

What on earth was he thinking of? With a hair-do and an uplift like that, she would be deemed unfit for duty at the induction examination. He decided she just fancied herself as a comedienne – probably did a nice line in bedroom repartee too.

See how she managed in the back of a taxi.

He remembered the name on the roof of the car. 'You must be Shirley,' he said, slipping his arm along the back of her seat.

'One of them,' she replied wearily, as though the gambit had been made a thousand times before.

Puzzled, Roger said: 'How many are there?'

Another white Ford complete with glowing roof sign flashed an acknowledgement as it passed in the opposite direction.

'Just two of us. I'm Elaine Shirley, and that,' she explained, jerking a thumb rearwards over her shoulder, 'was my husband Reg. Ever heard of him?'

Roger shook his head dumbly.

She was aghast. 'Never heard of Shagger Shirley? Never seen him wrestling on the telly? I tell you, he's your actual local hero, love. He retired while he was still on top and set up this little business.'

She gunned the car out of the brightly lit speed-limit zone. 'We haven't been going long but I reckon we'll do all right. Reg put it all in a nutshell the other day. "Only two cabs, El," he said. "But we got the world at our feet." Wasn't that a nice thing to say?'

'Sensible forward planning,' Roger observed sourly. His hopes and desires receded at an alarming rate. He discreetly removed his arm from behind her.

'Got a heart of gold, old Reg has . . .' she mused. Suddenly she threw him a pointed glance. Caught in the beams of passing cars, the expression on her face was definitely humourless. 'Mind you, he hasn't got a suntan, and he's not what you'd call pretty to look at, but you ought to see the muscles on him. D'you know, I saw him tear our street door off its hinges with his bare hands one night. All because we'd forgot to take the key out with us. I suppose his temper's his only weakness. With his strength he could easy kill someone when he only meant to push them around a bit. D'you know what I mean?'

'Quite,' Roger barked. Message received loud and clear. Obviously the erudite, dainty, intellectual Shagger was The Man in her life. Equally obvious was the need to attend weight-lifting and karate classes if he proposed to seduce the female proletariat.

In the aftermath of retarded lust, his stomach began a lazy downward spiral as the taxi sped him ever nearer the house.

Elaine – Mrs Shirley – broke a lengthy silence to ask in a lightly conversational manner: 'Did you hear about the council rubbish dump?'

Rubbish dump? His stomach hit bottom.

'No, what about it?' he asked casually. He wanted to grab her by the throat and beat every last scrap of information about the rubbish dump out of her, but she would never have guessed from the tone of his voice.

'Something weird's happened out there. It's been in the *Echo* for a couple of weeks. Have a look in the parcel tray, this week's is in there somewhere.' She switched the interior light on.

Roger found the local paper and stared at the screaming headlines: EYESORE BECOMES AMENITY AREA WITHOUT PLANNING CONSENT. COUNCILLOR ALLEGES GRAFT.

He hastily digested the report beneath. It seemed that most of the rubbish tip had been miraculously transformed within a few weeks. It was now a haphazard paradise of woods and wild glades. The council was hopping mad because the mammoth task had been carried out without their knowledge or permission. A separate Parks Planning Committee would have to be formed to examine ways and means of restructuring and improving the new facility to meet the requirements of the general public. The existing Parks Planning Committee, overburdened as it was with work, had nevertheless managed to provide broad guidelines for the new Parks Planning Committee to work to. These were incorporated in a preliminary report and recommended, among other things, two car parks, ornamental gardens, a small shopping complex licensed to sell gifts and refreshments, and of course toilets. The Finance Committee, upon receipt of this preliminary report from the existing Parks Planning Committee, estimated that the cost of construction alone, before the salaries of administrators, landscape gardeners, park keepers, etc, would mean another two pence on the general rate. The Finance Committee though was prepared to wait for the detailed specification from the new Parks Planning Committee before attempting an accurate costing. The Housing Committee wanted the new land for council houses, and every other committee wanted it for every other purpose. The Cleansing and Sanitation Committee – naturally – wanted to keep it.

There followed inch after column inch of allegations of corruption in low places, denials, counter-allegations. The whole bureaucratic rat's nest was in uproar simply because a tiny piece of God's earth had reverted to its natural state without reference to, or regard for, the boss of the primates.

The last few paragraphs on the front page provided Roger with the comfort he badly needed:

According to observers at the tip, the mysterious philanthropist has abandoned his activities in the vicinity. However, a pointer to his present whereabouts is given in the current issue of the East Anglian Argus, *an Echo Group newspaper serving the area north of the R. Stour.*

The paper carries an account of council workers at the ultra-modern Lavenham Refuse Reception Centre finding their place of work overrun by young eucalyptus trees and elephant grass.

When informed of this new development, a spokesman for our own Cleansing Department said, 'Glad to hear it. This crank is their concern now and frankly I hope he stays there!'

Roger folded the newspaper thoughtfully. So, the Bushmaster had moved on to create pastures new. Jolly good luck to it.

'Interesting,' he said, his newly found ease permeating his

voice. The dingy interior light pointed up the all-encombassing slab of make-up on his driver's face. He decided that he didn't fancy her after all.

'I went out there to have a look for myself,' she said. 'But they've put a big fence up so you can't get in. You can still see some dirty great trees though – and big tall grass waving in the wind. Marvellous it is.'

The taxi swung into Roger's road.

'What I'd like to know is, how this filantrypissed bloke got it all to grow in just a couple of weeks.'

'Probably a hoax,' said Roger noncommittally. He retrieved his cases from the rear seat.

He paid the exact fare, omitting the generous tip which might have crossed her palm had she been more cooperative. The 'queer beach boy' remark still rankled too. He addressed her scowling face through the open window: 'Give my regards to Shagger.'

She executed a wild U-turn in the narrow road. The car mounted the opposite kerb, the offside wing passing inches from a solitary lamp-post. Then, with two wheels on the grass verge, it accelerated viciously away, throwing chunks of neatly trimmed sod behind it. Roger chuckled and shook his head reprovingly. Evidently it wasn't only Shagger who had a temper.

He faced the house, its bulk dimly outlined against the heavily overcast night sky. Shapeless, he concluded. Shapeless, miserable, characterless; a mediocre, *narrow* man's home. The sooner he moved the better.

The light from the lamp-post opposite suffered from the twin evils of inflation and a nit-picking Highways Department: each electricity-price increase heralded the arrival of three men and a lorry to replace the bulb with one of a lower wattage. Soon it would go out altogether. By courtesy of its feeble rays Roger made his way along the front path. He deposited his cases in the porch, selected the key, inserted it into the lock, turned it. Nothing happened. Annoyed, he realized he must have bolted the door from the inside and left via the kitchen door. Leaving his cases, he negotiated the lawn and flower border and jumped the low brick wall dividing the front garden from the driveway. He entered the rear garden through the gate in the fence near the garage.

Something large and solid on the dark patio directly in front of the kitchen door sent him sprawling. He sat on the concrete, mouthing obscenities, nursing a bruised shin, and fumbling in his pocket for his lighter.

The flame flickered briefly, then died . . . Out of gas . . . It was one of those nights, but he had seen enough to send his heart to his mouth. A brown paper parcel. He reached out. To touch it, feel it, identify it . . .

He knew what it was by its contours.

The VibraGlide. Returned, repaired, from the shop. The idiot delivery man, finding no one at home, had dumped it. Roger relaxed, exhaling heavily. He smiled. Apparently there had developed within him a phobia about large brown paper parcels.

He regained his feet, brushed himself down and selected by touch the long key to fit the mortise lock on the kitchen door. After a thirty-second grope for the keyhole, the lock turned but the door only opened a fraction, as though jammed by a carpet or some similar object.

Bushmaster! Now miles away. You just read it. Reassured, he pushed as hard as he dared with his shoulder against the frosted glass.

The door opened a little wider.

Cursing loudly, he used his foot as a battering-ram on the wide wooden surround until the door moved inwards sufficiently to let him squeeze through.

Once inside the pitch-black kitchen the noxious, pungent atmosphere brought tears to his eyes, threatened to choke him. Something swirled around his legs to prevent him from walking. Above, the ceiling creaked ominously, and from every direction came strange sibilant sounds, like the hiss of sand poured erratically through a hundred paper funnels.

Coughing, wheezing, thoroughly alarmed, Roger fought his way across the kitchen, maintaining an upright stance with extreme difficulty. Even as his clawing fingers found the light switch the echoes of Minnie's voice came sprouting through his turgid mind like a fungus in the night. He knew instinctively that the words were true. The fluorescent light now provided sickening confirmation:

Do you know – have you any idea . . .

Thick clouds of dust floated in the kitchen. He had been wading thigh-deep through dirt, fine black dirt with a topping of dust and fluff.

. . . what would happen in this house if I left it for any length of time? Well, have you?

Through the murk, he saw the quivering, sagging ceiling; the buckled polystyrene tiles and splintered joists causing gaps, open taps through which flowed streams of dirt from above. Some of the streams were liquid mud caused by the dirt mixing with water from fractured bathroom pipes.

This house would be so full of dirt . . .

The door between kitchen and hall had become detached from its frame and was lying, almost buried beneath the filth, on its edge against the dishwasher.

. . . that you wouldn't be able to get in the front door!

No need to turn the hall light on, even had he been able to reach it. From his position in the kitchen doorway he could see well enough what was happening. The dirt coming down the stairs had caused a drift so deep that the front door was completely obliterated. The subsequent back-up on the stairway had found an escape route over the top of the flush-panelled baluster and was pouring into the hall below. All the doors leading off had been torn from their hinges, allowing the dirt entry into the downstairs rooms. But for that, the hall would have been filled to the ceiling long before now.

Roger broke. With flailing, panic-stricken arms and legs he tried to retrace his passage across the kitchen to the garden and the life-saving VibraGlide out there on the patio.

He was halfway when the ceiling, and the countless tons of dirt behind it, fell on him.

As he suffocated in the quiet darkness he knew positively that he was about to die. Surprisingly the knowledge conveyed no terror; quite the contrary, for the pleasant, upward-floating sensation was soothing, restful.

He was being wafted gently towards a tiny light, far, far above. Gradually, as he drew nearer, the light took on shape and substance . . . a standing figure bathed in glorious incandescence.

It was Minnie, a tranquil, smiling Minnie attired in a delicate, flowing gown of virginal white. In one hand she held a golden bucket and a jewel-encrusted tin of Vim. Her other hand beckoned him lovingly.

The terror came then.

Roger tried to scream but his mouth and lungs were full of filth.

DE MORTUIS

John Collier

Dr Rankin was a large and rawboned man on whom the newest suit at once appeared outdated, like a suit in a photograph of twenty years ago. This was due to the squareness and flatness of his torso, which might have been put together by a manufacturer of packing cases. His face also had a wooden and a roughly constructed look; his hair was wiglike and resentful of the comb. He had those huge and clumsy hands which can be an asset to a doctor in a small upstate town where people still retain a rural relish for paradox, thinking that the more apelike the paw, the more precise it can be in the delicate business of a tonsillectomy.

This conclusion was perfectly justified in the case of Dr Rankin. For example, on this particular fine morning, though his task was nothing more ticklish than the cementing over of a large patch on his cellar floor, he managed those large and clumsy hands with all the unflurried certainty of one who would never leave a sponge within or create an unsightly scar without.

The doctor surveyed his handiwork from all angles. He added a touch here and a touch there till he had achieved a smoothness altogether professional. He swept up a few last crumbs of soil and dropped them into the furnace. He paused before putting away the pick and shovel he had been using, and found occasion for yet another sweep of his trowel, which made the new surface precisely flush with the surrounding floor. At this moment of supreme concentration the porch door slammed with the report of a minor piece of artillery, which, appropriately enough, caused Dr Rankin to jump as if he had been shot.

The doctor lifted a frowning face and an attentive ear. He heard two pairs of heavy feet clump across the resonant floor of the porch. He heard the house door being opened and the visitors enter the hall, with which his cellar communicated by a short flight of steps. He heard whistling and then the voices of Buck and Bud crying, 'Doc! Hi, Doc! They're biting!'

Whether the doctor was not inclined for fishing that day, or whether, like others of his large and heavy type, he experienced an especially sharp, unsociable reaction on being suddenly startled, or whether he was merely anxious to finish undisturbed the job in hand and proceed to more important duties, he did not respond immediately to the inviting outcry of his friends. Instead, he listened while it ran its natural course, dying down at last into a puzzled and fretful dialogue.

'I guess he's out.'

'I'll write a note – say we're at the creek, to come on down.'

'We could tell Irene.'

'But she's not here, either. You'd think *she'd* be around.'

'Ought to be, by the look of the place.'

'You said it, Bud. Just look at this table. You could write your name – '

'Sh-h-h! Look!'

Evidently the last speaker had noticed that the cellar door was ajar and that a light was shining below. Next moment the door was pushed wide open and Bud and Buck looked down.

'Why, Doc! There you are!'

'Didn't you hear us yelling?'

The doctor, not too pleased at what he had overheard, nevertheless smiled his rather wooden smile as his two friends made their way down the steps. 'I thought I heard someone,' he said.

'We were bawling our heads off,' Buck said. 'Thought nobody was home. Where's Irene?'

'Visiting,' said the doctor. 'She's gone visiting.'

'Hey, what goes on?' said Bud. 'What are you doing? Burying one of your patients, or what?'

'Oh, there's been water seeping up through the floor,' said the doctor. 'I figured it might be some spring opened up or something.'

'You don't say!' said Bud, assuming instantly the high ethical standpoint of the realtor. 'Gee, Doc, I sold you this property. Don't say I fixed you up with a dump where there's an underground spring.'

'There was water,' said the doctor.

'Yes, but, Doc, you can look on that geological map the Kiwanis Club got up. There's not a better section of subsoil in the town.'

'Looks like he sold you a pup,' said Buck, grinning.

'No,' said Bud. 'Look. When the Doc came here he was green. You'll admit he was green. The things he didn't know!'

'He bought Ted Webber's jalopy,' said Buck.

'He'd have bought the Jessop place if I'd let him,' said Bud. 'But I wouldn't give him a bum steer.'

'Not the poor, simple city slicker from Poughkeepsie,' said Buck.

'Some people would have taken him,' said Bud. 'Maybe some people did. Not me. I recommended this property. He and Irene moved straight in as soon as they were married. I wouldn't have put the Doc on to a dump where there'd be a spring under the foundations.'

'Oh, forget it,' said the doctor, embarrassed by this conscientiousness. 'I guess it was just the heavy rains.'

'By Gosh!' Buck said, glancing at the besmeared point of the pickaxe. 'You certainly went deep enough. Right down into the clay, huh?'

'That's four feet down, the clay,' Bud said.

'Eighteen inches,' said the doctor.

'Four feet,' said Bud. 'I can show you the map.'

'Come on. No arguments,' said Buck. 'How's about it, Doc? An hour or two at the creek, eh? They're biting.'

'Can't do it, boys,' said the doctor. 'I've got to see a patient or two.'

'Aw, live and let live, Doc,' Bud said. 'Give 'em a chance to get better. Are you going to depopulate the whole darn town?'

The doctor looked down, smiled, and muttered, as he always did when this particular jest was trotted out. 'Sorry, boys,' he said. 'I can't make it.'

'Well,' said Bud, disappointed, 'I suppose we'd better get along. How's Irene?'

'Irene?' said the doctor. 'Never better. She's gone visiting. Albany. Got the eleven-o'clock train.'

'Eleven o'clock?' said Buck. 'For Albany?'

'Did I say Albany?' said the doctor. 'Watertown, I meant.'

'Friends in Watertown?' Buck asked.

'Mrs Slater,' said the doctor. 'Mr and Mrs Slater. Lived next door to 'em when she was a kid, Irene said, over on Sycamore Street.'

'Slater?' said Bud. 'Next door to Irene? Not in *this* town.'

'Oh, yes,' said the doctor. 'She was telling me all about them last night. She got a letter. Seems this Mrs Slater looked after her when her mother was in the hospital one time.'

'No,' said Bud.

'That's what she told me,' said the doctor. 'Of course, it was a good many years ago.'

'Look, Doc,' said Buck. 'Bud and I were raised in this town. We've known Irene's folks all our lives. We were in and out of their house all the time. There was never anybody next door called Slater.'

'Perhaps,' said the doctor, 'she married again, this woman. Perhaps it was a different name.'

Bud shook his head.

'What time did Irene go to the station?' Buck asked.

'Oh, about a quarter of an hour ago,' said the doctor.

'You didn't drive her?' said Buck.

'She walked,' said the doctor.

'We came down Main Street,' Buck said. 'We didn't meet her.'

'Maybe she walked across the pasture,' said the doctor.

'That's a tough walk with a suitcase,' said Buck.

'She just had a couple of things in a little bag,' said the doctor.

Bud was still shaking his head.

Buck looked at Bud and then at the pick, at the new, damp cement on the floor. 'Jesus Christ!' he said.

'Oh, God, Doc!' Bud said. 'A guy like you!'

'What in the name of heaven are you two bloody fools thinking?' asked the doctor. 'What are you trying to say?'

'A spring!' said Bud. 'I ought to have known right away it wasn't any spring.'

The doctor looked at his cement-work, at the pick, at the large worried faces of his two friends. His own face turned livid. 'Am I crazy?' he said. 'Or are you? You suggest that I've – that Irene –

SHORT SHARP SHOCKS

my wife – oh, go on! Get out! Yes, go and get the sheriff. Tell him to come here and start digging. You – get out!'

Bud and Buck looked at each other, shifted their feet, and stood still again.

'Go on,' said the doctor.

'I don't know,' said Bud.

'It's not as if he didn't have the provocation,' Buck said.

'God knows,' Bud said.

'God knows,' Buck said. 'You know. I know. The whole town knows. But try telling it to a jury.'

The doctor put his hand to his head. 'What's that?' he said. 'What is it? Now what are you saying? What do you mean?'

'If this ain't being on the spot!' said Buck. 'Doc, you can see how it is. It takes some thinking. We've been friends right from the start. Damn good friends.'

'But we've got to think,' said Bud. 'It's serious. Provocation or not, there's a law in the land. There's such a thing as being an accomplice.'

'You were talking provocation,' said the doctor.

'You're right,' said Buck. 'And you're our friend. And if ever it could be called justified – '

'We've got to fix this somehow,' said Bud.

'Justified?' said the doctor.

'You were bound to get wised up sooner or later,' said Buck.

'We could have told you,' said Bud. 'Only – what the hell?'

'We could,' said Buck. 'And we nearly did. Five years ago. Before ever you married her. You hadn't been here six months, but we sort of cottoned to you. Thought of giving you a hint. Spoke about it. Remember, Bud?'

Bud nodded. 'Funny,' he said. 'I came right out in the open about that Jessop property. I wouldn't let you buy that, Doc. But getting married, that's something else again. We could have told you.'

'We're that much responsible,' Buck said.

'I'm fifty,' said the doctor. 'I suppose it's pretty old for Irene.'

'If you was Johnny Weissmuller at the age of twenty-one, it wouldn't make any difference,' said Buck.

'I know a lot of people think she's not exactly a perfect wife,' said the doctor. 'Maybe she's not. She's young. She's full of life.'

64

'Oh, skip it!' said Buck sharply, looking at the raw cement. 'Skip it, Doc, for God's sake.'

The doctor brushed his hand across his face. 'Not everybody wants the same thing,' he said. 'I'm a sort of dry fellow. I don't open up very easily. Irene – you'd call her gay.'

'You said it,' said Buck.

'She's no housekeeper,' said the doctor. 'I know it. But that's not the only thing a man wants. She's enjoyed herself.'

'Yeah,' said Buck. 'She did.'

'That's what I love,' said the doctor. 'Because I'm not that way myself. She's not very deep, mentally. All right. Say she's stupid. I don't care. Lazy. No system. Well, I've got plenty of system. She's enjoyed herself. It's beautiful. It's innocent. Like a child.'

'Yes. If that was all,' Buck said.

'But,' said the doctor, turning his eyes full on him, 'you seem to know there was more.'

'Everybody knows it,' said Buck.

'A decent, straightforward guy comes to a place like this and marries the town floozy,' Bud said bitterly. 'And nobody'll tell him. Everybody just watches.'

'And laughs,' said Buck. 'You and me, Bud, as well as the rest.'

'We told her to watch her step,' said Bud. 'We warned her.'

'Everybody warned her,' said Buck. 'But people get fed up. When it got to truck-drivers – '

'It was never us, Doc,' said Bud, earnestly. 'Not after you came along, anyway.'

'The town'll be on your side,' said Buck.

'That won't mean much when the case comes to trial in the country seat,' said Bud.

'Oh!' cried the doctor, suddenly. 'What shall I do? What shall I do?'

'It's up to you, Bud,' said Buck. 'I can't turn him in.'

'Take it easy, Doc,' said Bud. 'Calm down. Look, Buck. When we came in here the street was empty, wasn't it?'

'I guess so,' said Buck. 'Anyway, nobody saw us come down to the cellar.'

'And we haven't been down,' Bud said, addressing himself forcefully to the doctor. 'Get that, Doc? We shouted upstairs, hung around a minute or two, and cleared out. But we never came down into this cellar.'

'I wish you hadn't,' the doctor said heavily.

'All you have to do is say Irene went out for a walk and never came back,' said Buck. 'Bud and I can swear we saw her headed out of town with a fellow in a – well, say in a Buick sedan. Everybody'll believe that, all right. We'll fix it. But later. Now we'd better scram.'

'And remember, now. Stick to it. We never came down here and we haven't seen you today,' said Bud. 'So long!'

Buck and Bud ascended the steps, moving with a rather absurd degree of caution. 'You'd better get that . . . that thing covered up,' Buck said over his shoulder.

Left alone, the doctor sat down on an empty box, holding his head with both hands. He was still sitting like this when the porch door slammed again. This time he did not start. He listened. The house door opened and closed. A voice cried, 'Yoo-hoo! Yoo-hoo! I'm back.'

The doctor rose slowly to his feet. 'I'm down here, Irene!' he called.

The cellar door opened. A young woman stood at the head of the steps. 'Can you beat it?' she said. 'I missed the damn train.'

'Oh!' said the doctor. 'Did you come back across the field?'

'Yes, like a fool,' she said. 'I could have hitched a ride and caught the train up the line. Only I didn't think. If you'd run me over to the junction, I could still make it.'

'Maybe,' said the doctor. 'Did you meet anyone coming back?'

'Not a soul,' she said. 'Aren't you finished with that old job yet?'

'I'm afraid I'll have to have to take it all up again,' said the doctor. 'Come down here, my dear, and I'll show you.'

THE BRIGHT BOY

Arthur Machen

Young Joseph Last, having finally gone down from Oxford, wondered a good deal what he was to do next and for the years following next. He was an orphan from early boyhood, both his parents having died of typhoid within a few days of each other when Joseph was ten years old, and he remembered very little of Dunham, where his father ended a long line of solicitors, practising in the place since 1707. The Lasts had once been very comfortably off. They had intermarried now and again with the gentry of the neighbourhood and did a good deal of the county business, managing estates, collecting rents, officiating as stewards for several manors, living generally in a world of quiet but snug prosperity, rising to their greatest height, perhaps, during the Napoleonic Wars and afterwards. And then they began to decline, not violently at all, but very gently, so that it was many years before they were aware of the process that was going on, slowly, surely. Economists, no doubt, understand very well how the country and the country town gradually became less important soon after the Battle of Waterloo; and the causes of the decay and change which vexed Cobbett so sadly, as he saw, or thought he saw, the life and strength of the land being sucked up to nourish the monstrous excrescence of London. Anyhow, even before the railways came, the assembly rooms of the country towns grew dusty and desolate, the county families ceased to come to their 'town houses' for the winter season, and the little theatres, where Mrs Siddons and Grimaldi had appeared in their divers parts, rarely opened their doors, and the skilled craftsmen, the clock-makers and the furniture-makers and the like began to drift away to the big towns and to the capital city. So it was with Dunham. Naturally the fortunes of the Lasts sank with the fortunes of the town; and there had been speculations which had not turned out well, and people spoke of a heavy loss in foreign bonds. When Joseph's father died, it was found that there was enough to educate the boy and keep him in strictly modest comfort and not much more.

He had his home with an uncle who lived at Blackheath, and after a few years at Mr Jones's well-known preparatory school, he went to Merchant Taylors and thence to Oxford. He took a decent degree (2nd in Greats) and then began that wondering process as to what he was to do with himself. His income would keep him in chops and steaks, with an occasional roast fowl, and three or four weeks on the Continent once a year. If he liked, he could do nothing, but the prospect seemed tame and boring. He was a very decent classical scholar, with something more than the average schoolmaster's purely technical knowledge of Latin and Greek and professional interest in them: still, school mastering seemed his only clear and obvious way of employing himself. But it did not seem likely that he would get a post at any of the big public schools. In the first place, he had rather neglected his opportunities at Oxford. He had gone to one of the obscurer colleges, one of those colleges which you may read about in memoirs dealing with the first years of the nineteenth century as centres and fountains of intellectual life; which for some reason or no reason have fallen into the shadow. There is nothing against them in any way; but nobody speaks of them any more. In one of these places Joseph Last made friends with good fellows, quiet and cheerful men like himself; but they were not, in the technical sense of the term, the 'good friends' which a prudent young man makes at the university. One or two had the bar in mind, and two or three the civil service; but most of them were bound for country curacies and country offices. Generally, and for practical purposes, they were 'out of it': they were not the men whose whispers could lead to anything profitable in high quarters. And then, again, even in those days, games were getting important in the creditable schools; and there, young Last was very decidedly out of it. He wore spectacles with lenses divided in some queer manner: his athletic disability was final and complete.

He pondered, and thought at first of setting up a small preparatory school in one of the well-to-do London suburbs; a day-school where parents might have their boys well grounded from the very beginning, for comparatively modest fees, and yet have their upbringing in their own hands. It had often struck Last that it was a barbarous business to send a little chap of seven or eight away from the comfortable, and affectionate habit of his home to a strange place among cold strangers; to bare boards, an inky smell, and grammar on an empty stomach in the morning. But consulting with Jim Newman of his old college, he was warned by that sage to drop his scheme and leave it on the ground. Newman pointed out in the first place that there was no money in teaching unless it was combined with hotel-keeping. That, he said, was all right, and more than all right; and he surmised that many people who kept hotels in the ordinary way would give a good deal to practise their art and mystery under housemaster's rules. 'You needn't pay so very much for your furniture, you know. You don't want to make the boys into young sybarites. Besides, there's nothing a healthy-minded boy hates more than stuffiness: what he likes is clear fresh air and plenty of it. And, you know, old chap, fresh air is cheap enough. And then with the food, there's apt to be trouble in the ordinary hotel if it's uneatable; but in the sort of hotel we're talking of, a little accident with the beef or mutton affords a very valuable opportunity for the exercise of the virtue of self-denial.'

Last listened to all this with a mournful grin.

'You seem to know all about it,' he said. 'Why don't you go in for it yourself?'

'I couldn't keep my tongue in my cheek. Besides, I don't think it's fair sport. I'm going out to India in the autumn. What about pig-sticking?'

'And there's another thing,' he went on after a meditative pause. 'That notion of yours about a day prep school is rotten. The parents wouldn't say thank you for letting them keep their kids at home when they're all small and young. Some people go so far as to say that the chief purpose of schools is to allow parents a good excuse for getting rid of their children. That's nonsense. Most fathers and mothers are very fond of their children and like to have them about the house; when they're young, at all events. But somehow or other, they've got it into their heads that strange schoolmasters know more about bringing up a small boy than his own people; and there it is. So, on all counts, drop that scheme of yours.'

Last thought it over, and looked about him in the scholastic world, and came to the conclusion that Newman was right. For two or three years he took charge of reading parties in the long vacation. In the winter he found occupation in the coaching of backward boys, in preparing boys not so backward for scholarship examinations; and his little text-book, *Beginning Greek*, was found quite useful in lower school. He did pretty well on the whole, though the work began to bore him sadly, and such money as he earned, added to his income, enabled him to live in the way he liked, comfortably enough. He had a couple of rooms in one of the streets going down from the Strand to the river, for which he paid a pound a week, had bread and cheese and odds and ends for lunch, with beer from his own barrel in the cellar, and dined simply but sufficiently now in one, now in another of the snug taverns which then abounded in the quarter. And, now and again, once a month or so, perhaps, instead of the tavern dinners, there was the play at the Vaudeville or the Olympic, the Globe or the Strand, with supper and something hot to follow. The evening might turn into a little party: old Oxford friends would look him up in his rooms between six and seven; Zouch would gather from the Temple and Medwin from Buckingham Street, and possibly Garraway, taking the Yellow Albion bus, would descend from his remote steep in the northern parts of London, would knock at 14, Mowbray Street, and demand pipes, porter, and the pit at a good play. And, on rare occasions, another member of the little society, Noel, would turn up. Noel lived at Turnham Green in a red brick house which was then thought merely old-fashioned, which would now – but it was pulled down long ago – be distinguished as choice Queen Anne or Early Georgian. He lived there with his father, a retired official of the British Museum, and through a man whom he had known at Oxford, he had made some way in literary journalism, contributing regularly to an important weekly paper. Hence the consequence of his occasional descents on Buckingham Street, Mowbray Street, and the Temple. Noel, as in some sort a man of letters, or, at least, a professional journalist, was a member of Blacks' Club, which in those days had exiguous premises in Maiden Lane. Noel would go round the haunts of his friends, and gather them to stout and oysters, and guide them into some neighbouring theatre pit, whence they viewed excellent acting and a cheerful, nonsensical play, enjoyed both, and were ready for supper at the Tavistock. This done, Noel would lead the party to Blacks', where they, very likely, saw some of the actors who had entertained them earlier in the evening, and Noel's friends, the journalists and men of letters, with a painter and a black-and-white man here and there. Here, Last enjoyed himself very much, more especially among the actors, who seemed to him more genial than the literary men. He became especially friendly with one of the players, old Meredith Mandeville, who had talked with the elder Kean, was reliable in the smaller Shakespearean parts, and had engaging tales to tell of early days in county circuits. 'You had nine shillings a week to begin with. When you got to fifteen shillings you gave your landlady eight or nine shillings, and had the rest to play with. You felt a prince. And the county families often used to come and see us in the Green Room: most agreeable.'

With this friendly old gentleman, whose placid and genial serenity was not marred at all by incalculable quantities of gin, Last loved to converse, getting glimpses of a life strangely remote from his own: vagabondage, insecurity, hard times, and jollity; and against it all as a background, the lighted murmur of the stage, voices uttering tremendous things, and the sense of moving in two worlds. The old man, by his own account, had not been eminently prosperous or successful, and yet he had relished his life, and drew humours from its disadvantages, and made hard times seem an adventure. Last used to express his envy of the player's career, dwelling on the dull insignificance of his own labours, which, he said, were a matter of tinkering small boys' brains, teaching older boys the tricks of the examiners, and generally doing things that didn't matter.

'It's no more education than bricklaying is architecture,' he said one night. 'And there's no fun in it.'

Old Mandeville, on his side, listened with interest to these revelations of a world as strange and unknown to him as the life of the floats was to the tutor. Broadly speaking, he knew nothing of any books but play books. He had heard, no doubt, of things called examinations, as most people have heard of Red Indian initiations; but to him one was as remote as the other. It was interesting and strange to him to be sitting at Blacks' and actually talking to a decent young fellow who was seriously engaged in this queer business. And there were – Last noted with amazement – points at which their two circles touched, or so it seemed. The tutor, wishing to be agreeable, began one night to talk about the origins of *King Lear*. The actor found himself listening to Celtic legends which to him sounded incomprehensible nonsense. And when it came to the Knight who fought the King of Fairyland for the hand of Cordelia till Doomsday, he broke in: 'Lear is a pill; there's no doubt of that. You're too young to have seen Barry O'Brien's Lear: magnificent. The part has been attempted since his day. But it has never been played. I have depicted the Fool myself, and, I must say, not without some meed of applause. I remember once at Stafford . . .' and Last was content to let him tell his tale, which ended, oddly enough, with a bullock's heart for supper.

But one night when Last was grumbling, as he often did, about the fragmentary, desultory, and altogether unsatisfactory nature of his occupation, the old man interrupted him in a wholly unexpected vein.

'It is possible,' he began, 'mark you, I say possible, that I may be the means of alleviating the tedium of your lot. I was calling some days ago on a cousin of mine, a Miss Lucy Pilliner, a very agreeable woman. She has a considerable knowledge of the world, and, I hope you will forgive the liberty, but I mentioned in the course of our conversation that I had lately become acquainted with a young gentleman of considerable scholastic distinction, who was somewhat dissatisfied with the too abrupt and frequent entrances and exits of his present tutorial employment. It struck me that my cousin received these remarks with a certain reflective interest, but I was not prepared to receive this letter.'

Mandeville handed Last the letter. It began: 'My dear Ezekiel,' and Last noted out of the corner of his eye a glance from the actor which pleaded for silence and secrecy on this point. The letter went on to say in a manner almost as dignified as Mandeville's that the writer had been thinking over the circumstances of the young tutor, as related by her cousin in the course of their most agreeable conversation of Friday last, and she was inclined to think that she knew of an educational position shortly available in a private family, which would be of a more permanent and satisfactory nature. 'Should your friend feel interested,' Miss Pilliner ended, 'I should be glad if he would communicate with me, with a view to a meeting being arranged, at which the matter could be discussed with more exact particulars.'

'And what do you think of it?' said Mandeville, as Last returned Miss Pilliner's letter.

For a moment Last hesitated. There is an attraction and also a repulsion in the odd and the improbable, and Last doubted whether educational work obtained through an actor at Blacks' and a lady at Islington – he had seen the name at the top of the letter – could be altogether solid or desirable. But brighter thoughts prevailed, and he assured Mandeville that he would be only too glad to go thoroughly into the matter, thanking him very warmly for his interest. The old man nodded benignly, gave him the letter again that he might take down Miss Pilliner's address, and suggested an immediate note asking for an appointment.

'And now,' he said, 'despite the carping objections of the Moody Prince, I propose to drink your jocund health tonight.'

And he wished Last all the good luck in the world with hearty kindliness.

In a couple of days Miss Pilliner presented her compliments to Mr Joseph Last and begged him to do her the favour of calling on her on a date three days ahead, at noon, 'if neither day nor hour were in any way incompatible with his convenience.' They might then, she proceeded, take advantage of the occasion to discuss a certain proposal, the nature of which, she believed, had been indicated to Mr Last by her good cousin, Mr Meredith Mandeville.

Corunna Square, where Miss Pilliner lived, was a small, almost a tiny, square in the remoter parts of Islington. Its two-storied houses of dim, yellowish brick were fairly covered with vines and clematis and all manner of creepers. In front of the houses were small paled gardens, gaily flowering, and the square enclosure held little else besides a venerable, wide-spreading mulberry, far older than the buildings about it. Miss Pilliner lived in the quietest corner of the square. She welcomed Last with some sort of compromise between a bow and a curtsy, and begged him to be seated in an upright armchair, upholstered in horse-hair, Miss

Pilliner, he noted, looked about sixty, and was, perhaps, a little older. She was spare, upright, and composed; and yet one might have suspected a lurking whimsicality. Then, while the weather was discussed, Miss Pilliner offered a choice of port or sherry, sweet biscuits or plum cake. And so to the business of the day.

'My cousin, Mr Mandeville, informed me,' she began, 'of a young friend of great scholastic ability, who was, nevertheless, dissatisfied with the somewhat casual and occasional nature of his employment. By a singular coincidence, I had received a letter a day or two before from a friend of mine, a Mrs Marsh. She is, in fact, a distant connection, some sort of cousin, I suppose, but not being a Highlander or a Welshwoman, I really cannot say how many times removed. She was a lovely creature; she is still a handsome woman. Her name was Manning, Arabella Manning, and what possessed her to marry Mr Marsh I really cannot say. I only saw the man once, and I thought him her inferior in every respect, and considerably older. However, she declares that he is a devoted husband and an excellent person in every respect. They first met, odd as it must seem, in Pekin, where Arabella was governess in one of the legation families. Mr Marsh, I was given to understand, represented highly important commercial interests at the capital of the Flowery Land, and being introduced to my connection, a mutual attraction seems to have followed. Arabella Manning resigned her position in the attaché's family, and the marriage was solemnized in due course. I received this intelligence nine years ago in a letter from Arabella, dated at Pekin, and my relative ended by saying that she feared it would be impossible to furnish an address for an immediate reply, as Mr Marsh was about to set out on a mission of an extremely urgent nature on behalf of his firm, involving a great deal of travelling and frequent changes of address. I suffered a good deal of uneasiness on Arabella's account, it seemed such an unsettled way of life, and so unhomelike. However, a friend of mine who is in the City assured me that there was nothing unusual in the circumstances, and that there was no cause for alarm. Still, as the years went on, and I received no further communication from my cousin, I made up my mind that she had probably contracted some tropical disease which had carried her off, and that Mr Marsh had heartlessly neglected to communicate to me the

intelligence of the sad event. But a month ago, almost to the day –
Miss Pilliner referred to an almanac on the table beside her – I
was astonished and delighted to receive a letter from Arabella.
She wrote from one of the most luxurious and exclusive hotels in
the West End of London, announcing the return of her husband
and herself to their native land after many years of wandering. Mr
Marsh's active concern in business had, it appeared, at length
terminated in a highly prosperous and successful manner, and he
was now in negotiation for the purchase of a small estate in the
country, where he hoped to spend the remainder of his days in
peaceful retirement.'

Miss Pilliner paused and replenished Last's glass.

'I am so sorry,' she continued, 'to trouble you with this long
narrative, which, I am sure, must be a sad trial of your patience.
But, as you will see presently, the circumstances are a little out of
the common, and as you are, I trust, to have a particular interest in
them, I think it is only right that you should be fully informed –
fair and square, and all above board, as my poor father used to say
in his bluff manner.

'Well, Mr Last, I received, as I have said, this letter from
Arabella with its extremely gratifying intelligence. As you may
guess, I was very much relieved to hear that all had turned out so
felicitously. At the end of her letter, Arabella begged me to come
and see them at Billing's Hotel, saying that her husband was most
anxious to have the pleasure of meeting me.'

Miss Pilliner went to a drawer in a writing-table by the window
and took out a letter.

'Arabella was always considerate. She says: 'I know that you
have always lived very quietly, and are not accustomed to the
turmoil of fashionable London. But you need not be alarmed.
Billing's Hotel is no bustling modern caravanserai. Everything is
very quiet, and, besides, we have our own small suite of
apartments. Herbert – her husband, Mr Last – positively insists
on your paying us a visit, and you must not disappoint us. If next
Thursday, the 22nd, suits you, a carriage shall be sent at four
o'clock to bring you to the hotel, and will take you back to
Corunna Square, after you have joined us in a little dinner.'

'Very kind, most considerate; don't you agree with me, Mr
Last? But look at the postscript.'

Last took the letter, and read in a tight, neat script: 'PS. We have a wonderful piece of news for you. It is too good to write, so I shall keep it for our meeting.'

Last handed back Mrs Marsh's letter. Miss Pilliner's long and ceremonious approach was lulling him into a mild stupor; he wondered faintly when she would come to the point, and what the point would be like when she came to it, and, chiefly, what on earth this rather dull family history could have to do with him.

Miss Pilliner proceeded.

'Naturally, I accepted so kindly and urgent an invitation. I was anxious to see Arabella once more after her long absence, and I was glad to have the opportunity of forming my own judgment as to her husband, of whom I knew absolutely nothing. And then, Mr Last, I must confess that I am not deficient in that spirit of curiosity, which gentlemen have scarcely numbered with female virtues. I longed to be made partaker in the wonderful news which Arabella had promised to impart on our meeting, and I wasted many hours in speculating as to its nature.

'The day came. A neat brougham with its attendant footman arrived at the appointed hour, and I was driven in smooth luxury to Billing's Hotel in Manners Street, Mayfair. There a major-domo led the way to the suite of apartments on the first floor occupied by Mr and Mrs Marsh. I will not waste your valuable time, Mr Last, by expiating on the rich but quiet luxury of their apartments; I will merely mention that my relative assured me that the Sèvres ornaments in their drawing-room had been valued at nine hundred guineas. I found Arabella still a beautiful woman, but I could not help seeing that the tropical countries in which she had lived for so many years had taken their toll of her once resplendent beauty; there was a weariness, a lassitude in her appearance and demeanour which I was distressed to observe. As to her husband, Mr Marsh, I am aware that to form an unfavourable judgment after an acquaintance which has only lasted a few hours is both uncharitable and unwise; and I shall not soon forget the discourse which dear Mr Venn delivered at Emmanuel Church on the very Sunday after my visit to my relative: it really seemed, and I confess it with shame, that Mr Venn had my own case in mind, and felt it his bounden duty to warn me while it was yet time. Still, I must say that I did not take at all to Mr Marsh. I really can't say why. To me he was most polite; he could not have been more so. He remarked more than once on the extreme pleasure it gave him to meet at last one of whom he had heard so much from his dear Bella; he trusted that now his wandering days were over, the pleasure might be frequently repeated; he omitted nothing that the most genial courtesy might suggest. And yet, I cannot say that the impression I received was a favourable one. However, I dare say that I was mistaken.'

There was a pause. Last was resigned. The point of the long story seemed to recede into some far distance, into vanishing prospective.

'There was nothing definite?' he suggested.

'No, nothing definite. I may have thought that I detected a lack of candour, a hidden reserve behind all the generosity of Mr Marsh's expressions. Still, I hope I was mistaken.

'But I am forgetting in these trivial and I trust erroneous observations, the sole matter that is of consequence; to you, at least, Mr Last. Soon after my arrival, before Mr Marsh had appeared, Arabella confided to me her great piece of intelligence. Her marriage had been blessed by offspring. Two years after her union with Mr Marsh, a child had been born, a boy. The birth took place at a town in South America, Santiago de Chile – I have verified the place in my atlas – where Mr Marsh's visit had been more protracted than usual. Fortunately, an English doctor was available, and the little fellow throve from the first, and as Arabella, his proud mother, boasted, was now a beautiful little boy, both handsome and intelligent to a remarkable degree. Naturally, I asked to see the child, but Arabella said that he was not in the hotel with them. After a few days it was thought that the dense and humid air of London was not suiting little Henry very well; and he had been sent with a nurse to a resort in the Isle of Thanet, where he was reported to be in the best of health and spirits.

'And now, Mr Last, after this tedious but necessary preamble, we arrive at that point where you, I trust, may be interested. In any case, as you may suppose, the life which the exigencies of business compelled the Marshes to lead, involving as it did almost continual travel, would have been little favourable to a course of systematic education for the child. But this obstacle apart, I gathered that Mr Marsh holds very strong views as to the folly of premature instructions. He declared to me his conviction that many fine minds had been grievously injured by being forced to undergo the process of early stimulation; and he pointed out that, by the nature of the case, those placed in charge of very young children were not persons of the highest acquirements and the keenest intelligence. 'As you will readily agree, Miss Pilliner,' he remarked to me, 'great scholars are not employed to teach infants their alphabet, and it is not likely that the mysteries of the multiplication table will be imparted by a master of mathematics.' In consequence, he urged, the young budding intelligence is brought into contact with dull and inferior minds, and the damage may well be irreparable.'

There was much more, but gradually light began to dawn on the dazed man. Mr Marsh had kept the virgin intelligence of his son Henry undisturbed and uncorrupted by inferior and incompetent culture. The boy, it was judged, was now ripe for true education, and Mr and Mrs Marsh had begged Miss Pilliner to make enquiries, and to find, if she could, a scholar who would undertake the whole charge of little Henry's mental upbringing. If both parties were satisfied, the engagement would be for seven years at least, and the appointments, as Miss Pilliner called the salary, would begin with five hundred pounds a year, rising by an annual increment of fifty pounds. References, particulars of university distinctions would be required: Mr Marsh, long absent from England, was ready to proffer the names of his bankers. Miss Pilliner was quite sure, however, that Mr Last might consider himself engaged, if the position appealed to him.

Last thanked Miss Pilliner profoundly. He told her that he would like a couple of days in which to think the matter over. He would then write to her, and she would put him into communication with Mr Marsh. And so he went away from Corunna Square in a mood of great bewilderment and doubt. Unquestionably, the position had many advantages. The pay was very good. And he would be well lodged and well fed. The people were wealthy, and Miss Pilliner had assured him: 'You will have no cause to complain of your entertainment.' And from the educational point of view, it would certainly be an improvement on the work he had been doing since he left the university. He had been an odd-job man, a tinker, a patcher, a cobbler of other people's work; here was a chance to show that he was a master craftsman. Very few people, if any, in the teaching profession had ever enjoyed such an opportunity as this. Even the sixth-form masters in the big public schools must sometimes groan at having to underpin and relay the bad foundations of the fifth and fourth. He was to begin at the beginning, with no false work to hamper him: 'from A B C to Plato, Æschylus, and Aristotle,' he murmured to himself. Undoubtedly it was a big chance.

And on the other side? Well, he would have to give up London, and he had grown fond of the homely, cheerful London that he knew; his comfortable rooms in Mowbray Street, quiet enough down by the unfrequented Embankment, and yet but a minute or two from the ringing Strand. Then there were the meetings with the old Oxford friends, the nights at the theatre, the snug taverns with their curtained boxes, and their good chops and steaks and stout, and chimes of midnight and after, heard in cordial company at Blacks': all these would have to go. Miss Pilliner had spoken of Mr Marsh as looking for some place a considerable distance from town, 'in the real country.' He had his eye, she said, on a house on the Welsh border, which he thought of taking furnished, with the option of buying, if he eventually found it suited him. You couldn't look up old friends in London and get back the same night, if you lived somewhere on the Welsh border. Still, there would be the holidays, and a great deal might be done in the holidays.

And yet; there was still debate and doubt within his mind, as he sat eating his bread and cheese and potted meat, and drinking his beer in his sitting-room in peaceful Mowbray Street. He was influenced, he thought, by Miss Pilliner's evident dislike of Mr Marsh, and though Miss Pilliner talked in the manner of Dr Johnson, he had a feeling that, like a lady of the Doctor's own day, she had a bottom of good sense. Evidently she did not trust Mr Marsh overmuch. Yet, what can the most cunning swindler do to his resident tutor? Give him cold mutton for dinner or forget to pay his salary? In either case, the remedy was simple: the resident tutor would swiftly cease to reside, and go back to London, and not be much the worse. After all, Last reflected, a man can't compel his son's tutor to invest in Uruguayan silver or Java spices or any other fallacious commercial undertaking, so what mattered the supposed trickiness of Marsh to him?

But again, when all had been summed up and considered, for and against; there was a vague objection remaining. To oppose this, Last could bring no argument, since it was without form of words, shapeless, and mutable as a cloud.

However, when the next morning came, there came with it a couple of letters inviting him to cram two young dunderheads with facts and figures and verbs in *mi*. The prospect was so terribly distasteful that he wrote to Miss Pilliner directly after breakfast, enclosing his college testimonials and certain other commendatory letters he had in his desk. In due course, he had an interview with Mr Marsh at Billing's Hotel. On the whole, each was well enough pleased with the other. Last found Marsh a lean, keen, dark man in later middle age; there was a grizzle in his black hair above the ears, and wrinkles seamed his face about the eyes. His eyebrows were heavy, and there was a hint of a threat in his jaw, but the smile with which he welcomed Last lit up his grimmish features into a genial warmth. There was an oddity about his accent and his tone in speaking, something foreign, perhaps? Last remembered that he had journeyed about the world for many years, and supposed that the echoes of many languages sounded in his speech. His manner and address were certainly suave, but Last had no prejudice against suavity, rather, he cherished a liking for the decencies of common intercourse. Still, no doubt, Marsh was not the kind of man Miss Pilliner was accustomed to meet in Corunna Square society or among Mr Venn's congregation. She probably suspected him of having been a pirate.

And Mr Marsh on his side was delighted with Last. As appeared from a letter addressed by him to Miss Pilliner – 'or, may I venture to say, Cousin Lucy?' – Mr Last was exactly the type of man he and Arabella had hoped to secure through Miss Pilliner's recommendation. They did not want to give their boy into the charge of a flashy man of the world with a substratum of learning. Mr Last was, it was evident, a quiet and unworldly scholar, more at home among books than among men; the very tutor Arabella and himself had desired for their little son. Mr Marsh was profoundly grateful to Miss Pilliner for the great service she had rendered to Arabella, to himself, and to Henry.

And, indeed, as Mr Meredith Mandeville would have said, Last looked the part. No doubt, the spectacles helped to create the remote, retired, Dominie Sampson impression.

In a week's time it was settled, he was to begin his duties. Mr Marsh wrote a handsome cheque, 'to defray any little matters of outfit, travelling expenses, and so forth; nothing to do with your salary.' He was to take a train to a certain large town in the west, and there he would be met and driven to the house, where Mrs Marsh and his pupil were already established – 'beautiful country, Mr Last; I am sure you will appreciate it.'

There was a famous farewell gathering of the old friends. Zouch and Medwin, Garraway and Noel came from near and far. There was grilled sole before the mighty steak, and a roast fowl after it. They had decided that as it was the last time, perhaps, they would not go to the play, but sit and talk about the mahogany. Zouch, who was understood to be the ruler of the feast, had conferred with the head waiter, and when the cloth was removed, a rare and curious port was solemnly set before them. They talked of the old days when they were up at Wells together, pretended – though they knew better – that the undergraduate who had cut his own father in Piccadilly was a friend of theirs, retold jokes that must have been older than the wine, related tales of Moll and Meg, and the famous history of Melcombe, who screwed up the dean in his own rooms. And then there was the affair of the Poses Plastiques. Certain lewd fellows, as one of the dons of Wells College expressed it, had procured scandalous figures from the wax-work booth at the fair, and had disposed of them by night about the fountain in the college garden in such a manner that their scandal was shamefully increased. The perpetrators of this infamy had never been discovered: the five friends looked knowingly at each other, pursed their lips, and passed the port.

The old wine and the old stories blended into a mood of gentle meditation; and then, at the right moment, Noel carried them off to Blacks' and new company. Last sought out old Mandeville and related, with warm gratitude, the happy issue of his intervention.

The chimes sounded, and they all went their several ways.

Though Joseph Last was by no means a miracle of observation and deduction, he was not altogether the simpleton among his books that Mr Marsh had judged him. It was not so very long before a certain uneasiness beset him in his new employment.

At first everything had seemed very well. Mr Marsh had been right in thinking that he would be charmed by the scene in which the White House was set. It stood, terraced on a hill-side, high above a grey and silver river winding in esses through a lonely, lovely valley. Above it, to the east, was a vast and shadowy and ancient wood, climbing to the high ridge of the hill, and descending by height and by depth of green to the level meadows and to the sea. And, standing on the highest point of the wood above the White House, Last looked westward between the boughs and saw the lands across the river, and saw the country rise and fall in billow upon billow to the huge dim wall of the mountain, blue in the distance, and white farms shining in the sun on its vast side. Here was a man in a new world. There had been no such country as this about Dunham in the Midlands, or in the surroundings of Blackheath or Oxford; and he had visited nothing like it on his reading parties. He stood amazed, enchanted under the green shade, beholding a great wonder. Close beside him the well bubbled from the grey rocks, rising out of the heart of the hill.

And in the White House, the conditions of life were altogether pleasant. He had been struck by the dark beauty of Mrs Marsh, who was clearly, as Miss Pilliner had told him, a great many years younger than her husband. And he noted also that effect which her cousin had ascribed to years of living in the tropics, though he would hardly have called it weariness or lassitude. It was something stranger than that; there was the mark of flame upon her, but Last did not know whether it were the flame of the sun, or the stranger fires of places that she had entered, perhaps long ago.

But the pupil, little Henry, was altogether a surprise and a delight. He looked rather older than seven, but Last judged that this impression was not so much due to his height or physical make as to the bright alertness and intelligence of his glance. The tutor had dealt with many little boys, though with none so young as Henry; and he had found them as a whole a stodgy and podgy race, with faces that recorded a fixed abhorrence of learning and a resolution to learn as little as possible. Last was never surprised at this customary expression. It struck him as eminently natural. He knew that all elements are damnably dull and difficult. He wondered why it was inexorably appointed that the unfortunate human creature should pass a great portion of its life from the very beginning in doing things that it detested; but so it was, and now for the syntax of the optative.

But there were no such obstinate entrenchments in the face or the manner of Henry Marsh. He was a handsome boy, who looked brightly and spoke brightly, and evidently did not regard his tutor as a hostile force that had been brought against him. He was what some people would have called, oddly enough, old-fashioned; childlike, but not at all childish, with now and then a whimsical turn of phrase more suggestive of a humorous man than a little boy. This older habit was no doubt to be put down partly to the education of travel, the spectacle of the changing scene and the changing looks of men and things, but very largely to the fact that he had always been with his father and mother, and knew nothing of the company of children of his own age.

'Henry has had no playmates,' his father explained. 'He's had to be content with his mother and myself. It couldn't be helped. We've been on the move all the time; on shipboard or staying at cosmopolitan hotels for a few weeks, and then on the road again. The little chap had no chance of making any small friends.'

And the consequence was, no doubt, that lack of childishness that Last had noted. It was, probably, a pity that it was so. Childishness, after all, was a wonder world, and Henry seemed to know nothing of it: he had lost what might be, perhaps, as valuable as any other part of human experience, and he might find the lack of it as he grew older. Still, there it was; and Last ceased to think of these possibly fanciful deprivations, when he began to teach the boy, as he had promised himself, from the very beginning. Not quite from the beginning; the small boy confessed with a disarming grin that he had taught himself to read a little: 'But please, sir, don't tell my father, as I know he wouldn't like it. You see, my father and mother had to leave me alone sometimes, and it was so dull, and I thought it would be such fun if I learnt to read books all by myself.'

Here, thought Last, is a lesson for schoolmasters. Can learning be made a desirable secret, an excellent sport, instead of a horrible penance? He made a mental note, and set about the work before him. He found an extraordinary aptitude, a quickness in grasping his indications and explanations such as he had never known before – 'not in boys twice his age, or three times his age, for the matter of that,' as he reflected. This child, hardly removed from strict infancy, had something almost akin to genius – so the happy tutor was inclined to believe. Now and again, with his, 'Yes, sir, I see. And then, of course . . .' he would veritably take the coming words out of Last's mouth, and anticipate what was, no doubt, logically the next step in the demonstration. But Last had not been accustomed to pupils who anticipated anything – save the hour for putting the books back on the shelf. And above all, the instructor was captured by the eager and intense curiosity of the instructed. He was like a man reading *The Moonstone*, or some such sensational novel, and unable to put the book down till he had read to the very last page and found out the secret. This small boy brought just this spirit of insatiable curiosity to every subject put before him. 'I wish I had taught him to read,' thought Last to himself. 'I have no doubt he would have regarded the alphabet as we regard those entrancing and mysterious cyphers in Edgar Allan Poe's stories. And, after all, isn't that the right and rational way of looking at the alphabet?'

And then he went on to wonder whether curiosity, often regarded as a failing, almost a vice, is not, in fact, one of the greatest virtues of the spirit of man, the key to all knowledge and all the mysteries, the very sense of the secret that must be discovered.

With one thing and another: with this treasure of a pupil, with the enchantment of the strange and beautiful country about him, and with the extreme kindness and consideration shown him by Mr and Mrs Marsh, Last was in rich clover. He wrote to his friends in town, telling them of his happy experiences, and Zouch and Noel, meeting by chance at the Sun, the Dog, or the Triple Tun, discussed their friend's felicity.

'Proud of the pup,' said Zouch.

'And pleased with the prospect,' responded Noel, thinking of Last's lyrics about the woods and the waters, and the scene of the White House, 'Still, *timeo Hesperides et dona ferentes*. I mistrust the west. As one of its own people said, it is a land of enchantment and illusion. You never know what may happen next. It is a fortunate thing that Shakespeare was born within the safety line. If Stratford had been twenty or thirty miles farther west . . . I don't like to think of it. I am quite sure that only fairy gold is dug from Welsh gold-mines. And you know what happens to that.'

Meanwhile, far from the lamps and rumours of the Strand, Last continued happy in his outland territory, under the great wood. But before long he received a shock. He was strolling in the terraced garden one afternoon between tea and dinner, his work done for the day; and feeling inclined for tobacco with repose, drifted towards the stone summer-house – or, perhaps, gazebo – that stood on the verge of the lawn in a coolness of dark ilex-trees. Here one could sit and look down on the silver winding of the river, crossed by a grey bridge of ancient stone. Last was about to settle down when he noticed a book on the table before him. He took it up, and glanced into it, and drew in his breath, and turning over a few more pages, sank aghast upon the bench. Mr Marsh had always deplored his ignorance of books. 'I knew how to read and write and not much more,' he would say, 'when I was thrown into business – at the bottom of the stairs. And I've been so busy ever since that I'm afraid it's too late now to make up for lost time.' Indeed, Last had noted that though Marsh usually spoke carefully enough, perhaps too carefully, he was apt to lapse in the warmth of conversation: he would talk of 'fax,' meaning 'facts.' And yet, it seemed, he had not only found time for reading, but had acquired sufficient scholarship to make out the Latin of a terrible Renaissance treatise, not generally known even to collectors of such things. Last had heard of the book; and the few pages he had glanced at showed him that it thoroughly deserved its very bad character.

It was a disagreeable surprise. He admitted freely to himself that his employer's morals were no business of his. But why should the man trouble to tell lies? Last remembered queer old Miss Pilliner's account of her impressions of him; she had detected 'a lack of candour', something reserved behind a polite front of cordiality. Miss Pilliner was, certainly, an acute woman: there was an undoubted lack of candour about Marsh.

Last left the wretched volume on the summer-house table, and walked up and down the garden, feeling a good deal perturbed. He knew he was awkward at dinner, and said he felt a bit seedy, inclined to a headache. Marsh was bland and pleasant as usual, and Mrs Marsh sympathized with Last. She had hardly slept at all last night, she complained, and felt heavy and tired. She thought there was thunder in the air. Last, admiring her beauty, confessed again that Miss Pilliner had been right. Apart from her fatigue of the moment, there was a certain tropical languor about her, something of still, burning nights and the odour of strange flowers.

Marsh brought out a very special brandy which he administered with the black coffee; he said it would do both the invalids good, and that he would keep them company. Indeed, Last confessed to himself that he felt considerably more at ease after the good dinner, the good wine, and the rare brandy. It was humiliating, perhaps, but it was impossible to deny the power of the stomach. He went to his room early and tried to convince himself that the duplicity of Marsh was no affair of his. He found an innocent, or almost innocent explanation of it before he had finished his last pipe, sitting at the open window, hearing faintly the wash of the river and gazing towards the dim lands beyond it.

'Here,' he meditated, 'we have a modified form of Bounderby's Disease. Bounderby said that he began life as a wretched, starved, neglected little outcast. Marsh says that he was made into an office boy or something of the sort before he had time to learn anything. Bounderby lied, and no doubt Marsh lies. It is the trick of wealthy men; to magnify their late achievements by magnifying their early disadvantages.'

By the time he went to sleep he had almost decided that the young Marsh had been to a good grammar school, and had done well.

The next morning, Last awoke almost at ease again. It was no doubt a pity that Marsh indulged in a subtle and disingenuous form of boasting, and his taste in books was certainly deplorable: but he must look after that himself. And the boy made amends for all. He showed so clean a grasp of the English sentence, that Last thought he might well begin Latin before very long. He mentioned this one night at dinner, looking at Marsh with a certain humorous intention. But Marsh gave no sign that the dart had pricked him.

'That shows I was right,' he remarked. 'I've always said there's no greater mistake than forcing learning on children before they're fit to take it in. People will do it, and in nine cases out of ten the children's heads are muddled for the rest of their lives. You see how it is with Henry; I've kept him away from books up to now, and you see for yourself that I've lost him no time. He's ripe for learning, and I shouldn't wonder if he got ahead better in six months than the ordinary, early-crammed child would in six years.'

It might be so, Last thought, but on the whole he was inclined to put down the boy's swift progress rather to his own exceptional intelligence than to his father's system, or no system. And in any case, it was a great pleasure to teach such a boy. And his application to his books had certainly no injurious effect on his spirits. There was not much society within easy reach of the White House, and, besides, people did not know whether the Marshes were to settle down or whether they were transient visitors: they were chary of paying their calls while there was this uncertainty. However, the rector had called; first of all the rector and his wife, she cheery, good-humoured and chatty; he somewhat dim and vague. It was understood that the rector, a high wrangler in his day, divided his time between his garden and the invention of a flying machine. He had the character of being slightly eccentric. He came not again, but Mrs Winslow would drive over by the forest road in the governess car with her two children; Nancy, a pretty fair girl of seventeen, and Ted, a boy of eleven or twelve, of that type which Last catalogued as 'stodgy and podgy,' broad and thick set, with bulgy cheeks and eyes, and something of the determined expression of a young bulldog. After tea Nancy would organize games for the two boys in the garden and join in them herself with apparent relish. Henry, who had known few companions besides his parents, and had probably never played a game of any kind, squealed with delight, ran here and there and everywhere, hid behind the summer-house and popped out from the screen of the French beans with the greatest gusto, and Ted Winslow joined in with an air of protest. He was on his holidays, and his expression signified that all that sort of thing was only fit for girls and kids. Last was delighted to see Henry so ready and eager to be amused; after all, he had something of the child in him. He seemed a little uncomfortable when Nancy Winslow took him on her knee after the sports were over; he was evidently fearful of Ted Winslow's scornful eye. Indeed, the young bulldog looked as if he feared that his character would be compromised by associating with so manifest and confessed a kid. The next time Mrs Winslow took tea at the White House, Ted had a diplomatic headache and stayed at home. But Nancy found games that two could play, and she and Henry were heard screaming with joy all over the gardens. Henry wanted to show Nancy a wonderful well that he had discovered in the forest; it came, he said, from under the roots of a great yew-tree. But Mrs Marsh seemed to think that they might get lost.

Last had got over the uncomfortable incident of that villainous book in the summer-house. Writing to Noel, he had remarked that he feared his employer was a bit of an old rascal in some respects, but all right so far as he was concerned; and there it was. He got on with his job and minded his own business. Yet, now and again, his doubtful uneasiness about the man was renewed. There was a bad business at a hamlet a couple of miles away, where a girl of twelve or thirteen, coming home after dusk from a visit to a neighbour, had been set on in the wood and very vilely misused. The unfortunate child, it would appear, had been left by the scoundrel in the black dark of the forest, at some distance from the path she must have taken on her way home. A man who had been drinking late at the Fox and Hounds heard crying and screaming, 'like someone in a fit,' as he expressed it, and found the girl in a terrible state, and in a terrible state she had remained ever since. She was quite unable to describe the person who had so shamefully maltreated her; the shock had left her beside herself; she cried out once that something had come behind her in the dark, but she could say no more, and it was hopeless to try to get her to describe a person that, most likely, she had not even seen. Naturally, this very horrible story made something of a feature in the local paper, and one night, as Last and Marsh were sitting smoking after dinner, the tutor spoke of the affair; said something about the contrast between the peace and beauty and quiet of the scene and the villainous crime that had been done hard by. He was surprised to find that Marsh grew at once ill at ease. He rose from his chair and walked up and down the room, muttering 'horrible business, shameful business'; and when he sat down again, with the light full on him, Last saw the face of a frightened man. The hand that Marsh laid on the table was twitching uneasily; he beat with his foot on the floor as he tried to bring his lips to order, and there was a dreadful fear in his eyes.

Last was shocked and astonished at the effect he had produced with a few conventional phrases. Nervously, willing to tide over a painful situation, he began to utter something even more conventional to the effect that the loveliness of external nature had never conferred immunity from crime, or some stuff to the same inane purpose. But Marsh, it was clear, was not to be soothed by anything of the kind. He started again from his chair and struck his hand upon the table, with a fierce gesture of denial and refusal.

'Please, Mr Last, let it be. Say no more about it. It has upset Mrs Marsh and myself very much indeed. It horrifies us to think that we have brought our boy here, to this peaceful place as we thought, only to expose him to the contagion of this dreadful affair. Of course we have given the servants strict orders not to say a word about it in Henry's presence; but you know what servants are, and what very sharp ears children have. A chance word or two may take root in a child's mind and contaminate his whole nature. It is, really, a very terrible thought. You must have noticed how distressed Mrs Marsh has been for the last few days. The only thing we can do is to try and forget it all, and hope no harm has been done.'

Last murmured a word or two of apology and agreement, and the talk moved off into safer country. But when the tutor was alone, he considered what he had seen and heard very curiously. He thought that Marsh's looks did not match his words. He spoke as the devoted father, afraid that his little boy should overhear nauseous and offensive gossip and conjecture about a horrible and obscene crime. But he looked like a man who had caught sight of a gallows, and that, Last felt, was altogether a very different kind of fear. And, then, there was his reference to his wife. Last had noticed that since the crime in the forest there had been something amiss with her; but, again, he mistrusted Marsh's comment. Here was a woman whose usual habit was a rather lazy good humour; but of late there had been a look and an air of suppressed fury, the burning glance of a jealous woman, the rage of despised beauty. She spoke little, and then as briefly as possible; but one might suspect flames and fires within. Last had seen this and wondered, but not very much, being resolved to mind his own business. He had supposed there had been some difference of opinion between her and her husband; very likely about the rearrangement of the drawing-room furniture and hiring a grand piano. He certainly had not thought of tracing Mrs Marsh's altered air to the villainous crime that had been committed. And now Marsh was telling him that these glances of concealed rage were the outward signs of tender maternal anxiety; and not one word of all that did he believe. He put Marsh's half-hidden terror beside his wife's half-hidden fury; he thought of the book in the summer-house and things that were being whispered about the horror in the wood: and loathing and dread possessed him. He had no proof, it was true; merely conjecture, but he felt no doubt. There could be no other explanation. And what could he do but leave this terrible place?

Last could get no sleep. He undressed and went to bed, and tossed about in the half dark of the summer night. Then he lit his lamp and dressed again, and wondered whether he had better not steal away without a word, and walk the eight miles to the station, and escape by the first train that went to London. It was not merely loathing for the man and his works; it was deadly fear, also, that urged him to fly from the White House. He felt sure that if Marsh guessed at his suspicions of the truth, his life might well be in danger. There was no mercy or scruple in that evil man. He might even now be at his door, listening, waiting. There was cold terror in his heart, and cold sweat pouring at the thoughts. He paced softly up and down his room in his bare feet, pausing now and again to listen for that other soft step outside. He locked the door as silently as he could, and felt safer. He would wait till the day came and people were stirring about the house, and then he might venture to come out and make his escape.

And yet when he heard the servants moving over their work, he hesitated. The light of the sun was shining in the valley, and the white mist over the silver river floated upward and vanished; the sweet breath of the wood entered the window of his room. The black horror and fear were raised from his spirit. He began to hesitate, to suspect his judgment, to inquire whether he had not rushed to his black conclusions in a panic of the night. His logical deductions at midnight seemed to smell of nightmare in the brightness of that valley; the song of the aspiring lark confuted him. He remembered Garraway's great argument after a famous supper at the Turk's Head: that it was always unsafe to make improbability the guide of life. He would delay a little, and keep a sharp look out, and be sure before taking sudden and violent action. And perhaps the truth was that Last was influenced very strongly by his aversion from leaving young Henry, whose extraordinary brilliance and intelligence amazed and delighted him more and more.

It was still early when at last he left his room, and went out into the pure morning air. It was an hour or more before breakfast time, and he set out on the path that led past the wall of the kitchen garden up the hill and into the heart of the wood. He paused a moment at the upper corner, and turned round to look across the river at the happy country showing its morning magic and delight. As he dawdled and gazed, he heard soft steps approaching on the other side of the wall, and low voices murmuring. Then, as the steps drew near, one of the voices was raised a little, and Last heard Mrs Marsh speaking:

'Too old, am I? And thirteen is too young. Is it to be seventeen next when you can get her into the wood? And after all I have done for you, and after what you have done to me.'

Mrs Marsh enumerated all these things without remission, and without any quiver of shame in her voice. She paused for a moment. Perhaps her rage was choking her; and there was a shrill piping cackle of derision, as if Marsh's voice had cracked in its contempt.

Very softly, but very swiftly, Last, the man with the grey face and the staring eyes, bolted for his life, down and away from the White House. Once in the road, free from the fields and brakes, he changed his run into a walk, and he never paused or stopped, till he came with a gulp of relief into the ugly streets of the big industrial town. He made his way to the station at once, and found that he was an hour too soon for the London express. So there was plenty of time for breakfast; which consisted of brandy.

The tutor went back to his old life and his old ways, and did his best to forget the strange and horrible interlude of the White House. He gathered his podgy pups once more about him; crammed and coached, read with undergraduates during the long vacation, and was moderately satisfied with the course of things in general. Now and then, when he was endeavouring to persuade the podges against their deliberate judgment that Latin and Greek were languages once spoken by human beings, not senseless enigmas invented by demons, he would think with a sigh of regret of the boy who understood and longed to understand. And he wondered whether he had not been a coward to leave that enchanting child to the evil mercies of his hideous parents. But what could he have done? But it was dreadful to think of Henry, slowly or swiftly corrupted by his detestable father and mother, growing up with the fat slime of their abominations upon him.

He went into no detail with his old friends. He hinted that there had been grave unpleasantness, which made it impossible for him to remain in the west. They nodded, and perceiving that the subject was a sore one, asked no questions, and talked of old books and the new steak instead. They all agreed, in fact, that the steak was far too new, and William was summoned to explain this horror. Didn't he know that beefsteak, beefsteak meant for the consumption of Christian men, as distinguished from Hottentots, required hanging just as much as game? William, the ponderous and benignant, tasted and tested, and agreed; with sorrowful regret. He apologized, and went on to say that as the gentlemen would not care to wait for a fowl, he would suggest a very special, tender, and juicy fillet of roast veal, then in cut. The suggestion was accepted, and found excellent. The conversation turned to Choric metres and Florence St. John at the Strand. There was port later.

It was many years afterwards, when this old life, after crumbling for a long while, had come down with a final crash, that Last heard the real story of his tutorial engagement at the White House. Three dreadful people were put in the dock at the Old Bailey. There was an old man, with the look of a deadly snake; a fat, sloppy, deplorable woman with pendulous cheeks and a faint hint of perished beauty in her eyes; and to the utter blank amazement of those who did not know the story, a wonderful little boy. The people who saw him in court said he might have been taken for a child of nine or ten; no more. But the evidence that was given showed that he must be between fifty and sixty at the least; perhaps more than that.

The indictment charged these three people with an unspeakable and hideous crime. They were charged under the name of Mailey, the name which they had borne at the time of their arrest; but it turned out at the end of the trial that they had been known by many names in the course of their career: Mailey, Despasse, Lartigan, Delarue, Falcon, Lecossic, Hammond, Marsh, Haringworth. It was established that the apparent boy, whom Last had known as Henry Marsh, was no relation of any kind to the elder prisoners. 'Henry's' origins were deeply obscure. It was conjectured that he was the illegitimate son of a very high Englishman, a diplomatist whose influence had counted for a great deal in the Far East. Nobody knew anything about the mother. The boy showed brilliant promise from very early years, and the father, a bachelor, and disliking what little he knew of his relations, left his very large fortune to his son. The diplomatist died when the boy was twelve years old; and he had been aged, and more than aged when the child was born. People remarked that Arthur Wesley, as he was then called, was very short for his years, and he remained short, and his face remained that of a boy of seven or eight. He could not be sent to a school, so he was privately educated. When he was of age, the trustees had the extraordinary experience of placing a very considerable property in the hands of a young man who looked like a little boy. Very soon afterwards, Arthur Wesley disappeared. Dubious rumours spoke of reappearances, now here, now there, in all quarters of the world. There were tales that he had 'gone fantee' in what was then unknown Africa, when the Mountains of the Moon still lingered on the older maps. It was reported, again, that he had gone exploring in the higher waters of the Amazon, and had never come back; but a few years later a personage that must have been Arthur Wesley was displaying unpleasant activities in Macao. It was soon after this period, according to the prosecution, that – in the words of counsel – he realized the necessity of 'taking cover.' His extraordinary personality, naturally enough, drew attention to him and his doings, and these doings being generally or always of an infamous kind, such attention was both inconvenient and dangerous. Somewhere in the East, and in very bad company, he came upon the two people who were charged with him. Arabella Manning, who was said to have respectable connections in Wiltshire, had gone out to the East as a governess, but had soon found other occupations. Meers had been a clerk in a house of business at Shanghai. His very ingenious system of fraud obtained his discharge, but, for some reason or other, the firm refused to prosecute, and Meers went – where Arthur Wesley found him. Wesley thought of his great plan. Manning and Meers were to pretend to be Mr and Mrs Marsh – that seemed to have been their original style – and he was to be their little boy. He paid them well for their various services: Arabella was his mistress-in-chief, the companion of his milder moments, for some years. Occasionally, a tutor was engaged to make the situation more plausible. In this state, the horrible trio peregrinated over the earth.

The court heard all this, and much more, after the jury had found the three prisoners guilty of the particular offence with which they were charged. This last crime – which the press had to enfold in paraphrase and periphrase – had been discovered, strange as it seemed, largely as a result of the woman's jealousy. Wesley's – affections, let us call them, were still apt to wander, and Arabella's jealous rage drove her beyond all caution and all control. She was the weak joint in Wesley's armour, the rent in his cover. People in court looked at the two; the debauched, deplorable woman with her flagging, sagging cheeks, and the dim fire still burning in her weary old eyes, and at Wesley, still, to all appearance, a bright and handsome little boy; they gasped with amazement at the grotesque, impossible horror of the scene. The judge raised his head from his notes and gazed steadily at the convicted persons for some moments; his lips were tightly compressed.

The detective drew to the end of his portentous history. The track of these people, he said, had been marked by many terrible scandals, but till quite lately there had been no suspicion of their guilt. Two of these cases involved the capital charge, but formal evidence was lacking.

He drew to his close.

'In spite of his diminutive stature and juvenile appearance, the prisoner, Charles Mailey, *alias* Arthur Wesley, made a desperate resistance to his arrest. He is possessed of immense strength for his size, and almost choked one of the officers who arrested him.'

The formulas of the court were uttered. The judge, without a word of comment, sentenced Maily, or Wesley, to imprisonment for life, John Meers to fifteen years' imprisonment, Arabella Manning to ten years' imprisonment.

The old world, it has been noted, had crashed down. Many, many years had passed since Last had been hunted out of Mowbray Street, that went down dingily, peacefully from the Strand. Mowbray Street was now all blazing office buildings. Later, he had been driven from one nook and corner and snug retreat after another as new London rose in majesty and splendour. But for a year or more he had lain hidden in a by-street that had the advantage of leading into a disused graveyard near the Gray's Inn Road. Medwin and Garraway were dead; but Last summoned the surviving Zouch and Noel to his abode one night; and then and there made punch, and good punch for them.

'It's so jolly it must be sinful,' he said, as he pared his lemons, 'but up to the present I believe it is not illegal. And I still have a few bottles of that port I bought in ninety-two.'

And then he told them for the first time the whole story of his engagement at the White House.

BUT AT MY BACK I ALWAYS HEAR

David Morrell

She phoned again last night. At 3 A.M. the way she always does. I'm scared to death. I can't keep running. On the hotel's register downstairs, I lied about my name, address, and occupation, hoping to hide from her. My real name's Charles Ingram. Though I'm here in Johnstown, Pennsylvania, I'm from Iowa City, Iowa. I teach – or used to teach until three days ago – creative writing at the University. I can't risk going back there. But I don't think I can hide much longer. Each night, she comes closer.

From the start, she scared me. I came to school at eight to prepare my classes. Through the side door of the English building I went up a stairwell to my third-floor office, which was isolated by a fire door from all the other offices. My colleagues used to joke that I'd been banished, but I didn't care, for in my far-off corner I could concentrate. Few students interrupted me. Regardless of the busy noises past the fire door, I sometimes felt there was no one else inside the building. And indeed at 8 A.M. I often *was* the only person in the building.

That day I was wrong, however. Clutching my heavy briefcase, I trudged up the stairwell. My scraping footsteps echoed off the walls of pale-red cinderblock, the stairs of pale-green imitation marble. First floor. Second floor. The neon lights glowed coldly. Then the stairwell angled toward the third floor, and I saw her waiting on a chair outside my office. Pausing, I frowned up at her. I felt uneasy.

Eight A.M. for you, is probably not early. You've been up for quite a while so you can get to work on time or get your children off to school. But 8 A.M., for college students, is the middle of the night. They don't like morning classes. When their schedules force them to attend one, they don't crawl from bed until they absolutely have to, and they don't come stumbling into class until I'm just about to start my lecture.

I felt startled, then, to find her waiting ninety minutes early. She sat tensely: lifeless dull brown hair, a shapeless dingy sweater, baggy faded jeans with patches on the knees and frays around the cuffs. Her eyes seemed haunted, wild, and deep and dark.

I climbed the last few steps and, puzzled, stopped before her. 'Do you want an early conference?'

Instead of answering, she nodded bleakly.

'You're concerned about a grade I gave you?'

This time, though, in pain she shook her head from side to side. Confused, I fumbled with my key and opened the office, stepping in. The room was small and narrow: a desk, two chairs, a wall of bookshelves, and a window. As I sat behind the desk, I watched her slowly come inside. She glanced around uncertainly. Distraught, she shut the door.

That made me nervous. When a female student shuts the door, I start to worry that a colleague or a student might walk up the stairs and hear a female voice and wonder what's so private I want to keep the door closed. Though I should have told her to reopen it, her frantic eyes aroused such pity in me that I sacrificed my principle, deciding her torment was so personal she could talk about it only in strict secrecy.

'Sit down.' I smiled and tried to make her feel at ease, though I myself was not at ease. 'What seems to be the difficulty, Miss. . . ? I'm sorry, but I don't recall your name.'

'Samantha Perry. I don't like "Samantha" though.' She fidgeted. 'I've shortened it to – '

'Yes? To what?'

'To "Sam". I'm in your Tuesday-Thursday class.' She bit her lip. 'You spoke to me.'

I frowned, not understanding. 'You mean what I taught seemed vivid to you? I inspired you to write a better story?'

'Mr Ingram, no. I mean you *spoke* to me. You stared at me while you were teaching. You ignored the other students. You directed what you said to *me*. When you talked about Hemingway, how Frederic Henry wants to go to bed with Catherine – ' She swallowed. ' – you were asking me to go to bed with you.'

I gaped. To disguise my shock, I quickly lit a cigarette. 'You're mistaken.'

'But I *heard* you. You kept staring straight at *me*. I felt all the other students knew what you were doing.'

'I was only lecturing. I often look at students' faces to make sure they pay attention. You received the wrong impression.'

'You weren't asking me to go to bed with you?' Her voice sounded anguished.

'No. I don't trade sex for grades.'

'But I don't care about a grade!'

'I'm married. Happily. I've got two children. Anyway, suppose I did intend to proposition you. Would I do it in the middle of a class? I'd be foolish.'

'Then you never meant to – ' She kept biting her lip.

'I'm sorry.'

'But you speak to me! Outside class I hear your voice! When I'm in my room or walking down the street! You talk to me when I'm asleep! You say you want to go to bed with me!'

My skin prickled. I felt frozen. 'You're mistaken. Your imagination's playing tricks.'

'But I hear your voice so clearly! When I'm studying or – '

'How? If I'm not there.'

'You send your thoughts! You concentrate and put your voice inside my mind!'

Adrenaline scalded my stomach. I frantically sought an argument to disillusion her. 'Telepathy? I don't believe in it. I've never tried to send my thoughts to you.'

'Unconsciously?'

I shook my head from side to side. I couldn't bring myself to tell her: of all the female students in her class, she looked so plain, even if I wasn't married I'd never have wanted sex with her.

'You're studying too hard. You want to do so well you're preoccupied with me. That's why you think you hear my voice when I'm not there. I try to make my lectures vivid. As a consequence, you think I'm speaking totally to you.'

'Then you shouldn't teach that way!' she shouted. 'It's not fair! It's cruel! It's teasing!' Tears streamed down her face. 'You made a fool of me!'

'I didn't mean to.'

'But you did! You tricked me! You misled me!'

'No.'

She stood so quickly I flinched, afraid she'd lunge at me or scream for help and claim I'd tried to rape her. That damned door. I cursed myself for not insisting she leave it open.

She rushed sobbing toward it. She pawed the knob and stumbled out, hysterically retreating down the stairwell.

Shaken, I stubbed out my cigarette, grabbing another. My chest tightened as I heard the dwindling echo of her wracking sobs, the awkward scuffle of her dimming footsteps, then the low deep rumble of the outside door.

The silence settled over me.

An hour later I found her waiting in class. She'd wiped her tears. The only signs of what had happened were her red and puffy eyes. She sat alertly, pen to paper. I carefully didn't face her as I spoke. She seldom glanced up from her notes.

After class I asked my graduate assistant if he knew her.

'You mean Sam? Sure, I know her. She's been getting Ds. She had a conference with me. Instead of asking how to get a better grade, though, all she did was talk about you, pumping me for information. She's got quite a thing for you. Too bad about her.'

'Why?'

'Well, she's so plain, she doesn't have many friends. I doubt she goes out much. There's a problem with her father. She was vague about it, but I had the sense her three sisters are so beautiful that Daddy treats her as the ugly duckling. She wants very much to please him. He ignores her, though. He's practically disowned her. You remind her of him.'

'Who? Of her father?'

'She admits you're ten years younger than him, but she says you look exactly like him.'

I felt heartsick.

Two days later I found her waiting for me – again at 8 A.M. – outside my office.

Tense, I unlocked the door. As if she heard my thought, she didn't shut it this time. Sitting before my desk, she didn't fidget. She just stared at me.

'It happened again,' she said.

'In class I didn't even look at you.'

'No, afterward, when I went to the library.' She drew an anguished breath. 'And later – I ate supper in the dorm. I heard your voice so clearly, I was sure you were in the room.'

'What time was that?'

'Five-thirty.'

'I was having cocktails with the Dean. Believe me, Sam, I wasn't sending messages to you. I didn't even *think* of you.'

'I couldn't have imagined it! You wanted me to go to bed with you!'

'I wanted research money from the Dean. I thought of nothing else. My mind was totally involved in trying to convince him. When I didn't get the money, I was too annoyed to concentrate on anything but getting drunk.'

'Your voice – '

'It isn't real. If I sent thoughts to you, wouldn't I admit what I was doing? When you asked me, wouldn't I confirm the message? Why would I deny it?'

'I'm afraid.'

'You're troubled by your father.'

'*What?*'

'My graduate assistant says you identify me with your father.' She went ashen. 'That's supposed to be a secret!'

'Sam, I asked him. He won't lie to me.'

'If you remind me of my father, if I want to go to bed with you, then I must want to go to bed with – '

'Sam – '

' – my father! You must think I'm disgusting!'

'No, I think you're confused. You ought to find some help. You ought to see a – '

But she never let me finish. Weeping again, ashamed, hysterical, she bolted from the room.

And that's the last I ever saw of her. An hour later, when I started lecturing, she wasn't in class. A few days later I received a drop-slip from the registrar, informing me she'd cancelled all her classes.

I forgot her.

Summer came. Then fall arrived. November. On a rainy Tuesday night, my wife and I stayed up to watch the close results of the election, worried for our presidential candidate.

At 3 A.M. the phone rang. No one calls that late unless . . .

The jangle of the phone made me bang my head as I searched for a beer in the fridge. I rubbed my throbbing skull and swung alarmed as Jean, my wife, came from the living room and squinted toward the kitchen phone.

'It might be just a friend,' I said. 'Election gossip.'

But I worried about our parents. Maybe one of them was sick or . . .

I watched uneasily as Jean picked up the phone.

'Hello?' She listened apprehensively. Frowning, she put her hand across the mouthpiece. 'It's for you. A woman.'

'What?'

'She's young. She asked for Mr Ingram.'

'Damn, a student.'

'At 3 A.M.?'

I almost didn't think to shut the fridge. Annoyed, I yanked the pop-tab off the can of beer. My marriage is successful. I'll admit we've had our troubles. So has every couple. But we've faced those troubles, and we're happy. Jean is thirty-five, attractive, smart, and patient. But her trust in me was clearly tested at that moment. A woman had to know me awfully well to call at 3 A.M..

'Let's find out.' I grabbed the phone. To prove my innocence to Jean, I roughly said, 'Yeah, what?'

'I heard you.' The female voice was frail and plaintive, trembling.

'Who *is* this?' I said angrily.

'It's me.'

I heard a low-pitched crackle on the line.

'Who the hell is *me*? Just tell me what your name is.'

'Sam.'

My knees went weak. I slumped against the wall.

Jean stared. 'What's wrong?' Her eyes narrowed with suspicion.

'Sam, it's 3 A.M.. What's so damn important you can't wait to call me during office hours?'

'Three? It can't be. No, it's one.'

'It's three. For God sake, Sam, I know what time it is.'

'Please, don't get angry. On my radio the news announcer said it was one o'clock.'

'Where *are* you, Sam?'

'At Berkeley.'

'California? Sam, the time-zone difference. In the Midwest it's two hours later. Here it's three o'clock.'

'. . . I guess I just forgot.'

'But that's absurd. Have you been drinking? Are you drunk?'

'No, not exactly.'

'What the hell does *that* mean?'

'Well, I took some pills. I'm not sure what they were.'

'Oh, Jesus.'

'Then I heard you. You were speaking to me.'

'No, I told you your mind's playing tricks. The voice isn't real. You're imagining – '

'You called to me. You said you wanted me to go to bed with you. You wanted me to come to you.'

'To Iowa? No. You've got to understand. Don't do it. I'm not sending thoughts to you.'

'You're lying! Tell me why you're lying!'

'I don't want to go to bed with you. I'm glad you're in Berkeley. Stay there. Get some help. Lord, don't you realize? Those pills. They make you hear my voice. They make you hallucinate.'

'I . . .'

'Trust me, Sam. Believe me. I'm not sending thoughts to you. I didn't even know you'd gone to Berkeley. You're two thousand miles away from me. What you're suggesting is impossible.'

She didn't answer. All I heard was low-pitched static.

'Sam – '

The dial tone abruptly droned. My stomach sank. Appalled, I kept the phone against my ear. I swallowed dryly, shaking as I set the phone back on its cradle.

Jean glared. 'Who was that? She wasn't any "Sam". She wants to go to bed with you? At 3 A.M.? What games have you been playing?'

'None.' I gulped my beer, but my throat stayed dry. 'You'd better sit. I'll get a beer for you.'

Jean clutched her stomach.

'It's not what you think. I promise I'm not screwing anybody. But it's bad. I'm scared.'

I handed Jean a beer.

'I don't know why it happened. But last spring, at 8 A.M., I went to school and . . .'

Jean listened, troubled. Afterward she asked for Sam's description, somewhat mollified to learn she was plain and pitiful.

'The truth?' Jean asked.

'I promise you.'

Jean studied me. 'You did nothing to encourage her?'

'I guarantee it. I wasn't aware of her until I found her waiting for me.'

'But unconsciously!'

'Sam asked me that as well. I was only lecturing the best way I know how.'

Jean kept her eyes on me. She nodded, glancing toward her beer. 'Then she's disturbed. There's nothing you can do for her. I'm glad she moved to Berkeley. In your place, I'd have been afraid.'

'I *am* afraid. She spooks me.'

At a dinner party the next Saturday, I told our host and hostess what had happened, motivated more than just by need to share my fear with someone else, for while the host was both a friend and colleague, he was married to a clinical psychologist. I needed professional advice.

Diane, the hostess, listened with slim interest until halfway through my story, when she suddenly sat straight and peered at me.

I faltered. 'What's the matter?'

'Don't stop. What else?'

I frowned and finished, waiting for Diane's reaction. Instead she poured more wine. She offered more lasagna.

'Something bothered you.'

She tucked her long black hair behind her ears. 'It could be nothing.'

'I need to know.'

She nodded grimly. 'I can't make a diagnosis merely on the basis of your story. I'd be irresponsible.'

'But hypothetically . . .'

'And *only* hypothetically. She hears your voice. That's symptomatic of a severe disturbance. Paranoia, for example. Schizophrenia. The man who shot John Lennon heard a voice. And so did Manson. So did Son of Sam.'

'My God,' Jean said. 'Her name.' She set her fork down loudly.

'The parallel occurred to me,' Diane said. 'Chuck, if she identifies you with her father, she might be dangerous to Jean and to the children.'

'Why?'

'Jealousy. To hurt the equivalent of her mother and her rival sisters.'

I felt sick; the wine turned sour in my stomach.

'There's another possibility. No more encouraging. If you continue to reject her, she could be dangerous to you. Instead of dealing with her father, she might redirect her rage and jealousy toward you. By killing you, she'd be venting her frustration toward her father.'

I felt panicked. 'For the *good* news?'

'Understand, I'm speaking hypothetically. Possibly she's lying to you, and she doesn't hear your voice. Or, as you guessed, the drugs she takes might make her hallucinate. There could be many explanations. Without seeing her, without the proper tests, I wouldn't dare to judge her symptoms. You're a friend, so I'm compromising. Possibly she's homicidal.'

'Tell me what to do.'

'For openers, I'd stay away from her.'

'I'm, *trying*. She called from California. She's threatening to come back here to see me.'

'Talk her out of it.'

'I'm no psychologist. I don't know what to say to her.'

'Suggest she get professional advice.'

'I tried that.'

'Try again. But if you find her at your office, don't go in the room with her. Find other people. Crowds protect you.'

'But at 8 A.M. there's no one in the building.'

'Think of some excuse to leave her. Jean, if she comes to the house, don't let her in.'

Jean paled. 'I've never seen her. How could I identify her?'

'Chuck described her. Don't take chances. Don't trust anyone who might resemble her, and keep a close watch on the children.'

'*How?* Rebecca's twelve. Sue's nine. I can't insist they stay around the house.'

Diane turned her wine glass, saying nothing.

'. . . Oh, dear Lord,' Jean said.

The next few weeks were hellish. Every time the phone rang, Jean and I jerked, startled, staring at it. But the calls were from our friends or from our children's friends or from some insulation/magazine/home-siding salesman. Every day I mustered courage as I climbed the stairwell to my office. Silent prayers were answered. Sam was never there. My tension dissipated. I began to feel she no longer was obsessed with me.

Thanksgiving came – the last day of peace I've known. We went to church. Our parents live too far away for us to share the feast with them. But we invited friends to dinner. We watched football. I helped Jean make the dressing for the turkey. I made both the pumpkin pies. The friends we'd invited were my colleague and his wife, the clinical psychologist. She asked if my student had continued to harass me. Shaking my head from side to side, I grinned and raised my glass in special thanks.

The guests stayed late to watch a movie with us. Jean and I felt pleasantly exhausted, mellowed by good food, good drink, good friends, when after midnight we washed all the dishes, went to bed, made love, and drifted wearily to sleep.

The phone rang, shocking me awake. I fumbled toward the bedside lamp. Jean's eyes went wide with fright. She clutched my arm and pointed toward the clock. It was 3 A.M.

The phone kept ringing.

'Don't,' Jean said.

'Suppose it's someone else.'

'You know it isn't.'

'If it's Sam and I don't answer, she might come to the house instead of phoning.'

'For God's sake, make her stop.'

I grabbed the phone, but my throat wouldn't work.

'I'm coming to you,' the voice wailed.

'Sam?'

'I heard you. I won't disappoint you. I'll be there soon.'

'No. Wait. Listen.'

'I've been listening. I hear you all the time. The anguish in your voice. You're begging me to come to you, to hold you, to make love to you.'

'That isn't true.'

'You say your wife's jealous of me. I'll convince her she isn't being fair. I'll make her let you go. Then we'll be happy.'

'Sam, where are you? Still in Berkeley?'

'Yes. I spent Thanksgiving by myself. My father didn't want me to come home.'

'You have to stay there, Sam. I didn't send my voice. You need advice. You need to see a doctor. Will you do that for me? As a favour?'

'I already did. But Dr Campbell doesn't understand. He thinks I'm imagining what I hear. He humours me. He doesn't realize how much you love me.'

'Sam, you have to talk to him again. You have to tell him what you plan to do.'

'I can't wait any longer. I'll be there soon. I'll be with you.'

My heart pounded frantically. I heard a roar in my head. I flinched as the phone was yanked away from me.

Jean shouted to the mouthpiece, 'Stay away from us! Don't call again! Stop terrorizing – '

Jean stared wildly at me. 'No one's there. The line went dead. I hear just the dial tone.'

I'm writing this as quickly as I can. I don't have much more time. It's almost three o'clock.

That night, we didn't try to go back to sleep. We couldn't. We got dressed and went downstairs where, drinking coffee, we decided what to do. At eight, as soon as we'd sent the kids to school, we drove to the police.

They listened sympathetically, but there was no way they could help us. After all, Sam hadn't broken any law. Her calls weren't obscene; it was difficult to prove harassment; she'd made no overt threats. Unless she harmed us, there was nothing the police could do.

'Protect us,' I insisted.

'How?' the sergeant said.

'Assign an officer to guard the house.'

'How long? A day, a week, a month? That woman might not even bother you again. We're overworked and understaffed. I'm sorry – I can't spare an officer whose only duty is to watch you. I can send a car to check the house from time to time. No more than that. But if this woman does show up and bother you, then call us. We'll take care of her.'

'But that might be too late.'

We took the children home from school. Sam couldn't have arrived from California yet, but what else could we do? I don't own any guns. If all of us stayed together, we had some chance for protection.

That was Friday. I slept lightly. Three A.M., the phone rang. It was Sam, of course.

'I'm coming.'

'Sam, where are you?'

'Reno.'

'You're not flying?'

'No, I can't.'

'Turn back, Sam. Go to Berkeley. See that doctor.'

'I can't wait to see you.'

'Please – '

The dial tone was droning.

I phoned Berkeley information. Sam had mentioned Dr Campbell. But the operator couldn't find him in the yellow pages.

'Try the University,' I blurted. 'Student Counselling.'

I was right. A Dr Campbell was a university psychiatrist. On Saturday I couldn't reach him at his office, but a woman answered at his home. He wouldn't be available until the afternoon. At four o'clock I finally got through to him.

'You've got a patient named Samantha Perry,' I began.

'I did. Not anymore.'

'I know. She's left for Iowa. She wants to see me. I'm afraid. I think she might be dangerous.'

'Well, you don't have to worry.'

'She's not dangerous?'

'Potentially she was.'

'But tell me what to do when she arrives. You're treating her. You'll know what I should do.'

'No, Mr Ingram, she won't come to see you. On Thanksgiving night, at 1 A.M., she killed herself. An overdose of drugs.'

My vision failed. I clutched the kitchen table to prevent myself from falling. 'That's impossible.'

'I saw the body. I identified it.'

'But she called that night.'

'What time?'

'At 3 A.M. Midwestern time.'

'Or one o'clock in California. No doubt after or before she took the drugs. She didn't leave a note, but she called you.'

'She gave no indication – '

'She mentioned you quite often. She was morbidly attracted to you. She had an extreme, unhealthy certainty that she was telepathic, that you put your voice inside her mind.'

'I know that! Was she paranoid or homicidal?'

'Mr Ingram, I've already said too much. Although she's dead, I can't violate her confidence.'

'But I don't think she's dead.'

'I beg your pardon?'

'If she died on Thursday night, then tell me how she called again on *Friday* night.'

The line hummed. I sensed the doctor's hesitation. 'Mr Ingram, you're upset. You don't know what you're saying. You've confused the nights.'

'I'm telling you she called again on Friday!'

'And I'm telling you she died on *Thursday*. Either someone's tricking you, or else . . .' The doctor swallowed with discomfort.

'Or?' I trembled. '*I'm* the one who's hearing voices?'

'Mr Ingram, don't upset yourself. You're honestly confused.'

I slowly put the phone down, terrified. 'I'm sure I heard her voice.'

That night, Sam called again. At 3 A.M. From Salt Lake City. When I handed Jean the phone, she heard just the dial tone.

'But you know the goddamn phone rang!' I insisted.

'Maybe a short circuit. Chuck, I'm telling you there was no one on the line.'

Then Sunday. Three A.M. Cheyenne, Wyoming. Coming closer.

But she couldn't be if she was dead.

The student paper at the University subscribes to all the other major student papers. Monday, Jean and I left the children with friends and drove to its office. Friday's copy of the Berkeley campus paper had arrived. In desperation I searched its pages. 'There!' A two-inch item. Sudden student death. Samantha Perry. Tactfully, no cause was given.

Outside in the parking lot, Jean said, 'Now do you believe she's dead?'

'Then tell me why I hear her voice! I've got to be crazy if I think I hear a corpse!'

'You're feeling guilty that she killed herself because of you. You shouldn't. There was nothing you could do to stop her. You've been losing too much sleep. Your imagination's taking over.'

'You admit you heard the phone ring!'

'Yes, it's true. I can't explain that. If the phone's broken, we'll have it fixed. To put your mind at rest, we'll get a new, unlisted number.'

I felt better. After several drinks, I even got some sleep.

But Monday night, again the phone rang. Three A.M. I jerked awake. Cringing, I insisted Jean answer it. But she heard just the dial tone. I grabbed the phone. Of course, I heard Sam's voice.

'I'm almost there. I'll hurry. I'm in Omaha.'

'This number isn't listed!'

'But you told me the new one. Your wife's the one who changed it. She's trying to keep us apart. I'll make her sorry. Darling, I can't wait to be with you.'

I screamed. Jean jerked away from me.

'Sam, you've got to stop! I spoke to Dr Campbell!'

'No. He wouldn't dare. He wouldn't violate my trust.'

'He said you were dead!'

'I couldn't live without you. Soon we'll be together.'

Shrieking, I woke the children, so hysterical Jean had to call an ambulance. Two interns struggled to sedate me.

Omaha was one day's drive from where we lived. Jean came to visit me in the hospital on Tuesday.

'Are you feeling better?' Jean frowned, troubled.

'Please, you have to humour me,' I said. 'All right? Suspect I've gone crazy, but for God sake, humour me. I can't prove what I'm thinking, but I know you're in danger. I am too. You have to get the children and leave town. You have to hide somewhere. Tonight at 3 A.M. she'll reach the house.'

Jean stared with pity.

'Promise me!' I said.

She saw the anguish on my face and nodded.

'Maybe she won't try the house,' I said. 'She might come here. I have to get away. I'm not sure how, but later, when you're gone. I'll find a way to leave.'

Jean peered at me, distressed; her voice sounded totally discouraged. 'Chuck.'

'I'll check the house when I get out of here. If you're still there, you know you'll make me more upset.'

'I promise. I'll take Susan and Rebecca, and we'll drive somewhere.'

'I love you.'

Jean began to cry. 'I won't know where you are.'

'If I survive this, I'll get word to you.'

'But how?'

'The English department. I'll leave a message with the secretary.'

Jean leaned down to kiss me, crying, certain I'd lost my mind.

I reached the house that night. As she'd promised, Jean had left with the children. I got in my sports car and raced to the Interstate.

A Chicago hotel where at 3 A.M. Sam called from Iowa. She'd

heard my voice. She said I'd told her where I was, but she was hurt and angry. 'Tell me why you're running.'

I fled from Chicago in the middle of the night, driving until I absolutely had to rest. I checked in here at 1 A.M. In Johnstown, Pennsylvania. I can't sleep. I've got an awful feeling. Last night Sam repeated, 'Soon you'll join me.' In the desk I found this stationery.

God it's 3 A.M. I pray I'll see the sun come up.

It's almost four. She didn't phone. I can't believe I escaped, but I keep staring at the phone.

It's four. Dear Christ, I hear the ringing.

Finally I've realized. Sam killed herself at one. In Iowa the time-zone difference made it three. But I'm in Pennsylvania. In the East. A different time zone. One o'clock in California would be *four* o'clock, not three, in Pennsylvania.

Now.

The ringing persists. But I've realized something else. This hotel's unusual, designed to seem like a home.

The ringing?

God help me, it's the doorbell.

A WEIRD DAY FOR AGRO

J. Yen

Someone nudged my elbow. I turned to see the short figure of Agro, a half-pint of lager already in his hand.

'All right, John?' he greeted me, sipping his drink and grinning. He glanced furtively round the slowly filling bar. 'Oy,' he began excitedly, 'it was really weird today, right.'

Then he suddenly paused, pensive and doubtful.

'What was?'

'Aw,' he said, shaking his head, 'don't know, mate.'

'Go on,' I pressed him, 'tell me.'

'Well,' he resumed, 'you know the old geezer that lives in our 'ouse?'

'No,' I replied, 'I thought it was just you lot and some other kids.'

'No, 'e lives downstairs, right, but 'e's only there about once a month or somefin'. 'E's the only old bloke in a house full of young people, right, and 'e's always moanin' about the noise.'

I nodded, borrowing his drink.

''Cos I was playin' my guitar today, right, and it weren't even very loud, an' he came in my room an' started 'avin' a go at me.'

'How did he get in?'

'Well, I didn't 'ave my door locked or nuffin',' he explained. 'Anyway, 'e burst in, right, and says, "Please turn that racket down! Why must you people be so noisy?" ' he mimicked.

I laughed.

'It really made me jump, right, him comin' in like that, so I said, "Piss off, you stupid bastard," right, and I just carried on playin', finkin' he'd go, like. But 'e just stood there, right, an' 'e was shakin' an' all red in the face, an' I fought 'e was gonna cry or somefin',' he giggled, 'cos 'e's a real weedy-lookin' old bloke an' that. Then 'e says 'e's got an allergy to loud noise, right, an' 'e's bin in hospital for it, an' that I'd 'ave to stop or it'd bring on an allergic reaction in 'im or somefin', 'is doctor said.'

I frowned in consternation. 'What's he talkin' about?' I said. 'There's no such thing, surely.'

'Yeah, yeah; that's what I fought,' Agro agreed, taking a packet of ten Benson and Hedges from a pocket of his scuffed leather jacket. He paused to light one, and took only a small drag before continuing.

'Yeah, so I said, "Bollocks," right, and carried on playin'. Then 'e starts screamin', right, "It makes me mad, it makes mad," like that, gettin' really hysterical. An' I fought 'e was just tryin' to scare me, right, so I ignored 'im. Then 'e got really out of order. 'E started kickin' things and knockin' stuff over in my room; my other guitar an' the chair an' that. An' 'e kicked the glass case wiv Dan's lizards in, right; smashes all the glass, an' stamps on the little ones, right; squashes 'em. Then he picked up the new one, you know, the big one, and bits its 'ead off!'

'Oh no,' I gasped, incredulous, 'Really?'

'Yeah,' he laughed, 'bit its 'ead right off!'

'Christ!'

'Then 'e says that it's my fault for makin' such a noise, right. I was gonna hit 'im then, but 'e tried to make a dive for my amp, right, to turn it off, like. But I got there first, and pushed 'im away, like, and turned it up full volume. An' it was *really* loud, right. The window was all rattlin' an' the light was shakin'; there was tons of feedback, an' it was really deafenin'. And then . . . aww, I don't know . . .' he faltered.

'What?' I said impatiently.

'It was really weird, right . . .'

'Go on,' I encouraged him.

'Well, 'e was standin' there shoutin' about 'is allergy to noise, right; then 'e goes all purple, and foam starts comin' out of 'is mouth an' 'is nose starts bleedin'.' Agro spoke slowly, carefully; measuring his words. His shiny green eyes were averted in concentration. 'An' 'e was still shakin' an' that. Then 'e fell over, right, and, aww . . .' He shook his head again. 'It was weird, John . . . His 'ead an' 'is face started goin' all mushy an' like a blancmange or somefin'. An' 'e was screamin' an' that . . . then 'is whole body starts to collapse and sort of . . . shrivel up, witherin' away like a burst balloon. An' it smelt 'orrible; like rotten vegetables or somefin' . . . an', I dunno . . . it 'appened so quickly, like . . . 'e just sort of disintegrated.'

Agro ground his cigarette into the ashtray and reached for another. 'It really freaked me out, actually,' he finished.

'Jesus,' I mumbled. 'So what did you do then?'

'Well, I just fought: "Aww, no!" He clapped his hand to his forehead in an imitation of his own despair. ' "What's the matter wiv you, mate?" An' I didn't know what to do, right, so I just scooped up this bloke – or what was left of 'im – into a dustbin liner an' left 'im in 'is own room.'

'You didn't!' I guffawed.

'Yeah . . . Well, what else could I do?' he said reasonably. 'Then there's the lizards; Dan doesn't know yet. An' that new one cost 'im nine quid, didn't it? What am I gonna tell 'im, John?' Agro looked at me hopefully, a helpless bemused smile on his small face.

I shrugged. 'I dunno,' I admitted.

'I can't really tell 'im the truth about that bloke comin' in treadin' on 'em an' eatin' one of 'em an' that, can I? It's a bit too weird, really, innit?'

He puffed on his cigarette. 'Aww,' he groaned at length. 'I'll have to buy him some more, I s'pose. Bad one, eh?'

THE LITTER

James Kisner

Harriet had been acting strange all afternoon. She would run sideways with her back humped up at the least provocation, and she'd hiss and spit at anyone who came too close to her.

I know cats are ambivalent creatures with changeable natures, but Harriet was usually very affectionate and playful. She would even let our two kids, a six-year-old and a three-year-old, pull her tail and roughhouse with her for hours at a time without giving the least evidence she was displeased with their handling of her.

This Indian summer in early October, however, Harriet seemed to have the devil in her. I was about ready to pack her off to the vet when little Ted pointed out something to me that should have been obvious if I'd been more observant.

'Harriet real *fat*,' Ted said, pointing to the cat's sides.

She was pregnant. Her first time, too, which is probably why I didn't consider that a possible explanation for her erratic behaviour.

'Harriet's going to have kittens,' I told my son. 'That's why she won't let us touch her. Do you understand?'

Ted put his finger in his nose and shook his head. His big sister, Pam, nodded wisely. 'Harriet is going to be a mother,' she said seriously. 'What a responsibility!'

I laughed and went into the house to tell my wife all about it.

'I knew we waited too long to get Harriet fixed,' Jean said as she loaded the dishwasher. 'Now we'll have to find homes for a passel of cats.'

'It's not so bad,' I said, admiring the view I was getting of Jean bending over. At thirty-five Jean maintained her figure and made me the envy of a lot of other men in the neighbourhood whose wives were beginning to look frumpy. Her auburn hair and greenish eyes contributed to the overall effect of a woman who was becoming more beautiful with maturity.

She stood up and turned to face me. I was sitting at the kitchen table sipping a lukewarm diet root beer. 'You know, I don't even recall her going into heat,' she said. 'I wonder who the father is.'

'There are a lot of strays wandering around here,' I said. 'And Harriet's a good-looker. It wouldn't be hard for her to catch a man.'

'Oh, don't be silly,' Jean said, kissing me lightly on the cheek. 'I think you have sex on your mind constantly.'

'Are you complaining?'

Jean just smiled. 'How about some grilled cheese sandwiches for dinner? I don't feel like fixing a big meal.'

'All right. But about Harriet – don't you think it'll be an educational experience for the kids to witness the miracle of birth?'

She grimaced. 'I don't think they're old enough yet, especially Teddy. Maybe we should take the cat to the vet.'

'That's ridiculous. When I was growing up I saw animals being born all the time. There's no need to shelter the kids so much.'

'But you grew up on a farm, Ted.'

'Pam already knows where babies come from. I think she'll feel cheated if she doesn't get to see the big event.'

'I don't even want to see it myself.'

I was about to present a very convincing argument to her when Pam ran into the room. She was excited and out of breath.

'*Daddy!* Harriet's making a *mess* in the basement! Hurry up, or you'll *miss* it.'

'Too late,' I said. 'Okay, Pam, show me where Harriet is.'

The cat had made a nest of some dirty clothes in a corner of the basement a few feet behind the furnace. I winced because part of the nest was one of my favourite everyday shirts. Little Ted was standing close to the nest, his eyes wide open.

'Ted, go upstairs and see Mommy.'

'Harriet have babies?'

'Yes, Ted, but you shouldn't watch. Mommy says you're too young.' I looked at Pam who had a look of fierce determination; there was no way I would get her to leave, but I thought I should try in order to save myself an argument later. 'Pam, you take Ted up to the kitchen.'

'I want to see.'

'Okay,' I sighed; 'but take him upstairs first. Then you can come back – if Mommy lets you.'

She took her little brother by the hand and wordlessly led him up the stairs. I expected Ted to protest, but he seemed confused about what was going on and not all that curious.

I approached the cat cautiously and bent down to see if any kittens had been born yet. The light was dim in that area of the basement, but I could make out at least two writhing forms struggling to get to Harriet's teats. Harriet was a yellow cat with a little white on her underbelly but the two kittens were greyish-looking. I watched three more come out quickly, then the afterbirth flowed out. Harriet looked up at me and seemed to be pleading.

'Don't glare at me,' I said. 'I didn't get you into this.'

Pam had returned.

'Oh, I *missed* it!' she said.

'Well, it's all over. You'd better . . .'

'What's that?' She pointed to the afterbirth. 'It's *gross!*'

I couldn't think of a ready explanation. I turned to Pam, stooped down to be face to face with her and laid my hands on her shoulders. 'When animals have babies,' I said, not knowing where I was going, 'they . . .'

'Oh, *really* gross!' she said, adding a couple of extra syllables to the word 'gross', which had lately become one of the most commonly-used words in her vocabulary.

I looked back, expecting to see Harriet doing what came naturally to many animals; instead, I saw something I wasn't prepared for at all.

The kittens were eating the afterbirth.

'That *is* gross,' I agreed.

After taking Pam up to her mother, I returned to the basement for another look. This time I plugged in my trouble light and held it over Harriet's nest. The pupils of the cat's eyes almost instantly turned into tiny black dots. I was aware of a strange odour that's best described as a mixture of urine, blood and decay. I tried to breathe through my mouth, and crouched down, getting as close to the nest as I dared.

The afterbirth was gone. There were five animals in the litter, but I wouldn't call them 'kittens'. The grey colour I had guessed at earlier turned out to be the colour of their skins, because not one of them had any fur at all. Their eyes, which should have been closed, were all open wide and pinkish in colour. They had no tails, but they did have little claws. God, they didn't *look* like *cats* – they looked more like ugly hairless moles. Harriet hadn't bothered to lick them clean either, and they were caked with crusty blood. *Mutations*, I thought; *slimy little bastards*. That's why Harriet hadn't cleaned them; she would probably kill them when she realized what they were.

One of them was on its back, gaping at the ceiling with its feet thrashing wildly as if it couldn't turn itself back over. Its mouth was wide open and I noticed it possessed large teeth, more like those of an adult animal than a kitten, and they were sharp. My stomach was protesting. I thought I was going to lose my lunch any second.

'Ted, come up here,' Jean yelled down the stairs. 'George wants to see you.'

'Can't it wait? We've got a real mess down here.'

'He said it's important. He seems upset.'

'Damn! Okay, I'm coming.' I took the stairs two at a time and met Jean at the top. 'Whatever you do, don't let the kids go down there. I don't want to go into it right now, but Harriet has given us a present we don't want. And it's not a dead mouse.'

'What?'

I appraised her mood and added, 'You better not go down there either. You won't like it a bit.'

George was our next door neighbour. We lived in a subdivision where all the houses have aluminium siding and two-car garages. There were no fences and the homes were built close together, so you learned to get along with your neighbours.

George was a good guy, though. He was an engineer at one of the local electronics companies. I'm an accountant and I help George with his taxes every year, so we don't have many secrets between us.

He was waiting for me in front of his garage, one door of which was up. The station wagon had been backed out onto the driveway. George looked uneasy; he was sweating despite it being only fifty outside. He was about my age – almost forty – and his hair was starting to turn grey. He was in excellent physical condition and jogged every morning to maintain his weight and stay fit. I often kidded him about his running, because I kept healthy without having to exert myself.

'What's up, George?' I asked.

'Jesus, Ted, you won't believe it. Come in here and tell me what you think of this.'

He took me inside the garage and directed me to a corner where his Dalmatian bitch was lying. She was stretched out on a dirty old sleeping bag and whimpering softly. I could also hear the high-pitched whining of something else that was with her – a litter of – no, *not* puppies.

'Look at those goddamn things,' George said. 'Did you ever see anything like that in your life?'

I had. The animals to which the Dalmatian had given birth were *exactly the same* as the litter Harriet had delivered. They were slightly larger, but otherwise exact duplicates.

There were eight of them.

I don't know much about biology, but I do know certain things are supposed to be impossible. Cats have kittens; dogs have pups. Damn it, that's the way things are supposed to happen.

All kinds of ideas went through my mind, none of them offering any real acceptable answers to what I was seeing. Was it because of air or water pollution? Radiation? Something supernatural? Something from outer space?

I shook my head. I don't believe in all that kind of nonsense. I believe in numbers and science, at least as much of it as I can understand. If it doesn't compute, it can't happen.

'George,' I said, 'I may be going out of my mind, but I think this litter looks just like the one Harriet had.'

'Your *cat*?'

'Yeah. Do you think that's possible?'

'Are you trying to kid me? If so, I'm not in the mood.'

'All right, I'll show you. Have you got some gloves out here?'

'What for?'

'I'm going to pick one of the little bastards up, and we'll compare them with my "kittens". That's a starting-point, at least.'

He gave me a pair of heavy leather work gloves. I was able to lift one of the animals away from the rest without disturbing the dog, who really didn't seem to care.

I didn't blame her. Looking at the creature closely now, I could see just how ugly it really was. The skin was not only hairless; it was scaly. The strangest thing I noticed though was that it had no navel. Thinking back, I realized the cat's offspring had no umbilical evidence either that I could remember. There had been no cord anywhere.

'Let's go,' I said, holding the slimy thing out in front of me to get away from the smell as much as possible. 'Maybe we can figure this thing out together.'

'I'm coming, but I don't like it a bit,' George said. 'You know, Ted, this is really the goddamnedest thing.'

'What's that?'

'We had that dog spayed last spring.'

Jean stayed clear of us as we came into the kitchen to get to the basement. Her face was pale as she saw what I held in my gloved hands, but she said nothing. It was obvious she had seen the litter despite my having warned her not to. I don't know why she didn't ask me about the thing in my hands; maybe she was too stunned.

'I don't know what we're going to do, but why don't you take the kids and go visit someone?'

She nodded without saying a word. I think she was glad to have an opportunity to leave.

'Give me a couple of hours,' I said. 'Better yet, call before you come home; just in case.'

'But what are you. . . ?'

'I told you I don't know.' I tried to sound like I was in control of the situation, but was failing to impress Jean or myself. Something inside me was churning, perhaps some instinctual recognition of things gone wrong, of nature turned topsy-turvy or inside-out. I sensed an underlying urgency to our finding out what was going on here, exactly.

I went ahead of George down into the basement and directly to the nest. Harriet had left her offspring; I couldn't blame her for that.

I laid the 'pup' next to the five 'kittens'.

'What did I tell you, George? There's not a damn bit of difference.'

'Except yours are a little bigger,' George said. He looked unhappy; scared. 'This doesn't make any sense.'

'I know it. That's weird. You said mine are bigger, and they are. But they were *smaller* when I left them.'

'Come *on*, Ted! They wouldn't grow in ten minutes.'

'It's not my imagination. I tell you they're *bigger*.'

I looked down at the squirming mass of ugly, scaly things which were now even more slimy and gore-encrusted than before. I bent closer and noticed one of them was gnawing on something – it was a piece of meat with fur on it. I reached out and flipped one of the things over and saw more bits of meat, which the others immediately descended on. I pulled apart some of the rags and clothing that made up the nest and found something I was hoping I wouldn't find at all – at least, not there.

It was the *rest* of Harriet, her head which had been stripped of flesh down to the bone, her tail and one paw. Her eyes had been spared for some reason and they stared back at me accusingly. *Why did you leave me alone?* they asked.

That was too much. I turned away and threw up, heaving mightily all over the floor, splattering George's shoes and legs.

George jumped away from me, lost his balance, and fell into the nest. One of the animals attached itself to his bare arm at once, biting him almost to the bone.

'Goddamn!' George howled – 'get this sonofabitch *off* me!'

I recovered quickly and pulled myself together enough to help pry the thing from George's skin as he scrambled up from the nest. I squeezed the beast in my right hand as hard as I could; it kept trying to wriggle around and bite me. Fortunately, I still wore the heavy gloves George had given me or the thing would have had a piece of me. For something no bigger than a gopher, the creature was amazingly strong. I couldn't hold it any longer and dropped it on the floor. Without even thinking, acting on an instinct I had never before exercised, I crushed it under my foot, grinding it into the cement with all my weight.

It went *'pop'* like some kind of obscene balloon.

Now it was George's turn to be sick.

I lifted my foot and stared down at the smudge on the floor, an iridescent green-grey spot of shivering slime-ooze with a head that still snapped and moved. Gradually the amorphous blob rearranged itself and assumed its former shape – more or less.

George was finished heaving now. 'Christ, Ted, what are we going to do?'

'You *saw* what happened, didn't you? I came down on it with all my weight . . . oh, God! They ate Harriet . . . Jesus . . . *ate* the cat. Can't *kill*!' I was a half-step away from hysteria.

'Come on, snap out of it, Ted.' George was shaking too.

'They ate the *cat*, George! Don't you understand that? What do you think the ones in your garage are doing *right now*?'

'Good God! I hope I'm not too late.' He ran up the basement steps, tripping over his own feet two or three times.

After he was gone, I was almost scared out of my skin by the sound of glass breaking behind me. When I turned to investigate I saw two of the creatures up on the shelves where we kept the fruits and vegetables we canned each year. They had managed to push over a quart of tomatoes and break it open. The jar lay on its side slowly draining its contents, and while one of them attempted to overturn another jar, the other burrowed into the tomatoes. In the context of the moment it appeared as if it were gnawing and wriggling through gore; and as it dug through the pulpy meal, its hind legs splattered tomato-grue on my face. I was momentarily sickened, but somehow gained control of myself.

How the hell had they gotten up *there*? Unless they could fly. That thought jolted me. They might sprout wings any minute.

'That does it,' I said to the animals. I *had* to do something now. I kept a small trash can next to my work bench which I knew would hold them all. I dumped the wood shavings and sawdust out of it and returned quickly to the nest.

Shock waves of nausea rippled through me and the blood throbbed in my temples as I picked the two creatures off the shelves and lifted the others from the nest, one by one, and dropped them into the can. It was like handling chunks of putrid meat – they smelled so bad – and their odour seemed to increase with their size – and their apparently-growing hunger.

Yes; they had grown larger within minutes. They were still smaller than normal kittens would have been, but the increase was noticeable. It was not something I was imagining. *Was it?*

I also had to contend with the remains of Harriet, and suddenly the loss of the cat seemed like the worst thing that had ever happened to me in my entire life. Tears came and I realized I was no longer acting rationally – again, as if I were being driven by instincts and emotions I didn't know existed within me.

What the hell would I tell the kids? What would I tell Jean?

I found myself obsessed with counting, then. I decided I should count the things several times to make certain I had them all. There were five from my original litter, plus the one I brought over from George's batch. That made six. *Six.* Yes, I told myself, there are six in this can. One-two-threefourfivesix. *Six, damn it!* Count them slowly. Be sure you have them all. *Onetwothree. Fourfive. Six.* Did I count that one twice?

Six things. One dog. No cat. Six things. Two kids. One wife. Six . . .

George will count them for me again. He'll be glad to.

I was becoming too fuzzy-thinking and bleary-eyed to know what I was doing. I had to get out of there quickly, or somehow, I thought, those things would overpower me. I felt my will gradually weakening when I stared into the can at the squirming things – and knew abruptly yet another new emotion: the desire to kill.

I slammed the lid on the can and wrapped a couple of pieces of duct tape over it to keep the things inside until I could make it to George's garage.

George stood outside, waiting for me. Without asking, I knew he had failed to save his dog. He looked helpless.

'What have you got there?' he asked in a low voice.

'What the hell do you think I have? I've got *them*.'

'So what are you going to do?'

'*We've* got to do something quick, George. We have to destroy them before they get too big. Don't you see that? We don't have any choice.'

He stared at the spot on his arm where he had been bitten. It was already swollen and it dripped with a greenish pus-like substance that smelled of decay.

'Hurts,' George said.

'I know it hurts. We'll get you to a doctor – just as soon as we take care of these things. Okay? Are you *listening* to me?'

He gave me a blank look, as if he didn't understand. I set the can down, grabbed him by the shoulders and shook him. 'Come to your senses, George! You've *got* to help me!'

'Hey! Leave me alone.' He broke free of my grip and sat down on the ground next to the garage, covering his face with his hands as he kind-of folded into himself. 'What's the use?'

'I never knew you were such a goddamn wimp,' I said. Under other circumstances I would have been immediately ashamed of myself for treating a good friend so harshly, but my reactions weren't entirely my own. I was afraid and angry. But my anger wasn't directed only at the creatures and the hell they had wrought. It was focused specifically on George, as if he were somehow personally to blame for what had happened.

Perhaps his injury had affected his reason – or the shock of losing his prized Dalmatian. It didn't really make any difference, because he was useless to me at that moment.

'I can't go in there,' he whimpered.

I left him slumped outside and took the can into the garage where I confronted the other litter.

And half a dog.

I burned them.

I doused the little bastards in gasoline and lit them, and by that means I discovered their sole virtue: they were *highly* inflammable.

I made a pile of them behind George's garage and ignited them. I counted them, of course. Thirteen little fireballs that made no sound at all as they burned. *God*, I hope I never have to do anything like that again.

One of our neighbours called in because I'd violated a local ordinance against open burning. By the time the fire marshal arrived there was nothing left but a charred spot on the ground; there weren't even any bones. After a few minutes the odour of burnt sulphur had totally dissipated too.

It's been a few weeks now and things have returned to fairly normal. George doesn't speak to me very often, but I know he'll get over it. He's getting better every day, and I can see he's beginning to regain movement in his arm.

I don't know what he did with the carcass of the Dalmatian. I'm not ready to ask him.

Jean told our kids the cat died in 'childbirth' and the kittens had to be put to sleep. They seem to be accepting that explanation, though I'm not sure Pam really believes it. I refuse to elaborate and have promised them a new pet soon – another cat, if that's what they want.

Of course, even Jean doesn't know the full story. Her eyes are always questioning me. Maybe someday I'll tell her everything, when it's all at a comfortable enough distance from reality for me to talk about it without breaking down.

Looking back, I realize I should have saved one of the creatures to show someone. If I had been rational, I would have kept one and called the newspapers or the television people. Instead, I destroyed them mindlessly, and the memories of the awful emotions I had that day have been the hardest to eradicate.

For a while I worried about the possibility of other litters. I even heard that a family a couple of blocks away had a German shepherd that produced a litter of deformed puppies. I contacted the people, but they refused to say anything. I can't say that I blame them very much.

I also expected to see something in the papers or on TV. It was the kind of thing you'd normally find plastered in headlines all over the supermarket tabloids, but I have yet to find a story in any of them about strange animal litters. Nothing but the usual run of UFO babies and two-headed cows. I guess what happened in our neighbourhood was an isolated event.

Of course, I wonder about the animals in the woods, just north of our subdivision. There are a lot of raccoons up there – and rabbits and opossums. If any of them gave birth to weird critters, it would be a while before anyone discovered it.

I try to keep such thoughts out of my mind, and I succeed most of the time. I have more important things to occupy me.

Jean's pregnant. She's due any day now.

The doctor says it might be twins.

SHE'LL BE COMPANY FOR YOU

Andrea Newman

It was at Margaret's funeral that I first realized Barbara was dangerous. The event itself was a great success, if one may tastefully use such a word with reference to a funeral: I had kept Margaret's relatives to a minimum by insisting that they should stay at the local hotel and not in my house. Many of them, therefore, rapidly added train-fare to bed and breakfast and decided not to come. Those who did wore black, wept discreetly, and settled for a few rounds of drinks rather than the lavish wake they had hopefully anticipated. But Barbara remained. Dressed in green, hideously distinguished by dyed red hair and that huge mole on her cheek (which I had cheerfully removed many times by mental surgery as she sat over dinner with Margaret and me in earlier days), Barbara remained. There was no one left in the bar; last orders had been called; glasses were being collected. The black arm-band I had acquired for the occasion began to weigh on me with an almost tangible pressure, macabre emblem of a sorrow I could not feel, for surely Margaret's death, of all deaths, was the one for which the phrase 'a merciful release' had been invented.

'We must go,' I said to Barbara, 'before they throw us out.' I felt that to be forcibly ejected from a pub on the day of my wife's funeral would be unseemly, to say the least.

She drained her glass. She looked at me with those huge eyes that matched her funereal green. They glittered. I am aware that this word is ridiculous and must be inaccurate, but I can find no other word which remotely describes what Barbara's eyes did. It occurred to me that Barbara made me nervous. This too was ridiculous and I could not recall that it had happened before. But then I had not been quite so alone with Barbara before. The barmen had disappeared somewhere; the place was deserted.

And Margaret was dead; I had heard the earth drop on her coffin. At that moment, hearing that obscene sound, I had, for a second, wished her back, forgetting the pain to which I would have been sentencing her. For no one should hear such a sound, and I had not thought about it in advance.

'Let's go,' Barbara said. She stood up, and I noticed how tall she was, as if for the first time. I seemed to be newly aware of a great many details on this particular day, but I put it down to my heightened emotional state. We walked out of the pub together into the dark of the October evening and I shivered. Barbara's presence was something I could have done without. Sufficient that Margaret was dead and I was alone and the strain of the past years was ended. I was oppressed by relief and sorrow and anticlimax.

'Take me home,' Barbara said. I visibly blinked at her, thinking she meant London, a good hour's drive away, but she added, 'I must come back to the house. I can't go home till I've been in Maggie's room again.'

The nickname irked me, for it was one I had never used and its use always seemed affected, although I had heard her address Margaret in this fashion innumerable times. It suggested someone altogether younger and more sprightly than the bravely lingering invalid I remembered. I was tired and weak from the funeral; Barbara's car was at the house, and short of shoving her into it there was no means of escape. I made a feeble protest out of silence: we got into my car without speaking and drove to the house without exchanging a word, while I bitterly reflected that to revisit my dead wife's room tonight was a most unholy and extravagant request. Arriving home, with tyres crunching on the gravel, I felt extraordinarily lonely, in the way that is only possible in someone's company. The darkened windows glowered at me and I thought quite clearly and briefly what a fool I was not to have arranged to spend the night at an hotel.

'At last,' Barbara said. She seemed quite eager, impatiently tapping her foot on the step as I groped for my key 'All that,' she said contemptuously, 'all *that* at the cemetery, that didn't count.' Finding my key and inserting it into the lock occupied me so that I had no time to examine this extraordinary remark, but it registered nevertheless. We entered the house and I yawned and said pointedly, 'One drink, Barbara, and then I must go to bed. I'm very tired.'

She took off her coat. This I thought was a bad sign, suggesting a longer occupation than I had given her any right to expect. She hung it up and I noticed that her dress matched her coat, that they were very much an outfit, and I wondered what on earth had possessed her to choose such flagrant green to wear to my wife's funeral.

'I don't want a drink,' she said with a sort of self-possessed cheerfulness. 'I won't be long.' And she disappeared upstairs, smiling at me over the banisters in a way I found somehow sinister – or, getting a grip on myself, at least out of place. I went into the living room and poured myself a stiff whisky.

The room, thank God, did not remind me of Margaret: it was so long since she had spent any time downstairs. It had become very much a man's room, very much a study or a library: my room. I relaxed. With a little effort and some more whisky I could almost imagine Barbara was not upstairs and I was (as I should be and would have to be) alone in the house. I refilled my glass and put up my feet: it was uncanny to realize that I would no longer have to listen for Margaret's emergency bell.

I don't know if I dozed. I was certainly tired enough to do so. But the next thing I knew was Barbara appearing in the living room in front of me, green and glittering, her smile almost phosphorescent in the dim light. Or was I dreaming?

'That's done,' she said, in the tone of one who has accomplished an important task. 'Now I'll have that drink.' And she sank into an armchair opposite me.

It seemed churlish to remind her that she had earlier refused a drink, but I resented none the less her air of occupation. I poured her a whisky and wondered how long she would take over it; from my standpoint it was her first and her last. I began to feel light-headed and a little victimized. Surely on the day of Margaret's funeral I was entitled to a little consideration, even from her friends?

'The thing is,' Barbara said, as if we were in the middle of a conversation, 'I must get away. I can't bear it. Maggie was everything to me. You know that.' And she stared at me with her huge eyes.

I was transfixed. Tales of snakes and rabbits, hedgehogs in the glare of headlamps, filtered through my mind.

'You were great friends,' I said sententiously. My mind and my body were beginning to part company, whether through alcohol or emotion, or a combination of both, I had no idea.

'She was my life.' Barbara, taking an enormous draught of whisky, still held me fixed with her green and glittering glance. I actually began to tremble; I even wondered if perhaps I was about to go down with flu. The whole evening, the whole day, started to crumble. I felt I had an uncertain hold on my very sanity. 'But you, Henry. You shouldn't be alone.'

I wanted to say I could manage; could manage very nicely, in fact. I wanted to say that being alone was exactly what I needed or, alternatively, that it was I, rather than Barbara, who should get away. But I was mesmerized, and I said nothing.

'You must have been very tempted,' she said, fitting a cigarette into a long amber holder and lighting it, 'to help Maggie over the hill.'

Now I really began to shake. 'What?' I said. And my voice sounded squeaky even to myself.

'You know what I mean.' She actually smiled at me. I watched her teeth and wondered if they were her own. But I was appalled. The conversation had taken a new and unexpected turn. I couldn't answer.

'You can talk to me, Henry,' Barbara said. She inhaled deeply and I watched the smoke curling upwards as she breathed out. There were even a few impromptu smoke rings. 'Maggie and I had no secrets from each other. You can tell me.'

'No,' I said. 'No.' All social conventions seemed suspended. 'There's nothing to tell. Margaret was very ill. You know how ill she was. It was only a matter of time. The doctor said so.' I clung to this. The doctor had understood my position and the nature of Margaret's illness; it was absurd for Barbara to intervene. But she did.

'Maggie might have got better,' she said flatly, to my astonishment. 'I was praying for her. We used to pray together. You didn't know that, did you, Henry?'

Indeed I did not; there was no way I could have done. And I could not see any purpose in her telling me now. I raised my glass to my lips and noticed how heavy my arm was and what an effort the movement involved. I must be even more exhausted than I had realized.

'I had no idea,' I said, 'that either of you were religious. Margaret never mentioned it.'

'In our own way,' Barbara said. 'There was no need to mention it. We were very close.'

'Yes, of course,' I said. 'I know that.'

'Well.' Barbara turned her glass in her hand, catching the light from the lamp. She drew on her cigarette and watched me through the smoke as she exhaled. 'Your ordeal is over now, isn't it? You'll be much freer now, won't you, Henry? Able to go out and about. You might even take out that girl – what's her name? – June, from your office.'

'You must be mad,' I said faintly. I began to feel light-headed, as if I had drunk far more than I had. 'She's just a secretary. Probably got a dozen boyfriends her own age. I don't know a thing about her.'

'Ah,' said Barbara almost tenderly. 'But a man of your age, Henry. Let me see, what are you? Forty-five? In your prime. It's not good for a man like you to be alone.'

'I shall manage.' There was something so uncannily sinister about the way she used my name that I could hardly answer. 'I shall have to get used to it. You can't seriously imagine I intend to start chasing little girls.' The whole discussion, particularly on this very day, struck me as in the worst of taste.

'But you mustn't be alone yet,' Barbara said. 'Especially in this house, with all your memories. Just now, in Maggie's room, I felt she was very much alive. Still with us. But that's probably because we were so close, she and I.' She rose, stubbing out her cigarette and finishing her drink. 'So I shall help you, Henry. We shall help each other, in fact. I told you I must go away for a while, whereas you, I'm sure, need the routine of work to sustain you. But not to come home to an empty house. So I shall send you my cat. She'll be company for you.'

It is always a mystery how one agrees to do anything one does not want to do. I suppose I argued, albeit feebly. I do not care much for cats, while not actively disliking them. I think I suggested kennels, which were instantly rejected as unthinkable.

The fact remained that Barbara was going away and I was not, therefore what could be more appropriate than for me to look after her cat in her absence? Yes, she was grateful, and yet my overall impression is that I was made to feel that she – or indeed the cat – would be doing me a favour.

After she had gone, and I never watched anyone leave with more relief in my soul, I staggered back to the sofa with another whisky. It must have been a large one. I lay there in a state of complete exhaustion and pictured myself enjoying the luxury of my spare room bed: the warmth, the silence, the solace of sleep. And I woke in the same position, stiff and cold in my funeral clothes, with the living-room fire shrunk to a heap of ashes. It was then – my first waking thought of the day – that I remembered Barbara had actually accused me of murdering my wife.

And then it began. The cat arrived two days later in a large wicker basket and I had to collect it from the station. I had expected Barbara to bring it herself, and in daylight, sober and rested, I was prepared for some very plain speaking about her outrageous remarks of the other night. Instead there was a letter of instructions on cat care and a parcel of tins which had to be alternated with the best fish and liver and chicken and rabbit. She enclosed five pounds; I supposed it would be enough. But the whole performance sickened me and there was no way I could retaliate: the letter carried a postscript, 'I leave today.' Barbara had made good her escape.

The cat, when I finally opened the basket, was striped, and vaguely a cross between a tabby and marmalade in colour. It seemed perfectly normal. I had heard its yowling protests during its period of captivity and when I finally released it, it showed as much gratitude as cats ever show, looked round in surprise at its surroundings, and took off on a tour of inspection. I opened one of Barbara's tins, shuddered at the smell, and put a plate of the stuff on the kitchen floor by way of welcome. The cat – Barbara had told me it was called Jennet, but I could not bring myself to use such an eccentric name – the cat returned eventually, sniffed at the food, disdained it, and rubbed itself round my legs, a habit I dislike although it is supposed to indicate friendship. I had nowhere to go that evening – I am by nature rather a solitary person and I was beginning to appreciate the peace of my empty house – so I cooked for myself and ate, then settled down with television and a glass of whisky. The cat lay on the rug in front of the fire. It made no sound. All mewing had stopped the moment I opened the basket. Occasionally it rolled over and stretched in that totally relaxed and apparently boneless way they have, and regarded me with its huge yellow eyes. There is something peculiar about a cat's stare: they seem to gaze longer and harder than other animals. A long, unblinking look, so that I had to be the first to glance away. But that was nothing out of the ordinary. Just the usual feeling of being silently sized up which no one enjoys: in human terms similar to being introduced at a party, or meeting a prospective employer. But it was only a cat, I reminded myself. I did not have to respond to it; I could ignore it completely if I chose. So I kept my eyes fixed on the television and drank some more whisky.

By ten I was surprisingly tired, too tired even to continue watching a programme I usually enjoyed. I got up and went into the kitchen to make a warm drink to take to bed. The cat followed me at once, as if at a given signal. While I was busy at the stove it ate a little of its food, then stood at the back door expectantly. With a strange sensation of relief I let it out and watched it disappear into the night. When I closed the door I felt an unaccountable lift in my spirits. I had not realized before that its presence was in some way oppressive.

I reckoned it gone for the night, had a leisurely bath and went to bed about eleven, taking one of the pills the doctor had given me. At three I was awake – suddenly, abruptly awake. I had forgotten to draw my curtains and there was bright moonlight pouring into my room, enough to wake anyone. But it was more than that. There on the window ledge, with its face pressed against the glass, its yellow eyes luminous, was the cat.

My house is covered by wisteria, so it must have been an easy climb. I should not have been surprised; perhaps it had yowled at the back door for admittance and I had not heard it. I felt ashamed of the shock it had given me, for what could be more normal than for a cat to climb? But it is always alarming to be woken abruptly from a drugged sleep. A cat-flap in the kitchen door, I reflected, would soon put an end to this nonsense; then it could come and go as it pleased. I got up resentfully and opened the window. The cat jumped in at once. It seemed disturbed: standing in the middle of the floor and swishing its tail. It also seemed larger than I remembered it, but I thought that must obviously be due to my half-awake state, an illusion of the night. I closed the window and opened the door, saying idiotically, 'Go on then, good cat,' for I had no intention of allowing it to sleep in my room. It didn't budge. Its tail lashed from side to side and it went on standing, all four feet firmly planted, in the middle of my bedroom. I felt absurd and rather cold, in a draught, clad only in pyjamas, virtually pleading with an animal to leave me alone. 'Come on, puss,' I said, more absurdly than ever, for it looked nothing like a puss, that cosy childhood word: it seemed to be glaring at me. Its eyes were huge and – now I came to notice – rather like Barbara's, though hers were green: they both had the same unnerving stare. As it didn't move I went towards it, to shoo it out of the room, but with a certain ridiculous apprehension, as if it were a larger animal. The fur rose on its back and its tail, it made a strange sound in its throat, and then, before I could even react, it was gone, streaking through the open door and down the passage. I closed the door and leaned against it; I found myself damp with sweat. Those pills, I thought, those pills must be too strong for me. Perhaps I should have my prescription changed. I went back to bed, but I could not sleep for what seemed like hours, and when at last I did I dreamed strange dreams that in the morning I could not clearly remember, but which left me unrefreshed.

'That bloody cat is getting on my nerves,' I said to Bill in the pub three days later. The trouble was, I did not know how to explain. A cat-door had stopped the nocturnal visitation, but a pattern of other, equally unpleasant habits had emerged: sharpening its claws on the furniture, playing with its meat in a most obscene manner, greeting me in the morning with a row of dead mice on the kitchen floor. Its presence was everywhere: it stared at me as it lay on the rug, it followed me round the house. Would Bill take any of this seriously? And it had even taken, occasionally, to standing outside Margaret's door and mewing – not in protest but plaintively, almost conversationally, as if it were having a long, sad discussion with someone. 'It miaows outside Margaret's room,' I said.

'Let it in.' Bill was relighting his pipe and his conversation was punctuated by the sort of sucking noise I particularly dislike. But I had known him a long time and he was someone to have a drink with. I could not recall having been so irritated by the noise before. 'We had a cat once.' Suck. Puff. 'Couldn't stand a closed door. In, out, all the time. Drove us nearly mad. You're not using the room, are you?'

'Of course not.' The question shocked me a little.

'Then open the door and let it in.' Suck. 'Probably all it wants, just to have a look round. Damned curious animals, cats.'

'They certainly are.' But I did not mean it as he did. And the idea of opening Margaret's door somehow appalled me. I had not been in the room since the day of the funeral. 'This one, anyway. It's really a bit odd.' I longed for him to read my mind, to know what I meant as if he had seen the cat for himself. I knew I would never find the right words to tell him.

'Odd? In what way?' He sucked at his pipe; he did not seem really interested. I could almost hear him thinking, Henry's in a funny mood, going on about a cat. Poor chap's not himself again yet. Can't blame him, I suppose, in the circumstances, but still.

'It follows me round the house,' I said. I could not begin to describe its tigerish, sinewy walk as it sloped down the corridors after me. 'It stares at me. You know that bloody disconcerting stare they have. Only this one seems . . . worse somehow. And then all the miaowing. It gets on my nerves.' But I had not even begun to tell him the truth. I was too afraid of mockery.

Bill leaned back in his chair. 'Sounds as if you ought to get away, old man,' he said. 'Take a holiday. Get away from it all. You've had a lot of strain, you know. Probably went back to work too soon.'

'But I can't get away,' I said desperately. 'That's the whole point. Barbara got away first.'

'Barbara?' He looked blank; he never had been good at remembering relevant facts about other people. Too wrapped up in his own petty affairs.

'It's Barbara's cat,' I said. I was obscurely angered at being forced into speaking the words. 'I'm supposed to be looking after it while *she's* away.'

'Oh, well, in that case you're stuck, aren't you?' He drained his glass; he looked relaxed and casual. He simply did not see the seriousness of my position. 'How about another round?' he said cheerfully.

And then the postcards started to arrive from Barbara. One each day, and each from a different place. It gave me an odd pain to read her handwriting, as if fingers were squeezing my heart. 'As you see, I keep moving,' she wrote unnecessarily. 'Maggie is with me in spirit.' And, 'I hope by now you and Jennet have come to an understanding. It comforts me to know she is with you.' And again, 'This is a beautiful place. If only Maggie could have seen it.' Every day there was a postcard waiting for me when I returned home. I had taken to eating out, sampling my new freedom of movement, I suppose, or calling in at the pub on my way home for a few drinks instead of going out later, when I often felt too tired to move. I found that although I didn't enjoy alcohol as much I seemed to need it more. And I have to admit that even then, within a week of Barbara's departure, I felt a strange reluctance to enter my own house.

The postcards lay on the hall table where Mrs Coates, my daily, who came and went in my absence, always placed the mail. The cat watched me read them, dashing as it usually did into the hall when I arrived, not so much to welcome me, I felt, as to check up that I had in fact returned for the night. And it watched me tear them up viciously, each one, into tiny pieces, as it sharpened its claws on a broom, on a chair, on the leg of a table. I had tried chasing it away but it only moved on somewhere else and started again. How long its body was when it reached out full length! It seemed longer each day, and wider too, as if there were more space between the stripes. I rebuked myself for drinking too much: my imagination was getting the upper hand. Mrs Coates had noticed nothing; there could not be anything to notice. She even seemed to like the animal and had taken to feeding it during the day, leaving me little notes of reassurance that 'Pussy had some nice fish' or 'Pussy ate all her rabbit.' Yet it still demanded food from me at night and if I refused it would twine itself round my legs in the way that I dreaded, as if it knew I could not bear contact. So I fed it. Going into the kitchen and chopping up meat which I left it alone to eat: I had had enough of watching it pirouetting around its meat like some blasted ballet dancer, tossing it in the air and catching it in its claws, dropping it and starting again, as if the wretched meat were alive. And yet, despite all this food, in the morning there would be two or three field mice laid out, quite dead, quite unmarked, as if they had died of fright.

Barbara had been gone for a week, therefore I was halfway through my ordeal. But I was shocked to find myself thinking in terms of an ordeal. The cat never left me alone. All the time I spent in the house it spent with me: I simply could not get away from it. If I watched television, it watched me; lying on my rug, in front of my fire, it stared at me with its large golden eyes, yawned indolently, showing all its sharp white teeth, rolled over, flexed its muscles, stretched to its full length, and finally curled up again. Its presence filled the room. Was this what Barbara had meant by company? I could well have done without it. If I got up to fetch a book from another room or to make myself some coffee it followed me, silently padding along the corridor or up the stairs after me. I tried closing doors to shut it out but it only scratched at them until its claws seemed to be grating on my very nerves or until my automatic concern for the paintwork forced me to let it in. At least when with me it was silent. I tried going to bed early, but any time before midnight it seemed to resent, for then it would scratch at my bedroom door or miaow outside Margaret's for what felt like hours, until it finally slunk away, out into the night, regardless of the weather, to hunt.

My work was beginning to suffer – because I was not sleeping well, I supposed. I tried to explain to people at the office; they had been very patient with me since Margaret died, making allowances (which I hated, as I had always been known for my efficiency) and now the allowances became really necessary, not a mere generous gesture to show respect for my bereavement. I saw their surprise at the trivial mistakes I made and the way in which they quickly covered up. 'It's the cat,' I explained. 'It's getting on my nerves.' (I was beginning to visualize my nerves as the exposed roots of a plant, red raw, with the cat swinging on them.) But they didn't understand; I could see them look puzzled. And the image of the plant made me sweat, just a little, so that I felt hot and cold at once, shivering in my jacket, with drops of moisture on my face. 'Are you all right?' someone asked. 'You look a bit groggy to me.' I found it hard to focus on their faces, so I was not always sure exactly who was speaking to me.

But I was not going to pieces. Oh no. In fact, so far was I from going to pieces that one lunchtime I made an appointment with the optician. It was about time I had my eyes tested again: another of the routine jobs I had put off because of all the business with Margaret. Not that there was much wrong with my eyes. I only wore glasses for reading and could actually manage without them if I had to, except that I would eventually get a headache. Still, it was a good thing to have regular check-ups. The chap did all the usual tests and told me there was no need to alter my prescription, there had been no significant change. That's all *you* know, I thought. I tried to be casual; I said, 'Then I couldn't be seeing things . . . bigger, by any chance?' and he looked at me oddly and asked what I meant, what kind of things? I said, laughing it off, 'Oh, just things, you know . . . people, animals,' and grinned at him, to show it was all quite trivial and light-hearted. I felt a fool, to be honest. 'Not at all, quite impossible,' he said reassuringly, and yet I did not find it at all reassuring; his smile seemed false. 'But if you'd like me to make further tests . . .' he said. 'Oh no, no,' I said quickly. 'That won't be necessary.' I wanted to get out now. But he lingered at the door with me. 'You're probably a bit tired, a bit run down,' he said. 'Maybe you need a holiday. Have you been under any sort of strain lately? That might account for it.' I burst out laughing, backing away from him into the street, but I didn't like it. Account for what? It was not as if I had told him anything. 'Why not see your doctor?' he shouted after me, his face creased up into a frown, as I walked off, laughing, along the windy pavement.

But of course it was no laughing matter. No one knew that better than I. The thing was, to proceed with caution. No good coming right out with it. Ridiculous to suggest seeing a doctor; I had seen enough of them to last me a lifetime, during Margaret's illness, and if there was one thing I had learnt from living with a chronic invalid, it was how not to turn into a hypochondriac. There was nothing wrong with me, I knew that. I was fit as a fiddle. A touch of indigestion now and then if I ate or drank too much; well, everyone got that. The merest palpitations if I woke suddenly in the night; well, you could not expect to sleep quite normally with pills and it was much too soon to give them up. I would not sleep at all without them as long as that creature was prowling about, making a row. Nobody could. And it would be bad for me to lie awake, dwelling on memories. The past was the past and no one could change it, even if they wanted to.

So I was cunning. There was an RSPCA place near the office and I went in there next day in my lunch hour and asked them how big a cat should be and whether an adult cat could go on growing. I knew Barbara had had the cat for years. The girl behind the counter gave me rather an odd look, I thought, but she answered all my questions and we went into the animal's diet: maybe I was overfeeding it, just a little, but that could not possibly make it grow, only get fat; it was much too old, fully grown. Then how about boarding it out, I asked quickly, before she lost interest, just for a few days, till its owner came back. I was a busy man, it was rather a tie, I could not be bothered with it. I made all this as casual as possible. Her face became dubious, even suspicious; her answers confused. I could hardly make sense of what she said, but it seemed their own kennels were full up (that must be a lie, for a start) and why didn't I try my local branch or the vet in my area, although at such short notice it was doubtful if anyone could help and in any case it was unusual (or irregular – I cannot remember which word she used) to accept an animal from anyone other than its owner . . . something about the responsibility. I was outraged. Didn't she think I had had enough responsibility, what about me, did nobody care? Her eyes were alarmed; she muttered something about asking advice and backed away from me, as if to call someone, but I knew better than that and I walked off, out of the shop while she was still speaking. That would show her.

All the same, she had given me an idea. I went home early – they were quite willing to let me go – and phoned all the local branches and vets in my neighbourhood. The cat watched me do it, but I paid no attention. I had to pretend it was mine, which stuck in my throat, but it had to be done. Again they all claimed to be full. While I waited for each one to answer I stole quick, secret glances at the cat. It *was* bigger: there was no doubt about it. And yet, when I looked again . . . As if someone were switching images, showing me two different photographs. Before and after. One, two. Rather – now I came to think of it – like that miserable optician with his alternate lenses, testing me. They were all at it. Barbara was testing me. I was on trial.

When I put down the phone I was shivering. The last place had let me down too. They were all pretending to be full, all muttering about short notice. But it simply could not be true. End of October, near enough; there could not be that many people away, boarding their pets. Pets. That was a laugh. A pet was something pleasant to touch, something you could stroke. Something soft and warm and friendly and . . . small. But this gave me another, better idea. You can't say I gave up without a struggle. If I could only bring myself to touch the animal (I had avoided all contact since releasing it from its basket) I could get it *back* in its basket and out of the house. It would be my prisoner. I could put it in the car and take it along to the wretched RSPCA, who seemed to have no idea of their duty, and pretend it was ill. Then they would have to take it in. I could say anything I liked; after all it could hardly contradict me. I could say it was foaming at the mouth, or refusing to eat (that would be a nice ironic touch), or being sick every day. By the time they found out it wasn't so, Barbara would be back.

I resolved on action. No more delay. I was even a little proud of myself. Such a simple solution; why had I not thought of it before? I advanced towards the cat, noting the position of the basket in the hall, closing the doors of the rooms so it could not escape, placing myself between it and the stairs so it could not run away without passing me. I would have to be quick: a quick grab, before it knew what was happening. But crafty too. So I made myself talk to it in a low, soothing voice. 'Nice cat, good cat, come on pussy, there's a good pussy cat.' Rubbish like that. It made me feel sick, actually. I must act quickly, before horror of touching its fur took me over. It seemed definitely orange today, or was it just the contrast with the very black stripes? Its coat really did seem more sharply defined. I got nearer gradually. It never stopped watching me, swishing its tail; that was a bad sign, I knew. But I had to go on: I had no choice. It backed away a little, almost into the basket, as if it were playing into my hands. I kept up my idiotic false monologue. But the smell was beginning to bother me. As I got nearer the smell that had faintly pervaded the whole house since it came grew suddenly more noticeable. And yet it was not the ordinary cat smell I knew, but much stronger, and though I could not place it I recognized it.

It all happened so fast. Looking back, I don't know in what order. Did it bare its teeth first, before I grabbed, or did I grab first, making it growl? I think I half closed my eyes at the moment of contact. But I saw its mouth open, and I felt my hands close on fur. Then the sudden sharp pain. I had never felt pain so acute. I let go at once; I had to. A black and orange streak flashed past me, seeming enormous, smelling obscene. The hall was full of its snarl. And I was left half crouching over the empty basket, staring at my hands.

They were covered in blood. I had never seen scratches like that. Two or three on each hand. But deep. All over the backs of my hands. Blood.

I told the story at work, as a hero. In bright sunlight, with people around me, it seemed almost an adventure: I wanted admiration. But no one seemed to realize how brave I had been, or how much I had suffered. My hands were covered with Elastoplast. Was it possible they thought I was inventing the whole thing? Even June seemed to look at me oddly, with an air of disbelief, and shuffled some papers on her desk to show she had work to do. She had not been really friendly, not at all her old self, since Margaret died. No one had. It was almost as if Barbara had talked to them all, putting them against me. I was beginning to feel myself an outcast. Was there nowhere to go where someone would understand? Did nobody *care* what happened to me?

'It was nice as pie this morning,' I told her. 'All round my legs, asking for breakfast.' I was keen to make this clear (though I shuddered at the memory) because it seemed to prove normality.

'There you are then,' she said pointlessly.

I lingered by her desk. It was some time since I had managed to be alone with her; in fact I had begun to wonder if she was deliberately avoiding me. Perhaps everyone was, as though I had some dreadful disease that might be catching. But with June it was worse. I cleared my throat.

'I was wondering,' I said, 'if you'd like to have a drink with me after work?' My voice sounded odd, strained. 'Or dinner. If you're not doing anything, that is.'

She did not even look up. I gazed at her, the top of her shiny hair, her pretty hands on the typewriter, her pointed breasts in the tight pink sweater. I willed her to say yes. I was so tired of eating alone.

'I'm sorry,' she said without expression. 'I've got a date.'

'Oh.' I was absurdly disappointed. No, more than that, rejected. It had taken so long to get up my courage again. I felt a door had slammed in my face. 'Yes, of course,' I said. 'It *is* very short notice. How about tomorrow?'

'She replied tonelessly, as if she were quoting from a magazine, 'I always wash my hair on Fridays.'

I didn't know what to say. She was like another person, not June of the old days. I made my voice cheerful, casual. 'Maybe one day next week then?'

I expected polite agreement, however vague. After all, I was not pinning her down to a day. But she shook her head instantly, not even pausing to think for politeness's sake.

'I'm busy all next week,' she said.

I should have left it at that, but something snapped. I heard myself say, quite sharply, 'I'm not a leper, you know. You were happy enough before – '

Her hands paused on the machine. 'Pardon?'

I found myself trembling. Why should this slip of a girl be able to make me tremble? 'You've changed your tune,' I said slowly.

She resumed typing, her mouth set in a line I knew well. It was a look that meant leave me alone, can't you see I'm not in the mood? 'Things are a little different now,' she said smoothly.

'It was a merciful release.' I could not stop the words coming out. I even put my hand on her typewriter and repeated them. 'You must know that.'

Then at last she looked up. All the warmth I remembered had gone from her eyes. 'I beg your pardon?'

I was incensed. After all, I had left it as long as I could, waited a decent interval, whatever that was. Still I could not get my tongue round the words 'Margaret's death'. I started to say, 'You know very well what I mean,' but she stood up at once, as if at a given signal, and ripped the piece of paper out of her machine.

'Excuse me,' she said crisply, not looking at me. 'I must take Mr Hervey this letter to sign.' She moved right round the desk to avoid passing close to me.

I lost control at this and who can blame me. 'I came to the point abruptly, shouting after her, 'Do *you* like cats?' and she turned at the door, the merest crease of a frown disturbing the childish perfection of her skin. She was so ridiculously young. But hard, I was learning, the way perhaps only the young can afford to be.

'Well, do you?' I shouted. 'How would you like to live with a cat?' I felt the sweat break out cold on my forehead.

'It's rather urgent,' she said. 'So he'll probably want me to post it at once. I'll be going home early.'

When I got home the cat was small and meek, waiting for food. But I knew better than to be fooled by appearances. Inside it was mocking me, biding its time. Yet it looked so innocent, so harmless. Was it really the same animal that had clawed me so viciously?

I dreamed that night of June. June at the office, smiling, close to me. June in my bed, welcoming me, my hands on her breasts. But I could not move. I knew I was being watched. I thought in the dream it was Margaret but it might have been Barbara. There was someone in that room, watching us, but June did not know. I tried to tell her and she did not understand; she thought I was saying something else and she smiled even more encouragingly. I struggled to free myself, to point to the watcher, whoever it was, but my hands seemed glued to her body. I woke to a piercing noise, the unmistakable, unforgettable sound of Margaret's bell.

It stopped at once, but I was already, by old habit, halfway to the door of my room. I was panting and covered in sweat. Automatically I completed the movement and opened my door. But Margaret was dead. I had seen her dead, I had seen her buried, I had heard the earth drop on her coffin. She could not be more dead. It wasn't my fault; she had to understand that. I had acted from the best, always from the best of motives. I could not help myself. But Barbara did not understand. Barbara would not make allowances, like Margaret. Barbara wanted revenge. I hammered on Margaret's door, completely losing control, crying, sobbing for mercy, and into a patch of moonlight on the landing, as into a spotlight on stage, strolled the cat. I was not mistaken. It was not my imagination or my eyesight, simply all I had feared and been unable to say. Larger. Every day a little larger. It was turning into a tiger.

Next day old man Hervey called me into his office. I was haggard from lack of sleep, from a night mostly spent curled up on my bed in my dressing-gown, shivering, reliving the past, listening to the wind fairly howling outside. It had been gusty all week but it seemed much worse that night, like a full force gale, or perhaps it was just that I was awake to hear it. I had tried to make plans. As I could not get rid of the cat I should have to go away myself. I resented this. Driven from my own house by an animal. But anything was preferable. I should have packed there and then, and gone. But in the morning, in daylight, with the cat nowhere to be seen, it all seemed like a nightmare, no more, and my head ached, and I was late for the office.

Mr Hervey suggested a holiday. They would make it compassionate leave, sick leave, whatever I liked; it need not even come off my annual holiday. I was run down, he said. It was understandable. A lot of strain, I had come back too soon. He oozed sympathy, but I knew. He wanted to get rid of me, wash his hands of me. I was no one's responsibility. Get a bit of sun, he said, soon fix you up, but what he meant was you're going to pieces, man, and I'm not having that here, in my office. I nearly asked him how he felt about cats, but he didn't look that sort of man.

So I went home early. The weather was wild. Late October winds lashing the trees, leaves blowing everywhere. I walked in a kind of trance, passing some giggling children in masks, but hardly noticing them. I was very cold. I knew there were things to be done, yet I felt incapable of action. I dreaded my return to the house yet I longed to be there, as if in a refuge, though I knew it was no refuge. Most of all I felt like a puppet. As if I had always been a puppet but only just realized. All freedom of choice an illusion.

I let myself in, and the door slammed with a hollow sound; the place echoed like a tomb. I picked up the mail from the hall table and went into the living-room to pour myself a drink. When I looked at the letters I found a couple of bills and underneath them a postcard. I knew before I turned it over that it was from Barbara. 'Happy Hallowe'en,' was all it said.

Of course you will think me a fool not to realize before. But I had not been meant to realize. The thing was beyond my control.

I rushed from the room, dropping my glass and heading for the front door. My instincts still made me behave as if I had a chance. But it was futile, almost laughable. The cat was there in the hall, between me and the door, blocking my path.

It was enormous. It might have come straight from the jungle. It was any tiger you can see in a film, in the zoo, on safari. Vast and orange, dark-striped. It even smelt different, as if it had never been a cat: I got a sickening waft of the authentic circus smell. And it opened its jaws and roared. For a second I was paralysed by the sound, then I turned and ran.

You cannot say I was cowardly. Straight into the kitchen I went, in search of a weapon. But there on the floor in front of me was a mouse, and this time there was blood on its neck.

I picked up a knife. The cat had not moved, but it could be only a question of time. Perhaps it would play with me. I tried the back door, my hands slippery with sweat, but the key was missing. Mrs Coates being cautious. So I was forced into bravery. The kitchen door was useless, a mere sliding and folding affair, affording no protection. So back into the hall I went, brandishing my weapon.

The cat was in the doorway of the living-room. Lying down, watching me, just like a cat. Except that it was still a tiger. I could reach the stairs without passing it, but not the front door. I wanted to run but instead I moved slowly; as I drew level with it I suddenly waved my knife, either from impatience or bravado. Or perhaps I had the idea that if I could make it roar again, someone might hear, someone might come. Though at the same time I half believed that it was audible only to me.

It merely yawned. A huge sleepy yawn, showing all its teeth. It had all the time in the world.

Somehow this terrified me more than anything. I panicked, hurling myself at the stairs. Halfway up I slipped, missing my footing, flung out both my hands to save myself, and automatically dropped the knife. It fell through the banisters to the floor below and I watched it with sickening despair but no surprise, as if I had known this was meant to happen. The cat saw it too. And as I dragged myself back to my feet a sudden sharp pain told me I had injured my ankle.

Progress was slow now, but still the cat did not come for me. I hobbled along the passage to the upstairs phone, in Margaret's room. It was damp and chill when I entered it but there was no horror: I had known all along I must return here and when I did it was like coming home. But the phone was dead. Even this gave me no surprise; I had hardly expected it to work. The lines have blown down in the gale, if you want to be rational. What does it matter?

I am very cold. And there isn't much time left. It must happen before midnight, I am sure of that. Forgive me. June and her breasts cannot warm me now as I lie on your bed, Margaret, in your place, where you died. It's so cold. A pane in the window has blown in. But you know better than Barbara, don't you? She may know facts, or what she calls facts. But you know my motives. You know I acted for the best. Don't you?

It's coming. My watch has stopped but I should guess it is nearly midnight. That would be about right. I could bar the door with furniture but that would only delay it and I am too weak and my ankle pains me. Padding along the passage I can hear it, very steady and stealthy. It knows where to come. Oh, God, I'm so alone. Never more alone. My heart bursting, a blackness in front of my eyes. I hope it won't hurt too much.

A COMPLETE COLLECTION

Sydney J. Bounds

Michael Fox brooded over a pipe and a pint of lager in the lounge of London's Regal Hotel. From the hubbub of voices surrounding him, he carefully separated a few names: Chilvers – of course! – Guthrie, King, Chilvers again . . .

All the big names in the fantasy field, and Fox was attending the Annual World Fantasy Convention. The Guest of Honour speech had ended and fans crowded the lounge in the interval before the fancy dress ball was due to start. Some were already in costume; he saw a cloaked Dracula, a werewolf and witch together.

Fox took a long swallow and tried to convince himself it wasn't envy he felt. He'd been writing fantasy, on and off, for twenty odd years, yet he felt out of place here. The young writers specialized, wrote fantasy only, and they were like gods in this one tiny field. He wrote under half a dozen names in as many fields, and needed to; he was a professional and that way he stayed solvent.

He was feeling ignored in a sea of long-haired youth when a man with middle-aged spread covered by expensive suiting approached and asked: 'Mr Michael Fox?'

Fox wondered what a square was doing at a fantasy convention. He saw a business executive type, hair neatly trimmed and clean shaven, even a hint of starch in the shirt collar. The stranger had a book tucked under one arm. A publisher, perhaps?

'Yes, I'm Fox.'

'I'm happy to meet you, sir. May I offer to refill your glass?'

The 'sir' paralysed Fox and he could only nod dumbly.

'Jonathan Jamieson, sir. If you call me J.J. you'll be following a precedent. I'm a collector, with a high regard for your work.'

'That's nice,' Fox said. 'You've just made my day.'

Jamieson held out the book he carried: *Doorway to Hell*, in fine condition. 'One of your first, I believe. I managed to outbid competing collectors at the auction earlier. I'd be honoured if you'll autograph it for me.'

Fox unclipped a ball-point and wrote a suitable inscription on the title page as their drinks arrived. The lounge began to empty as people drifted towards the ballroom, and they found comfortable armchairs in a corner of the room.

'I remember the first story of yours I ever read, *The Curse of Khephra*, in *Terror Tales*. I have an interest in Egyptology and yours was the first story of this type I'd come across where an author had bothered to get his facts right. I was impressed, sir, and immediately started to collect your work. I may say that I'm well on the way to forming a complete collection. Perhaps I may enlist your aid?'

With several lagers inside him and an appreciative reader, Fox nodded happily. He gathered that Jamieson was a self-made man who'd struck it lucky with some kind of plastic gimmick; now he put in only a token appearance at his factory and had time and money to spend on his hobby.

Two days passed before the first letter arrived: where had *Voodoo Doll* first been published? As the weeks rolled by it seemed that every post brought its queries . . .

Do you have a spare copy of *Nightmare*?

Can you list your stories which appeared in the following magazines?

Is *Satan's Daughter* your earliest published work?

Fox's answers became shorter. They took valuable time and Jamieson began to worry him; this insistence on detail seemed more like an obsession than a harmless hobby.

When Jamieson got around to asking about pen-names, Fox smiled and admitted he had written westerns and crime novels under different names. That should slow him down, he thought.

A reply came back by return. 'Full details, if you please! I will admit you're giving me far more work than I had anticipated, but I am committed to completing my collection.'

Wearily, Fox racked his brain for details.

One evening, typing fast on the final chapter of a thriller, he cursed as the doorbell interrupted his flow of words. He ignored it, but the caller would not go away. Fox lit his pipe and went to the door to find Jamieson standing there.

A camera in a leather case hung from the strap around his neck and he held out a wine bottle. 'My apologies for calling unannounced sir. Please accept this as a token of the debt I owe you.'

Reluctantly, Fox invited him in and showed him his workroom. 'I'm busy, as you can see – a deadline to meet.'

'I shall not detain you long,' Jamieson said. He unfastened the leather case and produced a small cine-camera. 'May I . . . ?'

He panned slowly round the room, taking in the typewriter on an old kitchen table, the rack of reference books. As he filmed, he said: 'I am engaged upon a replica of your workroom in which to house my collection.'

Fox opened the wine and poured two glasses. 'You seem to be going to a lot of trouble.'

Jamieson smiled. 'I suppose I'm a perfectionist.' He took a sheet of screwed-up paper from the basket by the table. 'Ah, the author's rough work.' It disappeared into his pocket along with an empty ball-point.

Fox stared in fascination. He'd met collectors before, but this one was in a class of his own; he felt slightly repelled by so complete a surrender to an obsession. But his sense of unease was reduced by his need to get the last chapter finished.

Jamieson apparently read his mind. 'I shan't disturb you longer, sir.' His gaze lit on an old pipe with a cracked bowl. 'I wonder if I might – '

'Take it by all means,' Fox said hastily.

Jamieson left, apparently satisfied with his filming and the odds and ends he'd collected.

After that, Fox didn't hear from him for some time. A letter arrived just after he'd finished a rush job and was feeling the need for a break.

'I have just read your latest story and enjoyed it immensely. Perhaps you can find the time to spend a weekend with me? I hope so – I now have something interesting to show you.'

Fox quickly decided that a weekend in the country was just what he needed, and wrote a letter of acceptance. Late on Friday afternoon he caught a local up to London and a main line train out through Chelmsford and Colchester. It was dark when he arrived at his destination and he was the only passenger to alight at the small country halt.

The place seemed desolate, with a salt wind blowing in from the sea.

Jamieson was waiting with a car. 'Let me take your bag. It is a fair distance, I'm afraid, and this is a lonely part of the country.'

He drove carefully over empty roads that wound between dark fields. The moon came up to reveal a light mist. Presently they came to a high stone wall and Jamieson turned into a drive bordered by gaunt trees. The house was big and Victorian. As the car's headlights swept across it, a spark struck in Fox's mind: a Gothic, now, there was a market for that kind of story. He began to look forward to exploring the interior of the house.

Behind diamond-shaped glass, a single light burned. They climbed stone steps to the front door, a slab of solid timber. Jamieson used his key and ushered Fox inside.

'I live here alone, sir, except for some help from a lady in the nearest village. Unfortunately she is not well just at the moment and I'm doing for myself. But I promise to look after you.'

He set down Fox's suitcase in the hall.

'We'll have a drink to start the evening, but first I must show you this.'

He took another key from his pocket and opened a door in the passage. Steps led down to what had once been a cellar and had now been converted.

Fox thought he was back home. It was a strikingly successful replica of his own workroom; the table and chair appeared identical, the typewriter was the same model he used himself, even the reference books were the same.

There was one big difference. Along one wall stretched a glass bookcase containing all his published writings.

'Your collected works, sir.' Jamieson's voice held a note of pride. 'Complete, I believe.'

Fox said weakly, 'I'm impressed.'

'We'll take that drink now,' Jamieson said.

Fox followed him up the steps and along the passage. His nose wrinkled at an acrid smell.

His host noticed and said: 'Trouble with the drains – it's an old house.'

The room they entered was large and fitted with comfortable armchairs. A log fire burned in the grate. The bookcase was filled with books on ancient Egypt, and Fox recognized titles he'd used in his own research.

Jamieson poured two glasses of wine, handed one to Fox. 'I believe I mentioned I had an interest in Egyptology?' He raised his glass. 'May your reputation increase.'

Fox drank. His stomach burned and he doubled over; pain engulfed him. He collapsed on the carpet, consciousness fading.

Jonathan Jamieson watched silently. After a few minutes he checked for a pulse: none.

Now he moved swiftly, before the body had time to stiffen. He carried Fox into the kitchen and laid him out on a stainless steel table, stripped the clothes away. His tools were set out in preparation.

He glanced at the text of an Egyptian book headed: *His body shall endure.*

Already Fox's eyes had dulled; soon the skin would chill. With a kitchen knife he made an incision in the left flank and removed the internal organs. The natron was ready to hand. Jamieson's eyes gleamed with excitement; no one knew more about preserving bodies than the ancient Egyptians.

As he stuffed the body, he imagined Michael Fox seated at the table downstairs, hands forever poised over a typewriter keyboard. His collection was finally complete: the author *and* his works.

DEAD WEEK

Leonard Carpenter

From 6.00 PM until 11.00 PM, Cassy slept the sleep of the hunted. She awoke still dressed, stiff and cold on her cot, and lay for a long time in a semicomatose state watching the ghosts of car lights creep across the ceiling.

Sleeping odd hours was a method she used to cope with her roommates' erratic study habits, and their taste for bluegrass music played loud and long. Now the house below her was finally quiet. The long night lay ahead for a last-ditch effort to prepare for finals next week.

Cassy couldn't understand why no one else ever needed to study. Between her full load of classes, the cafeteria job to supplement her meagre scholarship, and the lab requirements for the advanced biology programme, she had no time left. The endless talking, socializing, and kicking back that the others engaged in were luxuries she couldn't afford. By accepting a steep increase in rent she had managed to get a room to herself – not a room really, just a cramped vestibule atop the back stairway, probably rented out in violation of fire regulations. But she needed it to study in peace.

Her first task, the one she had been dreading, was to clean off her desk. It was an unexplored drift of papers reflecting the disorder of her own mind – books, lecture notes, handouts, reading lists, and who-knew-what-else dumped there in moments of exhaustion during the semester. Now she would need to review all her course requirements in order to cram efficiently. She dragged herself up, switched on the naked bulb overhead, plugged in her coffee pot, and went to work.

The job went faster than she expected. Most of the papers could be arranged by course number and date or thrown away. The notes were legible, if sparse, and she had really only fallen behind in her reading a few weeks before – so maybe things weren't so bad.

Then she found something. Near the bottom of the mess was a pink, printed card with the hours and days of a week blocked out like a calendar, bearing the motto 'Courtesy of the Berkeley Student Bookstore'. The card itself wasn't strange – the times of Cassy's classes, labs, and work shifts were sketched into it with the care of someone mapping out a glorious new life, long before it turned into a murderous routine.

The strange thing was that on Tuesday and Thursday afternoons at 3.00 PM – right in the middle of her cherished library study time – were pencilled blocks labelled 'Demo 168'.

It looked like her writing, but it puzzled her. She certainly wasn't taking any courses in demonology. Maybe it was demolitions – she laughed, thinking that would make a good poli-sci course. On an impulse she picked up her dog-eared schedule and directory and thumbed through the alphabetical listings. There it was, in tiny computer print, underscored in red pencil. 'Demography Dept. – Demo 168–133 Dwinelle Hall – TTh 3.'

Intrigued and a little disturbed, she plunged into the thick yellow course catalogue. 'Demography 168. 3 units. The Limits of Population. An exploration of the theoretical and practical limits to population growth, with special emphasis on the roles of birth and death controls in restoring equilibrium. Professors Thayer and Munck.'

Slowly, with the elusive quality of a dream, it came back to her. She had indeed considered taking the course in February, nearly five months before. She'd even attended one or two lectures. The subject had sounded interesting – and relevant, she had thought, to the populations of microbes she would be working with in bio. She'd heard that it was a smart precaution to sign up for extra classes in case your first preferences were too crowded.

But the professor had indicated that the course would focus on human populations, using a social-science approach. That was the main reason Cassy had dropped it.

At least she seemed to recall dropping it. She began hunting through the desk drawers. There it was – the green carbon copy of the enrollment card, signed by her faculty advisor. As she read it her heart plunged and her fingertips felt numb. It listed five courses; the fifth one was Demo 168.

But that was crazy! How could she be taking a course without even knowing it? She was sure she hadn't bought any of the texts – at some point she must have just stopped attending and forgotten all about it.

Frantically she searched through the last of the clutter on the desktop. A single sheet, mimeographed in pale purple, came to light. It read, 'Demography 168 – Course Requirements. The grade will be based sixty percent on the final exam and forty percent on the term paper, to be handed in at the last class meeting. Lecture attendance is recommended. Required reading: *Man against the Ceiling* by Storvich and Smith, Sutton House, 1973; *The Dynamics of Death Control* by E.C. Festung, 1978 ed.; *Sower and Reaper* by G. Hofstaedler, Vendome, 1979. Additional readings to be assigned periodically.'

Cassy felt a great, sinking despair. The chance of catching up so late in the semester was nil. She would have to request some kind of administrative relief. Whether it would affect her scholarship, she didn't know.

There was certainly nothing to be done so late at night – and no one she could talk to. She tried to study for other classes, but thoughts of the phantom class kept twisting through her brain. As the night dragged on she accomplished nothing more. Sleep was unattainable.

The most upsetting thing was the realization of her own mental lapse – somehow, under all the demands and stress, her mind had slipped gears. Was it the first time? Would it be the last?

The Berkeley campus seemed deserted the following day as Cassy walked to the Admin Building. Dead Week, students called it – week of anguished repentance for thoughtless months of procrastination. The sky was steely grey with the fog that can make San Francisco Bay summers colder than its winters. Swishing sprinklers transected the lawns.

Cassy's route passed Barrows Hall, the eight-storey maths building. She involuntarily glanced at the demolished shrub where a grad student had dived from the roof a few days before. He had been the second suicide to choose the boxlike building this term, the fourth this school year. They were keeping the roof doors locked now.

Sproul Hall loomed impassive on the left, seemingly built of sugar cubes. The plaza wasn't deserted – its bizarre bazaar never ceased. Two die-hard disc throwers, a vagrant guitar player, a revivalist preacher ranting to nobody, and an odd assortment of street people were all doing their things. Cassy hurried through. Somehow the sight of the anonymous social transactions taking place here only intensified her loneliness.

Cassy had friendships, of course – smooth working relation- ships with the people in her major, her job, and her house. But she felt there was some kind of sustenance she wasn't getting. She knew that she didn't fit the conventional beauty standard; the schoolkid puns about 'Cassy's chassis' had stopped being funny after her chassis became a little too stout for most boys' liking. And though she had definitely and finally determined that she was not 'pigfaced', it was depressing to have to remind herself of it each time she looked into a mirror.

Not that she wanted a delirious romance. Her schedule didn't allow for it. Summer loomed ahead, with two accelerated class sessions, more hours at the cafeteria, and a visit or possibly two with her mom. She would have liked to do more dating and partying, but lately the guys who approached her always seemed a little slimy. 'Let's talk about you,' they said; 'Tell me about yourself' – willing to give only as much as they absolutely had to. Their attention shifted too easily. The latest one, Howie, had been that way. He had left a message for her a few weeks ago, but she had forgotten to return his call.

Inside Sproul Hall there were long lines at the administration window in spite of Dead Week – students fighting their bureaucratic battles to the bitter end. No one in her line said anything to her; Cassy vainly opened up her biochem text and stared at the chapter on protein synthesis.

When her turn came she tried to explain her situation. The clerk, a bored girl who looked younger than Cassy herself, pointed to an orange bulletin under the glass countertop. 'I'm sorry, the last day to add or drop classes was March third.'

'But I never really took this class. I mean, I didn't mean to!' She felt herself getting in deeper. 'I don't need it . . . I only took it by mistake.'

'I'm sorry. The only way to drop now would be to withdraw from the University.' The girl peered over Cassy's shoulder to summon the next one in line.

'But that's impossible . . . my other classes. My scholarship! I want to talk to someone else, please.'

'You could ask the instructor for a grade of Incomplete.'

'Please let me talk to someone else.'

'Very well. You'll have to make an appointment to see the Dean. His office is on the second floor, in front of you as you leave the stairwell. Next.'

After waiting in the Dean's anteroom and making an appointment for the following day. Cassy didn't have time to go home before her work shift. Instead she went to the Graduate Social Sciences Library in Stevens Hall. There, at the back of a yellow-lit aisle in the soundless stacks, she was able to find one of the books on the Demo 168 reading list, the Festung text. It was a hardcover maroon volume two inches thick, and it looked as if no one had ever opened it. The glossy pages were densely printed, with graphs of sociological data.

The chapter titles made it sound pretty heavy: 'Nature's Inexorable Balance', 'Death Controls Versus Human Ingenuity', 'The Pathology of Crowding', 'The Role of the Unconscious', and so on. The graphs dealt mainly with crime rates and deaths from various causes as functions of population density, in an endless series of uptailing curves. The prose was impenetrable – written in Berkeleyese, a pretentious academic style that tries earnestly to make itself immune to all criticism and ends up qualifying itself into meaningless obscurity.

Typical social sciences material, Cassy thought. There was no hope of making sense of it without the lectures and the teacher's help, if she did end up having to do the coursework.

That was one reason Cassy had majored in biology. It had no shortage of cumbersome facts and figures to grapple with, but there was also the laboratory work – real, concrete procedures that could show the truth or untruth of the theories in solid, life-or-death terms. She was good in the lab, and it was largely on the strength of this aptitude that she'd been accepted into the advanced bio programme.

Of course, it had put unexpected demands on her time and cut into her other activities – but she didn't mind. It made her feel good to be valued as a researcher. Much of it was routine work and errand-girl stuff – growing and feeding cultures, caring for test animals, and delivering specimens – still, she was learning a great deal about immunology research. Some of it was quite advanced; she suspected that the lab programmes were tied to defence – though her instructors would never admit that, with the current sentiment on campus.

Returning home in a haze of fatigue. Cassy cut across the grassless front lawn and climbed the porch steps of her house. It was a worn, gaudily painted Victorian building perched on a roaring one-way street. The front door stood open and an acrid smell drifted out. She headed down the hall, past the communal kitchen, and heard voices raised.

'There she goes now.' It was an angry-sounding female, Vickie or Connie, speaking from one of the rooms. An intense murmur interrupted her, and then the voice shrilled. 'Well, somebody's got to tell the creep!'

Cassy turned as Dave's tee-shirted figure, built square for soccer, appeared in the kitchen doorway. His face was set grimly. 'Cassy, come here.' He jerked his head in the direction of the kitchen.

Cassy complied. Dave stepped back to reveal the room. The acrid smell was heavier here, and the ceiling was smoke-stained. The blackened, ill-scrubbed stove with scorched and blistered cabinets above it resembled an altar.

'We had the fire department here this morning, Cassy,' Dave said. 'After you left. Did you forget to turn off the burner?'

Cassy felt numb, confused. 'Well, maybe . . . I'm not sure . . .'

'Sure she did.' Vickie, dressed in tight jeans and Dave's sweatshirt, came through the door that joined their room to the kitchen. 'It was her crap piled up on the stove that caught fire. If Bruce hadn't smelt it, we would've all burned to death in our sleep.' She thumped across the floor in bare beet and confronted Cassy. 'What's with you anyway?'

156

'I'm sorry . . .' Cassy had only a vague, recollection of her hurried breakfast of coffee, toast, and doughnuts. 'I've been so busy lately . . .'

'Busy – jeez!' Vickie threw up her hands violently. 'We could be dead right now, and you're busy!' She rolled her eyes ceilingward. 'How do we know you won't do it again tomorrow? You sneak around here, and never talk to anybody . . .'

Dave put a hand on her shoulder, gingerly. 'Vickie, I think she gets the idea.'

'Butt out, Dave.' Vickie twisted out from under his hand and went on, 'You stay up all night. You know, we can hear you moving around up there. When you walk back and forth, it makes the whole house creak.'

Cassy reddened. 'Well, that's better than some of the things I've heard coming from your room!' She turned and started down the hall.

Vickie ran out of the kitchen after her. 'Bullshit! You almost burned us alive! You leave your coffee grounds all over – and the weird stuff you eat takes up most of the space in the fridge!'

Dave was physically restraining her. 'That's enough, Vick.'

'I don't care,' she screamed. As Cassy started up the back stairs, Vickie was yelling. 'Why don't you just move out!'

Next day Cassy sat in the office of Dean Moody while he thumbed through her master file. Over his shoulder, visible through the venetian blind, the soaring ivory tower of the Campanile chimed out eleven o'clock. He looked up and pinched his clean-shaven lips into a smile.

'Just an oversight, you say? Well, whatever the cause, I think we can make an exception in view of your excellent academic record. It can be written up as a late drop for health reasons. All that will be required are the signatures of the instructor and your faculty advisor.' He took a card from his desk drawer, partially filled it in, and handed it to her. 'You can hand it in at the window downstairs.'

Cassy had no difficulty getting the signature of her advisor, Professor Langenschiedt. He was so busy between the affairs of the Medical Physics Department and the Academic Senate, that he scarcely listened to her explanation before expressing every confidence in her good judgment, signing the form, and hurrying her out.

The approval of the course instructor was another matter. Cassy had some uneasiness about approaching him to tell him she'd lost interest in his class. Every academician takes his job seriously; she didn't really suppose that he'd consider her case important enough to warrant withholding his signature, but she anticipated an unpleasant encounter.

She had reconstructed a fairly clear mental picture of Professor Thayer from the beginning of the term: tall, tweedy, with squared-off tortoiseshell glasses and grey hair sculptured around his brow. His lectures had been dry and dispassionate, giving no hint of his general disposition.

She looked up his office number and went in search of it. Her quest took her through the cavernous lobby of Dwinelle Hall and into its dim, labyrinthine recesses. In building the hall and adding Dwinelle Annex, the designers had violated some basic law of architectural geometry, or else one of human perception. Angular corridors and half-flights of stairs created baffling and often frightening missteps for those who ventured inside. The sickly-brown light reflecting off the floor added to the eerie effect. But after many detours and hesitations. Cassy found the indicated door, number 1521, and knocked. 'Come in!'

As she opened the door a flood of daylight came through, so that she could see only the outline of the man behind the desk. The tall window looked out on a tree-filled quadrangle, and the north wall opposite was bright with sun.

Professor Thayer closed the book before him and motioned Cassy to a chair. 'Hello, Miss . . . uh, I'm pleased to see you. Aren't you in one of my classes?'

'Well, yes I was . . . I mean I am. That's sort of what I needed to talk to you about. I stopped going after the second lecture.'

'Why, that's funny – I thought I'd seen you more than that. I recognize your bangs.'

Cassy blushed. Although she had been busy all day formulating excuses, they evaporated now. Cassy told him simply and truthfully what had happened. There was something so reassuring in his manner that she went into more detail than she had done with anyone, and she finished with a lump in her throat. She took the drop card out of her book bag and placed it on his desk.

Professor Thayer nodded at it, but didn't seem in any hurry to sign.

'Tell me,' he asked, 'how many units are you taking?'

'Fifteen. Besides your class, I mean.'

'That's quite a load. You also work part-time?'

'Yes sir. At the Meals Facility. And my lab requirement is six hours a week, but I usually spend more time than that.' Cassy didn't mean to sound abject, but somehow she didn't feel like holding anything back.

'You must be under great stress. I can see how it might cause, uh, a slip of the kind you describe.' He smiled. 'Oh course I'll be glad to sign your card.' But instead of reaching for it, the professor folded his arms, leaned back in his chair, and began to profess.

'It's a shame, in a way, that you couldn't have taken my class. It would have given you some insight into a problem that's affecting you – and affecting us all, whether we know it or not.

'The course deals with overpopulation. It's been controversial in the Demography Department, since it probably should be called a sociology or population-ecology course instead; some of my colleagues don't approve of my taking what amounts to a moral stance, by saying just how much population is too much. But since the class deals specifically with human society, and most of the data are here, I've kept it in the department.

'We explore the correlation of increased population density with all the classes of effects – from high rents to disrupted living conditions, stress, violent crime, suicide, *et cetera*. One of the key factors at work is *anomie* – the insecure, faceless "lonely crowd" feeling discussed by Durkheim and Riesman. It's hard to define an emotion like that scientifically, but it's easy to see its results; they fill the front pages of our newspapers – with gruesome statistics.' Professor Thayer prodded a fat green softcover volume of census figures at the side of his desk, so that it flopped shut of its own weight.

'Of course, when you're discussing overpopulation, there's no better example of it than the student body of a large school like

Berkeley. In this case, the population pressure is artificial – resulting from the crush of students to a favoured institution – but it's intense enough to develop all the classic effects: high rents, crowded living conditions, the overload of facilities, and above all, stress. An interesting microcosm.' Professor Thayer gazed speculatively at Cassy for a moment, then resumed.

'The intriguing approach is to view all these social problems not just as ill effects, but as attempts by a dynamic system to balance itself. "Death controls", in E. C. Festung's phrase.

'When a population exceeds natural limits, it definitely will be reduced – if not by birth control, then by death controls such as famine and disease. The human species is uniquely fortunate in having the power to choose – though we don't seem to be using that power.

'Festung identified a wide range of behaviour peculiar to man as death controls: war, terrorism, violent crime, transportation accidents, cult suicides, nuclear "events" ' – the professor drew imaginary brackets around the word with two pairs of fingers – 'all the unique disasters we take for granted today. He maintains that they all stem from an instinct, inborn in mankind far beneath the level of rational thought, to reduce a population that, unconsciously, we perceive as too large. Like caged birds in the five-and-dime pecking each other to death. In effect, crowding is seen to induce irrational and aggressive behaviour. A fascinating theory.' This time his pause was punctuated by the sound of sparrows chirping outside in the quad.

'Unfortunately, it all tends to sound very morbid. Many students can't work with it – too depressing. They'd rather just shrug it off, at least until it becomes too big to ignore. Like so many contemporary issues, it's a hard one to face – I've seen some fine minds become paralyzed by a sort of ecological despair.' He massaged his chin a moment. 'In a way, your little bout of forgetfulness parallels the attitude of all Western society toward the population issue, ever since the time of Malthus. The initial warnings were just too grim, so we thrust it away to the back of our minds. Unfortunately that doesn't alleviate the problem.'

The professor lapsed into silence and stared out the window for a while, hands folded. Then he bestirred himself and looked at his watch. 'Oh my, I've run on for quite a while. You ended up

taking my course anyway – the special condensed version. Hope I
didn't bore you. Or depress you. Here, I'll sign this.'

In a few moments Cassy was being ushered out the door. She
didn't regret having spent so long with Professor Thayer. He was
cute, though long-winded – and a lot of what he said sounded
awfully unscientific.

Leaving Dwinelle she headed for the lab. After that, home, to
do some serious cramming!

So Dead Week ended, if not quite happily, then at least hurriedly.
Although the menace of the phantom class was laid to rest, Cassy
knew that the distraction and delay had hurt her study effort –
perhaps seriously. So she halved her sleep time and doubled her
coffee intake to catch up, and in a while agony faded to mere
numbness. Perhaps it didn't matter anyway – she had always
found that final grades bore no recognizable relationship to her
effort of understanding.

To complicate matters, there was a flurry of last-minute
activity at the lab. An ill-timed biochemical breakthrough had
Cassy making special trips around the campus to deliver files and
samples when she should have been doing a dozen other things.
In the department she sensed excitement and an unspoken
pressure to keep the matter quiet – if not permanently, then at
least until the summer break, when the majority of the students
would have gone home and the chance of protest lessened.

On Wednesday the lunch crowd in the Meals Facility was only
slightly smaller than usual. A few of the diners moved with the
sanctified air of having finished their final exams; others carried
stacks of books on their trays and looked haggard. Cassy stood
behind the counter doling out portions of stew, chicken, and
enchiladas.

A familiar face appeared in the customer line. 'Hello,
Profession Thayer,' she said brightly.

'Why, hello, Cassy! Oh, that's right – you told me you worked
here, didn't you?' The professor put on a playfully pensive look.
'Hmmm. I wonder what's good today.'

'Everyone's having the Caesar salad,' said Cassy, smiling. 'It ought to be good – I helped make it.' she reached for a clean bowl and began to dish up an especially generous helping.

At that moment she noticed the Erlenmayer flask right there before her – from the lab. It was nearly empty of bacterial toxins, type K. It really didn't look much different from the salad dressing cruet – but that was over on the table by her purse, and it was still full. Again that lightheaded feeling, of gears slipping somewhere.

Cassy and the professor heard a tray crash and looked out across the expanse of tables. Something was happening. A man near the window lurched, fell across a table, and rolled to the floor. There were violent movements elsewhere in the room, and out on the terrace.

Then the screaming began.

MISS SMITH

William Trevor

One day Miss Smith asked James what a baby horse was called, and James couldn't remember. He blinked and shook his head. He knew, he explained, but he just couldn't remember. Miss Smith said:

'Well, well; James Machen doesn't know what a baby horse is called.'

She said it loudly so that everyone in the class-room heard. James became very confused. He blinked and said:

'Pony, Miss Smith?'

'Pony! James Machen says a baby horse is a pony! Hands up everyone who knows what a baby horse is.'

All the right arms in the room, except James's and Miss Smith's, shot upwards. Miss Smith smiled at James.

'Everyone knows,' she said. 'Everyone knows what a baby horse is called except James.'

James thought: I'll run away. I'll join the tinkers and live in a tent.

'What's a baby horse called?' Miss Smith asked the class, and the class shouted:

'Foal, Miss Smith.'

'A foal, James,' Miss Smith repeated. 'A baby horse is a foal, James dear.'

'I knew, Miss Smith. I knew but . . .'

Miss Smith laughed and the class laughed, and afterwards nobody would play with James because he was so silly to think that a baby horse was a pony.

James was an optimist about Miss Smith. He thought it might be different when the class went on the summer picnic or sat tightly together at the Christmas party, eating cake and biscuits and having their mugs filled from big enamel jugs. But it never

163

was different. James got left behind when everyone was racing across the fields at the picnic, and Miss Smith had to wait impatiently, telling the class that James would have to have his legs stretched. And at the party she heaped his plate with seed cake, because she imagined, so she said, that he was the kind of child who enjoyed such fare.

Once James found himself alone with Miss Smith in the class-room. She was sitting at her desk correcting some homework. James was staring in front of him, admiring a fountain pen that the day before his mother had bought for him. It was a small fountain pen, coloured purple and black and white. James believed it to be elegant.

It was very quiet in the class-room. Soundlessly, Miss Smith's red pencil ticked and crossed and underlined. Without looking up, she said: 'Why don't you go out and play?'

'Yes, Miss Smith,' said James. He walked to the door, clipping his pen into his pocket. As he turned the handle he heard Miss Smith utter a sound of irritation. He turned and saw that the point of her pencil had broken. 'Miss Smith, you may borrow my pen. You can fill it with red ink. It's quite a good pen.'

James crossed the room and held out his pen. Miss Smith unscrewed the cap and prodded at the paper with the nib. 'What a funny pen, James!' she said. 'Look, it can't write.'

'There's no ink in it,' James explained. 'You've got to fill it with red ink, Miss Smith.'

But Miss Smith smiled and handed the pen back. 'What a silly boy you are to waste your money on such a poor pen!'

'But I didn't . . .'

'Come along now, James, aren't you going to lend me your pencil sharpener?'

'I haven't got a pencil sharpener, Miss Smith.'

'No pencil sharpener? Oh James, James, you haven't got anything, have you?'

When Miss Smith married, James imagined he had escaped her for ever. But the town they lived in was a small one and they often met in the street or in a shop. And Miss Smith, who at first found marriage rather boring, visited the school quite regularly. 'How's

James?' she would say, smiling alarmingly at him. 'How's my droopy old James?'

Then, when Miss Smith had been married for about a year she gave birth to a son, which occupied her a bit. He was a fine child, eight pounds six ounces, with a good long head and blue eyes. Miss Smith was delighted with him, and her husband, a solicitor, complimented her sweetly and bought cigars and drinks for all his friends. In time, mother and son were seen daily taking the air: Miss Smith on her trim little legs and the baby in his frilly pram. James, meeting the two, said: 'Miss Smith, may I see the baby?' But Miss Smith laughed and said that she was not Miss Smith any more. She wheeled the pram rapidly away, as though the child within it might be affected by the proximity of the other.

'What a dreadful little boy that James Machen is!' Miss Smith reported to her husband. 'I feel so sorry for the parents.'

'Do I know him? What does the child look like?'

'Small, dear, like a weasel wearing glasses. He quite gives me the creeps.'

Almost without knowing it, James developed a compulsion about Miss Smith. At first it was quite a simple compulsion: just that James had to talk to God about Miss Smith every night before he went to sleep, and try to find out from God what it was about him that Miss Smith so despised. Every night he lay in bed and had his conversation, and if once he forgot it James knew that the next time he met Miss Smith she would probably say something that might make him drop down dead.

After about a month of conversation with God James discovered that he had found the solution. It was so simple that he marvelled he had never thought of it before. He begun to get up very early in the morning and pick bunches of flowers. He would carry them down the street to Miss Smith's house and place them on a window-sill. He was careful not to be seen, by Miss Smith or by anyone else: he knew that if anyone saw him the plan couldn't work. When he had picked all the flowers in his own garden he started to pick them from other people's gardens. He became rather clever at moving silently through the gardens, picking flowers for Miss Smith.

Unfortunately, though, on the day that James carried his thirty-first bunch of blooms to the house of Miss Smith he was observed. He saw the curtains move as he reached up to lay the flowers on the window-sill. A moment later Miss Smith, in her dressing-gown, had caught him by the shoulder and pulled him into the house.

'James Machen! It would be James Machen, wouldn't it? Flowers from the creature, if you please! What are you up to, you dozey James?'

James said nothing. He looked at Miss Smith's dressing-gown and thought it was particularly pretty: blue and woolly, with an edging of silk.

'You've been trying to get us into trouble,' cried Miss Smith. 'You've been stealing flowers all over the town and putting them at our house. You're an underhand child, James.'

James stared at her, and then ran away.

After that, James thought of Miss Smith almost all the time. He thought of her face when she caught him with the flowers, and how she had afterwards told his father and nearly everyone else in the town. He thought of how his father had had to say he was sorry to Miss Smith, and how his mother and father had quarrelled about the affair. He counted up all the things Miss Smith had ever said to him, and all the things she had ever done to him, like giving him seed cake at the Christmas party. He hadn't meant to harm Miss Smith as she said he had. Giving people flowers wasn't unkind; it was to show them you liked them and wanted them to like you.

'When somebody hurts you,' James said to the man who came to cut the grass, 'what do you do about it?'

'Well,' said the man, 'I suppose you hurt them back.'

'Supposing you can't,' James argued.

'Oh, but you always can. It's easy to hurt people.'

'It's not, really,' James said.

'Look,' said the man, 'all I've got to do is to reach out and give you a clip on the ear. That'd hurt you.'

'But I couldn't do that to you. Because you're too big. How d'you hurt someone who's bigger than you?'

'It's easier to hurt people who are weaker. People who are weaker are always the ones who get hurt.'

'Can't you hurt someone who is stronger?'

The grass-cutter thought for a time. 'You have to be cunning to do that. You've got to find the weak spot. Everyone has a weak spot.'

'Have you got a weak spot?'

'I suppose so.'

'Could I hurt you on your weak spot?'

'You don't want to hurt me, James.'

'No, but just could I?'

'Yes, I suppose you could.'

'Well then?'

'My little daughter's smaller than you. If you hurt her, you see, you'd be hurting me. It'd be the same, you see.'

'I see,' said James.

All was not well with Miss Smith. Life, which had been so happy when her baby was born, seemed now to be directed against her. Perhaps it was that the child was becoming difficult, going through a teething phase that was pleasant for no one; or perhaps it was that Miss Smith recognized in him some trait she disliked and knew that she would be obliged to watch it develop, powerless to intervene. Whatever the reason, she felt depressed. She often thought of her teaching days, of the big square schoolroom with the children's models on the shelves and the pictures of kings on the walls. Nostalgically, she recalled the feel of frosty air on her face as she rode her bicycle through the town, her mind already practising the first lesson of the day. She had loved those winter days: the children stamping their feet in the playground, the stove groaning and cracking, so red and so fierce that it had to be penned off for safety's sake. It had been good to feel tired, good to bicycle home, shopping a bit on the way – home to tea and the wireless and an evening of reading by the fire. It wasn't that she regretted anything; it was just that now and again, for a day or two, she felt she would like to return to the past.

'My dear,' Miss Smith's husband said, 'you really will have to be more careful.'

'But I am. Truly I am. I'm just as careful as anyone can be.'

'Of course you are. But it's a difficult age. Perhaps, you know, you need a holiday.'

'But I've had difficult ages to deal with for years . . .'

'Now now, my dear, it's not quite the same, teaching a class of kids.'

'But it shouldn't be as difficult. I don't know . . .'

'You're tired. Tied to a child all day long, every day of the week, it's no joke. We'll take an early holiday.'

Miss Smith did feel tired, but she knew that it wasn't tiredness that was really the trouble. Her baby was almost two, and for two years she knew she had been making mistakes with him. Yet somehow she felt that they weren't her mistakes. It was as though some other person occasionally possessed her: a negligent, worthless kind of person, who was cruel, almost criminal, in her carelessness. Once she had discovered the child crawling on the pavement beside his pram: she had apparently forgotten to attach his harness to the pram hooks. Once there had been beads in his pram, hundreds of them, small and red and made of glass. A woman had drawn her attention to the danger, regarding curiously the supplier of so unsuitable a plaything. 'In his nose he was putting one, dear. And may have swallowed a dozen already. It could kill a mite, you know.' The beads were hers, but how the child had got them she could not fathom. Earlier, when he had been only a couple of months, she had come into his nursery to find an excited cat scratching at the clothes of his cot; and on another occasion she had found him eating a turnip. She wondered if she might be suffering from some kind of serious absentmindedness, or blackouts. Her doctor told her, uncomfortingly, that she was a little run down.

'I'm a bad mother,' said Miss Smith to herself; and she cried as she looked at her child, warm and pretty in his sleep.

But her carelessness continued, and people remarked that it was funny in a teacher. Her husband was upset and unhappy, and finally suggested that they should employ someone to look after the child. 'Someone else?' said Miss Smith. 'Someone *else*? Am I then incapable? Am I so wretched and stupid that I cannot look after my own child? You speak to me as though I were half crazy.' She felt confused and sick and miserable. The marriage teetered beneath the tension, and there was no question of further children.

Then there were two months without incident. Miss Smith began to feel better; she was getting the hang of things; once again she was in control of her daily life. Her child grew and flourished. He trotted nimbly beside her, he spoke his own language, he was wayward and irresponsible, and to Miss Smith and her husband he was intelligent and full of charm. Every day Miss Smith saved up the sayings and doings of this child and duly reported them to her husband. 'He is quite intrepid,' Miss Smith said, and she told her husband how the child would tumble about the room, trying to stand on his head. 'He has an aptitude for athletics,' her husband remarked. They laughed that they, so unathletic in their ways, should have produced so physically lively an offspring.

'And how has our little monster been today?' Miss Smith's husband asked, entering the house one evening at his usual time.

Miss Smith smiled, happy after a good, quiet day. 'Like gold,' she said.

Her husband smiled too, glad that the child had not been a nuisance to her and glad that his son, for his own sake, was capable of adequate behaviour. 'I will just take a peep at him,' he announced, and he ambled off to the nursery.

He sighed with relief as he climbed the stairs, thankful that all was once again well in the house. He was still sighing when he opened the nursery door and smelt gas. It hissed insidiously from the unlit fire. The room was sweet with it. The child, sleeping, sucked it into his lungs.

The child's face was blue. They carried him from the room, both of them helpless and inadequate in the situation. And then they waited, without speaking, while his life was recovered, until the moment when the doctor, white-coated and stern, explained that it had been a nearer thing than he would wish again to handle.

'This is too serious,' Miss Smith's husband said. 'We cannot continue like this. Something must be done.'

'I cannot understand . . .'

'It happens too often. The strain is too much for me, dear.'

'I cannot understand it.'

Every precaution had been taken with the gas fire in the nursery. The knob that controlled the gas pressure was a key and the key was removable. Certainly, the control point was within the child's reach, but one turned it on or off, slipped the key out of its socket, and placed it on the mantelpiece. That was the simple rule.

'You forgot to take out the key,' Miss Smith's husband said. In his mind an idea took on a shape that frightened him. He shied away, watching it advance, knowing that he possessed neither the emotional nor the mental equipment to fight it.

'No, no, no,' Miss Smith said. 'I never forget it. I turned the fire off and put the key on the mantelpiece. I remember distinctly.'

He stared at her, drilling his eyes into hers, hopelessly seeking the truth. When he spoke his voice was dry and weary.

'The facts speak for themselves. You cannot suggest there's another solution?'

'But it's absurd. It means he got out of his cot, turned the key, returned to bed and went to sleep.'

'Or that you turned off the fire and idly turned it on again.'

'I couldn't have; how could I?'

Miss Smith's husband didn't know. His imagination, like a pair of calipers, grasped the ugly thought and held it before him. The facts were on its side, he could not ignore them: his wife was deranged in her mind; consciously or otherwise, she was trying to kill their child.

'The window,' Miss Smith said. 'It was open when I left it. It always is, for air. Yet you found it closed.'

'The child certainly could not have done that. I cannot see what you are suggesting.'

'I don't know. I don't know what I am suggesting. Except that I don't understand.'

'He is too much for you, dear, and that's all there is to it. You must have help.'

'We can't afford it.'

'Be that as it may, we must. We have the child to think of, if not ourselves.'

'But one child! One child cannot be too much for anyone. Look, I will be extra careful in future. After all, it is the first thing like this that has happened for ages.'

'I'm sorry, dear. We must advertise for a woman.'

'Please . . .'

'Darling, I'm sorry. It's no use talking. We have talked enough, and it has got us nowhere. This is something to be sensible about.'

'Please let's try again.'

'And in the meanwhile? In the meanwhile our child's life must be casually risked day in day out?'

'No, no.'

Miss Smith pleaded, but her husband said nothing further. He pulled hard on his pipe, biting it between his jaws, unhappy and confused in his mind.

Miss Smith's husband did indeed advertise for a woman to see to the needs of their child, but it was, in fact, unnecessary in the long run to employ one. Because on his second birthday, late in the afternoon, the child disappeared. Miss Smith had put him in the garden. It was a perfectly safe garden: he played there often. Yet when she called him for his tea he did not come; and when she looked for the reason she found that he was not there. The small gate that led to the fields at the back of the house was open. She had not opened it; she rarely used it. Distractedly, she thought he must have managed to release the catch himself. 'That's quite impossible,' her husband said. 'It's too high and too stiff.' He looked at her oddly, confirmed in his mind that she wished to be rid of her child. Together they tramped the fields with the police, but although they covered a great area and were out for most of the night, they were utterly unsuccessful.

When the search continued in the light of the morning it was a search without hope, and the hopelessness in time turned into the fear of what discovery would reveal. 'We must accept the facts,' Miss Smith's husband said, but she alone continued to hope. She dragged her legs over the wide countryside, seeking a miracle, but finding neither trace nor word of the direction of her child's wanderings.

A small boy, so quiet she scarcely noticed him, stopped her once by a sawmill. He spoke some shy salutation, and when she blinked her eyes at his face she saw that he was James Machen. She passed him by, thinking only that she envied him his life, that for him to live and her child to die was proof indeed of a mocking Providence. She prayed to this Providence, promising a score of resolutions if only all would be well.

But nothing was well, and Miss Smith brooded on the thought that her husband had not voiced. *I released the gate myself. For some reason I have not wanted this child. God knows I loved him, and surely it wasn't too weak a love? Is it that I've loved so many other children that I have none left that is real enough for my own?* Pathetic, baseless theories flooded into Miss Smith's mind. Her thoughts floundered, and collapsed into wretched chaos.

'Miss Smith,' James said, 'would you like to see your baby?'

He stood at her kitchen door, and Miss Smith, hearing the words, was incapable immediately of grasping their meaning. The sun, reflected in the kitchen, was mirrored again in the child's glasses. He smiled at her, more confidently than she remembered, revealing a silvery wire stretched across his teeth.

'What did you say?' Miss Smith asked.

'I said, would you like to see your baby?'

Miss Smith had not slept for a long time. She was afraid to sleep because of the nightmares. Her hair hung lank about her shoulders, her eyes were dead and seemed to have fallen deeper into her skull. She stood listening to this child, nodding her head up and down, very slowly, in a mechanical way. Her left hand moved gently back and forth on the smooth surface of her kitchen table.

'My baby?' Miss Smith said. 'My baby?'

'You have lost your baby,' James reminded her.

Miss Smith nodded a little faster.

'I will show you,' James said.

He caught her hand and led her from the house, through the garden and through the gate into the fields. Hand in hand, they walked through the grass, over the canal bridge and across the warm, ripe meadows.

'I will pick you flowers,' James said, and he ran to gather poppies and cow parsley and blue, beautiful cornflowers.

'You give people flowers,' James said, 'because you like them and you want them to like you.'

She carried the flowers, and James skipped and danced beside her, hurrying her along. She heard him laughing; she looked at him and saw his small weasel face twisted into a merriment that frightened her.

The sun was fierce on her neck and shoulders. Sweat gathered on her forehead and ran down her cheeks. She felt it on her body tightening her clothes to her back and thighs. Only the child's hand was cool, and beneath her fingers she assessed its strength, wondering about its history. Again the child laughed.

On the heavy air his laughter rose and fell; it quivered through his body, and twitched lightly in his hand. It came as a giggle, then a breathless spasm; it rose like a storm from him; it rippled to gentleness; and it pounded again like the firing of guns in her ear. It would not stop. She knew it would not stop. As they walked together on this summer's day the laughter would continue until they arrived at the horror, until the horror was complete.

THE GRIEF CONDITION

Conrad Hill

The animals are starving. They have been shut in the kitchen since the woman who feeds them had fallen down here on the floor and been taken away. They have waited patiently through one period of lightness and two periods of darkness; soon, another period of lightness will begin.

They know that the man who lives with the woman who feeds them is in the house; he returned during the first darkness. They have listened hopefully to the irregular shuffling footfalls of the man but he hasn't come to feed them.

During the last lightness they heard the chiming of the door bell, knowing that it wasn't the woman. Only the rattling of her key in the lock combined with the comforting, 'Cooee, I'm home!' call is associated with her arrival. Instead, they heard the feet of the man coming down the stairs to the front door, the murmur of conversation followed by the movement of many feet along the passage to the room at the end. More murmurings, and then the same multiple, squeaky-leather feet moving, faster now, back along the passage and then crunching on the gravel outside; the thud of closing doors, the departure of a vehicle. Silence, save for the slow heavy tread of the man as he visited different parts of the house. But not the kitchen; he didn't come to feed them.

The stocky brown mongrel has managed to open an ill-fitting cupboard door and drag out a tin – one of the tins from whence comes the food. Despite the compact power of his jaws and the sawing action of his teeth, he has succeeded merely in denting the centre of the container. Shreds of blue label litter the floor amidst piles of hardening excrement. He gnaws monotonously at the metal, pausing occasionally to pinpoint the position of the cat prowling the work surfaces above him in the darkness. He both resents and respects her agility and silent speed. To take her for granted is dangerous. To kill and eat her will be difficult.

Beyond the reach of the dog, the ginger cat scours the smooth formica, searching vainly for any microscopic pieces of food she may have previously overlooked. She envies the dog his strength, yet is contemptuous of his clumsiness and his total dependence upon the woman who feeds them. Her tail whips restlessly through the cold stale air as she waits for the dog's teeth to breach the side of the food can. Then she will strike swiftly and precisely; her speed combined with the element of surprise should be sufficient to wrest a little food from the dog. She knows there must be no error. An error is death between those stubby jaws.

The long-standing domestic truce between cat and dog is breaking down.

The man is wrapped in loneliness, preoccupied with his grief. The dark and freezing sitting room is the hub of his crumbling universe.

From time to time he wanders lethargically to other parts of the house: to stand on an unlit landing, creating in his mind a familiar, friendly, loving figure on the stairs; or to sit at a dressing table tentatively fingering bottles and tubes and jars, a mother-of-pearl handled mirror . . . hoping to find in their smooth contours and protuberances a residual vibrancy – some small indication that she once existed.

He feels nothing.

Now he weeps before the black bulk of the wardrobe. Almost desperately he clutches at the hanging dresses, hearing only their empty rustling obsolescence. They are as cold, as useless, as inanimate . . . as dead as she, herself, is dead down there in the sitting room . . .

But always, he returns to where she has lain since yesterday afternoon. He has studied her face for hours: from the time the men brought her in the brick-red light of a dying winter sun, until the gloom obliterated her. And beyond, for he requires no light to illuminate features known and loved by him for years. The face is peacefully white, almost translucent save for the beguiling rosiness of the cheeks. He acknowledges with a grateful shudder the skill of the mortician who, with mallet, pliers and needle transformed the slate-blue skin, the staring eyes and the mouth twisted by racking pain into the symmetrical serenity of sleep. She would be grateful to be consigned to the earth with some semblance of dignity. It is a small comfort. Minimal.

In the black bleak hours of a new day the man is unaware of the condensation ice that grimly clings to the insides of the window panes or the bitter wind that slashes through leafless trees and infiltrates the house in a hundred tiny places. To him, it is just another natural appurtenance of her death. He would expect nothing less.

He slumps in an armchair near the coffin. He knows that opposite him in the darkness is the other armchair – her armchair, unfilled now or ever again.

Should he sit her in her armchair just once before they come to take her from the house?

For a moment the idea fascinates him but is quickly swamped beneath a tide of revulsive guilt: such desecration of her final hours horrifies him. That he could even *think* of popping her into her armchair is a warning indicator of his mental and physical condition. No food has passed his lips and no sleep has come to anaesthetize his grief since they removed her from the kitchen. How many hours, how many *days* ago was that?

The cold. All over the house the raw air blankets everything. The man endures the cold, enjoys it almost, because the concept of warmth is intolerable to him when she is as cold as it is possible to be. Dead cold. But food and rest – these are essential if he is to be rational during the forthcoming interment. Afterwards it doesn't matter, but for now, he must be seen to participate in the ceremonial mouthings and the empty ritual of accepted procedure. He would have preferred to bury her in the garden near the rhododendron bushes or cremate her in the little wooden summer house. But that was not the proper way; she liked things done in the proper way no matter how futile and uncomfortable they might be.

He knows he is obliged to contend with the mourners. Entertain them afterwards, endure their patronizing sympathy, see the tears that flow only from the eyes, the pinched faces and the sad, brave little smiles. Worst of all, perhaps, will be their insensitive reminiscences about her whilst they guzzle his liquor:

'Do you remember when she . . .' All of them bright-eyed, animated and inebriated when they leave, having come to terms with their loss, but none of them concerned with *her* loss – the greatest loss of any. Everybody privately thankful that this time death had passed *them* by and was someone else's problem. As they shake hands with him and mouth platitudes like, 'Chin up, Charles. Life goes on.' relief will be uppermost in their minds, relief that the interment is done with, and that nobody created a scene by wailing and head-banging, Middle-Eastern fashion, at the graveside, or toppled ostentatiously into the pit. The relief will be enhanced by the pleasurable anticipation of departure from this dismal house and its melancholic occupant.

The man knows they will be like this, but who can blame them?

Slowly and stiffly he rises from the armchair and makes his way through the darkness to the place at the other end of the passage where she started her death.

He opens the kitchen door oblivious to the purred and grunted greetings of the animals. The atmosphere is foetid and lacks the intoxicating warmth of her beloved stove. He switches on the light, his eyes narrowed protectively against the assault of the fluorescent glare. They widen gradually to survey the cold and cheerless space: the enslimed crockery protruding from the plastic bowl, the massive cooker, heatless and redundant now for want of solid fuel; the pedal bin upturned with contents strewn across the floor, intermingled with the faeces of the animals and the battered tin of dog food . . .

The man experiences no repugnance or surprise at the room's deterioration; it seems appropriate that the place where she collapsed should itself collapse. All that matters now is the sitting room. And the sitting room is clean and tidy.

He stops at the spot where she lay. She was just alive then, clinging on with a rattling throat and foaming, scummy bubbles dribbling from her lips. Her eyes were the worst – full of the pain inside her, yet still conscious of him and wanting to tell him something. But he couldn't understand what she was trying to say because the awful pain wiped out the message too quickly. Those eyes watching him from the floor had been bluer than he had ever seen them; bluer than any sky; bluer than the bits of dog food label that lie there now . . .

The man cries silently. The tears drip into the black trenches beneath his eyes and run down his cheeks.

With an effort he staves off total breakdown, wrestling with his despair, forcing it to the back of his mind to form an unstable backdrop against which his trivial monologue of self-interest can be resumed.

Food. He opens a cupboard door and takes out a round tin with a flower-painted lid. For the first time, he notices the animals: the cat mewing and purring at him from the kitchen table; the dog nuzzling at his leg. He focusses his attention upon them. The fact that she is dead means nothing to these soulless creatures. They care only for their stomachs and the furtherance of their hedonism. These brutes who, until now, have always disregarded him have suddenly become his friends. This transference of affection from her to him is appalling. He detests them for deceiving her, for letting her believe that her love for them was reciprocal. He resolves to get rid of them after the funeral. He experiences a prickling of pleasure – the first he has had since she fell dying to the floor.

His fumbling fingers prise the lid off the tin, revealing dainty domed cakes, each with its ruffle of crinkled greaseproof paper. The friendly brownness of them suggests a warmth, a freshness, an intimation that she might have made them yesterday instead of last week. He picks one up. It is as cold and hard as . . . To eat it would be unbearable. He returns it reverently to the tin and crosses to the refrigerator.

The cat is a ginger blur as she dashes from table – to floor – to worktop where the open cake tin sits so invitingly. Incensed and outwitted by the cat's sudden access to food, the dog leaps snarling, in a vain attempt to reach the tin. The cat spits at him once before tearing at the cakes.

The man turns at the sound of the commotion to see the loathsome cat contaminating *her* cakes with its rotten mouth. In three strides he is at the worktop, his clenched white fist smashing into the ginger body. The impact of the punch hurls the cat to the floor and sends her skidding, her claws frantically seeking a grip on the smooth tiles. Stunned and hurting, she crawls through the doorway and then makes her way along the passage towards the open door at the other end . . .

Pleased at the cat's disgrace, and now confident of food, the brown mongrel jumps joyfully around the man. Thus the massive kick, delivered slightly above the little white patch on his chest is unexpected. He yelps with the surprise and pain of it, crashes over on his back and slides head-first into the base of the stove. He rights himself and cowers flat, whimpering softly.

The man has punished the defilers; for the second time he feels pleasure. He looks forward to disposing of them when the pleasure will be keener. Now that *she* is dead, surely they don't expect their lives to continue unchanged? He replaces the lid on the cake tin. His hands are trembling and his heavy breaths condense in the unwarmed air. He takes a carton of orange juice and a piece of cheese from the refrigerator, pulls a chair from beneath the table and sits to strip the cellophane wrapping from the yellow block. The cold cheese becomes an amorphous lump in his mouth, barely acceptable to palate or throat – swallowed only with the aid of an occasional swig of juice.

Gradually the punched cat's throbbing pain is subsiding. She emerges from beneath the sofa to wash herself and restore her dignity. Sometimes she pauses to scan the black sitting room through dilated pupils, and analyse the jumble of small sounds and scents carried to her on eddys of bitter air. She hears the squeak and scurry of mice, safe behind their skirting board fortresses, and, in the distance, the slurping sound of the man who hurts her. She detects the stench of him, so strong that it almost overwhelms the pungent smell of the frightened dog.

There is something else . . . Something closer . . . A fragile, indefinable odour that interests her, teases her . . .

She raises her head until her delicately twitching nostrils are the highest point of her body. The alien wafting scent is slightly stronger; she can trace it now to the long dark shape towering above her. The decision to investigate is made instantly. She computes the distance from the floor to the top surface of the shape. She jumps.

The cat is on the lidless coffin.

Instead of the expected top surface, she finds merely a narrow wooden ledge, and below that, something white and presumably solid. For a few moments she teeters, undecided whether to walk along the ledge or risk the broad expanse beneath. She extends her front paws down the inner side of the container, the unsheathed claws acting as a brake by digging into the shiny quilted lining. Now she is in a head-down, almost vertical, position, but with rear paws still in contact with the ledge. By stretching out an exploratory left front paw to touch the bulky whiteness, she verifies its solidity and allows her sinuous body to settle upon it.

Here she waits, watching and listening for any movement within the container.

The elusive odour has become a smell fragrant and cloying; not at all unpleasant. It seems to be stronger towards the other end of the container – beyond where the sides widen.

She moves. The softly rustling material underfoot envelops something firm, but with difficult contours and depressions, so she treads with care to ensure a balanced progress. She pauses to sniff at the exposed hands. They possess some of the tantalizing scent she seeks, but she knows the main source is further up towards the end of the container . . .

The man empties the juice carton, swilling the last of the tasteless cheese down his throat. He sits exhausted in the hard-backed chair under the harsh fluorescent light. His lustreless eyes see nothing, transmit no fresh stimuli to his brain. His mind is operating near the subconscious, seeking to dredge up complete sections of past experience and convert them into vivid imagery; living memories of her which will erase reality. But there are only little pictures which form and vanish like bubbles in a molten lava bed: a face absorbed in a newspaper, freckled skin on speckled sand, the swirling hem of a new dress, a distant figure in a summer-scented garden . . . All disjointed scraps. Nothing tangible to grip.

The cat has reached the head.

She crouches, sniffing the jaw, not recognizing the face of the woman who feeds her, not recognizing it as any face at all. To her it represents a small quest completed. Her abrasive tongue removes layers of cosmetic from a small area below the lips. The taste is sweet, the texture powdery-dry, but worth enduring for the skin beneath is mildly salty. She digs deeper, her paw becoming a clawed excavator shovel returning small pieces of tissue to her mouth for testing. The meat is old and tough and cold, not of the quality to which she is accustomed; but, for the starving, the act of mastication lends succulence.

She springs onto the face turning deftly so that her rear feet find ideal supports in the lidded indentations of the eye sockets. She eats.

The brown dog shivers and salivates, doleful eyes watching the empty orange juice carton on the table. He doesn't understand why the man who hurts him will not feed him. He misses the woman who feeds him; for as long as he can remember, she has never been away for this long. He needs her, for, apparently, only her hand can extract his food from its metal prison. He can detect vague scents of her, but they are ancient fading scents almost overpowered by the stink of the man who hurts him. Yet spiralling through the misery in his dim little mind is the hope that the woman will return, or, failing that, that the man will provide him with food. So he waits and watches quietly the motionless figure at the table.

The man's eyes slowly close. His head sinks forward to his chest. The haggard features relax. He sleeps.

Beyond the kitchen window, the new day progresses. In the lessening darkness, a few snowflakes dance on the turbulent wind.

The dog softly snuffles the floor beneath the man's chair. The particles of cheese he finds serve only to intensify his dreadful hunger. He remembers the cat – the warm, *comestible* cat . . .

With a glance at the sleeping man, he moves, snake-like, from the kitchen into the passage. He stops to listen, his ears no longer flattened back and down, but straining erect, pointed save for the little curls at the tips. He listens for the cat.

The sound he hears is incompatible with his knowledge of the house: *food in the room at the end of the passage*. The cat has found food where there should be none. Food is only available in the kitchen. His flaring jealous rage propels him along the passage and into the sitting room.

From somewhere above him the sound of chewing and ragged

purring ceases. He allows his eyes to adjust to the dark room enabling him to locate the cat. She is high, too high for him to reach her – or the food. Again, he resents the innate agility that allows her to feed with impunity just a few feet away from him. He tries to get closer by standing on his hind legs with his front paws propped against the polished wooden side of the coffin, but the cat slashes viciously at him, compelling him to return to the floor. He climbs onto an armchair which, although some distance away from the coffin, gives him a better view of the cat as she feeds. His ordered and harmonious existence has been violently disrupted: the woman has gone; the man hurts him instead of feeding him; the cat eats food denied to him – food in the sitting room. He misses the woman, he fears the man, he detests the cat, but, above all, he is hungry. He watches the ginger shape in the coffin, twin tassels of saliva hanging from his mouth like a broken, enslimed silver necklace.

The man dreams of a funeral, a hideous parody of a funeral. The grave is a frozen black hole in a cemetary of wizened trees and sagging headstones. The mourners are stunted dark shapes clustering around the yawning rectangle. Grotesque pallbearers with animal heads support a matchwood coffin with their hairy arms. He shrinks from their bestial faces as they pass him to halt at the graveside. He hears the mocking incantation of a faceless antipriest and the ribald laughter of the crooked mourners. Then the grinning pall-bearers hurl the coffin into the pit. Talons grip his arms, thrusting him forward to the edge to watch the coffin shatter into pieces at the bottom. He recognizes the clotted, putrid thing that lies screaming thinly in the wreckage. He falls down . . . down towards her until he can feel her writhing glutinously in his arms. He gazes upward. The grave is a funnel with the distant mocking faces at its rim. Earth, heavy damp and cold, splatters down upon him. He chokes beneath the cloying clay . . .

The man wakes, shuddering and moaning. Despite the cold, his face drips with desperate perspiration. His neck and back ache, the pain seeps insidiously through his numb body. For an exhilarating instant, he believes he still dreams, that the foul nightmare was only a dream within a dream. The ecstasy dissolves when he sees the light of the new morning hovering outside the kitchen window competing reluctantly with the fluourescent light, diminishing the intensity of the dead white tube with its soft matt greyness.

He has slept but is unrefreshed; the hard kitchen chair has caused his bones to ache. Soon, he will have to prepare himself, make himself presentable for his last journey with her. But he must sit with her first. The ghastly dream has left him with a feeling of unease, some small and tremulous apprehension. *He must sit with her.* She needs the reassurance of his protective presence.

He struggles to his feet. One of his shoes scuff a pile of excrement, extracting little pieces of dog food label to the sole. Unaware and imbued now with a sense of urgency, he totters along the dawn-tinted passage to where she rests lonely and quiet.

The sitting room is a cave of brooding darkness isolated from the burgeoning daylight by heavy curtains. The man gropes for the wall switch to flood her face with electric light.

But there is no face. There is only the sleek shape of the ginger cat crouching on raw, scarlet gristle. Hanging by an organic thread from her mouth is an eye of cerulean blue . . .

The huge scream originating from the man's soul is choked in his throat by streams of erupting vomit. It sprays from his mouth and nostrils as he lunges for the cat. She turns from the head to run quickly along the shroud, leaving russet pawprints on the white purity of the material. She soars from the end of the coffin to find safety on the floor beneath the sofa. The man throws himself to the carpet, his hand groping desperately for the cat, to shatter, crush and smash . . . But she huddles beyond his reach, observing his efforts with inpenitent eyes.

The man sobs convulsively, senseless words gurgling from his lips. His tears mingle with the vomit on the soft pile of the carpet.

Bewildered and fearful, yet encouraged by the man's disinterest in him, the brown dog slips uncertainly from the armchair to approach the man who moans so loudly on the floor. He flinches when the man's arm sweeps around his thin frame, but the gesture is friendly, as though the man seeks comfort from another living creature. The dog's tail wags hesitantly. He cleans the man's face, savouring the sour and salty wetness on his tongue. The previous hurt is past and food becomes a possibility after all. He basks in the man's favour, proud of his close proximity to him – whereas the hated cat is in mortal danger. Perhaps the man who lives with the woman who feeds him will kill the cat and give him the carcass.

Under the sofa the cat inches along the carpet seeking an escape route whilst the prostrate figure of the man cuddles the loathsome, obsequious dog and weeps uncontrollably. The brown mongrel continues to nuzzle the man automatically, but his attention is fixed wholly on the creeping ginger shape. He growls softly, warning the man of the cat's imminent flight. Unheeding, uncaring, the man continues to sob pitiably.

As she makes her break for freedom from beneath the end of the sofa, the cat underestimates the speed of the dog. He tears free from the man's encircling arm to ambush the cat in her race to the door. They fight – a snarling, snapping, hissing battle that rages across the sitting room. The man rolls onto his back screaming curses at the animals as they fight furiously. He swings ineffectual fists at them whenever they come within range, receiving bites and scratches in return. Then the battle finishes as quickly as it began. The cat rolls away, beaten by superior size and strength. She arches her back, spitting venom and frustration at the dog. The man, moaning mindlessly, struggles to a sitting position and punches wildly at the victorious mongrel. One blow strikes home and, for the dog, one blow is all that is required: he knows suddenly that the man will not feed him and will continue to hurt him. He has vanquished the cat; the time has come to vanquish the man . . .

He launches himself at the exposed neck of the man, his desperate jaws puncturing flesh and clamping down on ruptured pipe and artery, warm blood jetting triumphantly against the roof of his mouth.

The man offers surprisingly little resistance, but the fangs continue to retain their mighty grip until the limbs cease to jerk and twitch.

The cat circles warily, her ears flat, her tail bushy. She seeks an opportunity to taste *warm* meat.

The animals stare at each other – soft brown eye into bland green eye; not communicating, yet instinctively reaching an understanding. The cat leaps lightly onto the coffin, retracing her steps to the meal at the end of the shroud. The dog turns back to the body on the floor. He eats noisily, ravenously, warmly.

For the moment, the domestic truce between cat and dog is restored.

THE OTHER WOMAN
R. A. Hall

He woke up covered in sweat, his pyjamas sticking to him, and lay there for several minutes trembling very slightly, making no effort to control it. The sweat suddenly felt cold and he eased himself out of bed and went into the bathroom, leaving both doors open so that their closing should not wake the sleeping woman. He stripped off the damp pyjamas and rubbed himself down with a rough towel. To find other pyjamas he would have to go back into the bedroom and turn on the light. After a moment's thought he groped in the airing-cupboard for a shirt and underpants, put these on, tucking the shirt into the pants, and went back into the bedroom, leaving the bathroom door open but closing the bedroom door very gently. He eased himself back between the damp sheets without waking his wife. The ticking of the alarm-clock loud in his ears he lay there, not thinking, waiting for daybreak.

Looking at the receptionist John decided that, whatever other changes he might find, Alan's taste in women had remained completely static: they had to be tall, painfully thin, ash-blonde. As she picked up the phone to announce him he found himself wondering whether his old friend had ever taken time to analyse himself and find the reason for this strange clinging to one shape, size and colour of woman: lovely as they were in their way, it must surely become boring. Then the door behind her was thrown open and Alan came out, grinning from ear to ear, took him by the hand and shoulder and propelled him into the other room. As the door closed behind them John was amused to catch a glimpse of the receptionist's startled face. Obviously an older Alan was not usually so informal.

It was a beautifully thought-out room; combining without clash the necessities of an office and the comfort of a lounge. In addition to a very large, very modern desk, there was a small, low occasional table with a cluster of elegant chairs round it. Alan lowered him into one of these, crossed to a battered old bookcase, which somehow fitted perfectly into the otherwise modern decor, and brought back a bottle of whisky, a soda-siphon and two glasses.

'You still drink this poison at any hour of the day and night, I suppose.'

'Try me,' grinned John, the familiar, almost tangible warmth of his friend's personality filling him with ease. 'I see your taste in women hasn't changed, either. Doesn't it get a bit boring, leaving a woman at the office and finding virtually the same woman waiting for you when you get home? How is Jean, by the way?'

Alan finished putting together the whisky and soda, taking his time, his face expressionless.

'I gathered that you wanted to see me professionally,' he said at last, pushing one glass across the unpolished mahogany towards John. 'For yourself, or for someone else?'

'I'm probably wasting your time,' said John, trying to smile, but merely twisting his mouth, 'but I do badly need some advice.'

'You know I'm no longer a practising psychiatrist, merely an admin type – a pen-pusher, as you so elegantly put it. Although, mind you, it takes a psychiatrist to try to get any sense out of this load of nuts; psychiatrists they call themselves – they need analysing to a man.' He sipped his drink, his eyes above the glass intent for a moment on John's long, dark face.

'What's the trouble, John? I gather you seem to have dropped most of your old friends. Roger tells me he hasn't really seen you for nearly a year. It must be nearly three years since I last actually saw you to talk to – although that's partly my fault . . . this job . . .'

John hunched his shoulders and relaxed them again, going over yet again in his mind the form in which he had planned to present his problem to his old friend.

Receiving no comment, Alan continued talking to fill the gap. 'There's no trouble at home, is there? Jean saw Sue . . . I suppose it must have been just after Christmas . . . I gathered you had both settled down nicely since the move. Work going all right? I never see your rag, of course, but trade journals can't help thriving, can they?'

John hardly heard any of this. The genuine warmth of his friend's interest made it impossible for him to go through the elaborate chain of half-truths which he had so carefully forged. He knew he was going to tell the story unvarnished. The thought appalled him, and he was still desperately anxious that Alan should not think that he was *seriously* worried. He wanted to give the impression that he was simply curious for an explanation.

He looked squarely at Alan for the first time since entering the room, noticing the clusters of grey in his tight, jet black curls, and the wrinkles across the forehead, now deepened by concern. The brown eyes behind the heavy glasses were red-rimmed but bright with intelligence. John drank the rest of the whisky and put down the glass. Alan refilled it.

'You remember Alice Northwood,' began John, a statement rather than a question. 'Yes, of course, of course,' he put in quickly, as Alan's expression turned to mild amusement. Alan had introduced them.

'Well, there was something about her death which never came out. It was so silly, so far-fetched, that there was simply no point in bringing it up at the time. But it has nagged at me on and off ever since, and now . . .'

Alan's expression had turned to one of intense concern, his professional calm forgotten. Several times he began to speak and stopped, but John somehow understood what he was shying from asking.

'No, no, Alan. I was in the clear, I had nothing to do with it, but . . .'

'Of course you didn't,' interrupted Alan, anxious to make amends for his momentary doubt. 'Sue testified . . . not only testified but told me personally – it was impossible to doubt her – that you were by her side all that night. What's worrying you?'

'Alan, as far as I know, and I've thought about it again and again, Alice was completely faithful to me. What I said in evidence was perfectly true: as far as I know there was no other man in her life, but . . . well . . . it's hard to explain . . .'

'It was a great pity it all had to come out,' mused Alan, lifting his glass and looking through it towards the window. 'I honestly thought Sue wasn't going to get over it. You did the right thing in moving away from there.' He finished his drink and poured two more.

They were silent for a while, each following wisps of memory.

'I'm almost positive there was no other man,' John said quietly, sounding his memory of events as he spoke; 'and yet I had a series of the most uncanny dreams you ever came across.' He grinned wearily as Alan suddenly radiated attention.

'Dreams? What dreams?'

John put down his untouched drink and for the first time in many months allowed his mind to wander through the months of his time with Alice.

'You know, the strangest thing about that whole business was how close she and I lived together. What? Two hundred yards? I must have seen her dozens of times around the artists' colony, and she must have seen me. Yet when you introduced us at your party I fell, hook, line and sinker, and it hit her just as badly. Terry had been dead little more than a year at that time, and she had loved him very much – I suppose you know more about that than I do; you knew them both. He was pretty gifted, wasn't he?'

Alan nodded, and his eyes turned briefly to a small picture on the wall beside his desk. John assumed that this was the work of Alice's husband, but said nothing.

'Anyhow, here she was, not much more than a year later, in love again – that tiny, uncomplicated little woman, hardly a year later, and feeling guilty about it. As much in love as we were, she just wouldn't sleep with me. Remember me asking you to analyse her? All the time she said that it was because I was married, unwilling to give the real reason, even when I spelled it out for her. But finally, as you know, it began to make me ill – physically ill. Seeing so much of her, knowing she wanted me as much as I wanted her . . . and nothing. Well, we did become lovers, and if you knew how unsatisfactory it was at first, you'd wonder why we continued. But it improved with time, until in the end . . . But, what the hell, I bored you with all this at the time . . . no, no,' he added as his friend protested his willingness to listen, 'the point is this . . .' He sat for a moment marshalling his thoughts, taking an untasted sip of his drink.

'One day I saw her coming out of a restaurant with a man.' He shifted in his chair, uncomfortable at the memory. 'It was the strangest thing: we were always running into each other unexpectedly, which makes one think that all the time we didn't know each other we must have passed each other in the street hundreds of times. But this was something else. She hadn't noticed me and I followed them for a few minutes, then got sick of myself and turned into a side street and went back to the office. I was sick with jealousy and disappointment. We both of us always knew what the other was doing, even if we didn't see each other for several days: who we were lunching with, our plans for the weekend. But she had never mentioned this man to me. They hadn't seemed very intimate as they walked along, but somehow, by the time I reached my office, I had managed to convince myself that they were either lovers or were about to become lovers.

'I didn't phone her that day, or the next, but just as I was about to leave the office that evening she phoned me. I tried to be distant with her and refused to explain my coldness, but her voice broke, and the next thing I knew I was gabbling my hurt into the phone, nearly hysterical.'

He grinned ruefully at the memory.

'It turned out that she *had* told me about this chap: Robin someone or other. He wanted to buy two of Terry's paintings. But I used to know a girl called Robin, knew her very well, and I, probably not paying much attention in any case, had assumed that she was talking about a woman. That was our first quarrel, or misunderstanding if you like, and after it we were, if anything, closer than ever. Then, about a week later, I had my first dream.'

Alan shifted impatiently in his chair, and taken up though he was with his own thoughts, John smiled involuntarily at his friend's Pavlovian reaction to the mention of dreams.

'They were the weirdest dreams I have ever had. I say weird, but that's just what they were not. The terrifying thing about them was their complete normality. Like watching a film, or a TV play, and taking a part at the same time. Or, to be more exact, two parts.'

The phone rang and they both jumped. Almost spitting with annoyance Alan was at the door in two long strides, tore it open and said in a mild, reasonable voice: 'Jane, I'm not to be disturbed.' Closing the door quietly and going back to his seat he gulped down the rest of his drink. John followed suit, but waved away the bottle when Alan made to fill his glass.

'That's what it was like,' said John, as if there had been no interruption: 'like watching a TV serial. I dreamed that Alice met a man at a party. He said that he had heard of her husband's work and would like to see it. But all the time I knew, and she knew, that he was merely looking for a way of quickly establishing a relationship. They arranged for him to call at the colony the next evening. Something woke me up at this point, but I dreamed parts of the dream again during the night. It was so vivid next day still, that when I was about to phone her, I found myself fuming, hating her. I deliberately arranged to meet her that evening, although at such short notice it was a little difficult for both of us. And all the time I knew that I was doing this so as to prevent any possibility of her meeting this other man.'

John smiled unconvincingly, his eyes sad, and searched his friend's face for reactions. Alan smiled back with just the right balance of amusement and concern.

'What makes it so daft, was that the other man was me! That's the one element in these dreams which was definitely dream-like. The other man was me. I knew it but Alice didn't. His approach was the typical cynical one of the practised womanizer; making his approach slickly and with the minimum of fuss. And what made it so horrible for me was that I knew he was going to succeed, and easily. Whereas I loved the woman and had gone through torments for months before we finally went to bed. Somehow that was humiliating.

'Well, I met her that evening, and within minutes things were back to normal. She had a wonderful effect on me, you know. Whenever I was with her, there was this wonderful warmth and ease . . . by God, Alan, I loved her . . . I still love her . . . I don't know how I go on from day to day, knowing that I will never see her again . . . every so often I think I see her in the street, and it's like a punch to the stomach . . . the phone goes and I expect to hear her voice . . . I see a part of London I last saw with her . . . But the dreams went on. About every third or fourth night the story unfolded. They didn't make love that first evening, although she was perfectly willing. Somebody called and made it impossible. But she arranged to meet him in town and then a few days later at another party. After the party they went and spent the night at his place. There were elements of fantasy here too, because his place was my place, and Susan and the children were somewhere in the house.

'I had continued to see her, of course, but each time it became more and more difficult to behave normally with her. I knew on a conscious level that this was only a series of incredibly vivid dreams, but some expression would cross her face, or she would say something she had said in one of the dreams, and I would find myself hating her, as if the dreams were real.

'She thought I was cooling towards her, and her bruised dignity about it, after the initial bewilderment, made me love her more and more. You've noticed that? How you think you can't love any more deeply, any more widely, but then you find you can? It reached the point in the dreams when I told her that she must choose between him and me. She laughed at me, enjoying my pain. I gave her a back-handed slap across the face which sent her reeling across the room. She was such a tiny little thing. The sense of relief was enormous. I woke up next morning feeling cheerful for the first time in weeks. We had lunch together and I told her about the dreams. She practically cried with relief and we arranged to spend the next evening together at her place. Then, next day, shortly before I was about to leave the office to go to her, she phoned, putting me off, and was vague about the reason. I assumed that someone was in the office with her and that she couldn't speak freely, but I was miserably disappointed. By the time I reached home I was convinced that she was going to spend the night with my other self, as if he really existed. I tried hard to shake off the feeling. I was desperate to leave the house and go along to the colony, but it was impossible; there was no possible excuse. If only I had! Well, you know the rest. It came out in the police enquiries. I think I *could* do with another drink.'

Alan poured two more drinks, his movements automatic, preoccupied with the implications of his friend's dreams. He handed John a drink.

'That was the night she died, I suppose?'

'Yes, but this is where I come to the really frightening part. That night I dreamed that I killed her. Strangled her in exactly the way she was found. I dreamed that I got out of bed, put trousers over my pyjamas, put on an overcoat, left the house, walked to the colony in my slippers, found her sleeping alone, but with signs of someone having slept with her, and I strangled her.

'When I put my hands round her little throat, inserting my fingers between her neck and the pillow, she opened her eyes, startled and then full of joy when she recognized me. At that moment, in my dream, I knew that the dreams were not true, that I was suffering from some horrible hallucination, but I pressed my hands together and choked her to death.

'The dream didn't show me how I got back to my bed. I woke up dripping with sweat, Sue fast asleep beside me. The dream had been so vivid that I don't know how I forced myself to remain in bed. I wanted so desperately to go to the colony and make certain she was all right.

'When I phoned her office next morning and she hadn't arrived, and had sent no message, I was hysterical with foreboding. I phoned her home and one of the police people answered. It was ghastly.'

Alan put a hand on his shoulder, then, embarrassed by the gesture, stood up and went and adjusted a book on his desk.

'That was three years ago,' continued John; 'almost exactly three years. I still love her. I still miss her horribly. And every so often I find myself convinced that I killed her. I've tried so hard to lead a normal life, but it's empty, quite empty.'

Alan waited a long time for his friend to continue, but it was as if John had forgotten where he was and that someone else was with him.

'But my dear, dear laddy,' said Alan at last from the desk. 'It was proved beyond doubt that there was another man with her that evening, and no one saw him leave. I don't believe myself that she was playing around, and whoever it was may not have been the man that killed her, but one thing is certain: it wasn't you!'

'I know,' said John with a sigh, 'but what worries me is that I've started to dream again.'

'What?'

'Yes, exactly the same kind of dream. About a woman living a little way down the road. Her name's Margaret Owen.'

'You mean you're having an affair with her?'

'No, no, Alan; there's been no-one since Alice. No. I can see what started it, but I can't see why it goes on. This woman is a widow, older than Alice, but much the same shape and size, but very dark and foreign looking, whereas Alice . . . Looking at her from a distance sometimes the resemblance is quite striking. Being a little, rounded woman she holds herself and walks very like Alice. When she first moved in a few months ago my heart was in my mouth every time I caught a glimpse of her. But then she and Sue became friends very quickly and I saw quite a lot of her. She's so completely different from Alice, I can't think why I continue to identify them.

'I think what must have started the dreams was seeing a man come out of her place late one night. It set me thinking about whoever it was that killed Alice. Presumably he's still around somewhere, living a normal life, unsuspected. That night I dreamed about Margaret. I met her at a party, exactly as I met Alice. You introduced us. She *was* Alice, but she was also Margaret. The difference was that I fell in love and she didn't. Oh, she was quite prepared to have an affair, but she kept me waiting – as Alice had done, but not for the same reason: deliberately torturing me, getting pleasure out of it. In dream after dream what had happened between Alice and me was repeated, but distorted almost beyond recognition. It has been so vivid that when I meet Margaret I find myself puzzled that an occasional glance does not pass between us. It seems impossible that she can be unaware of what is going on.

'Then, about a fortnight back, I had a dream which was an exact replica of the first one I had about Alice. She met a man at a party. The man was me and was someone else. The woman was both Margaret Owen and Alice. Every other night or so the sequence of dreams has followed, exactly as before. And, Alan, you'll probably think I'm mad, but in the next dream I shall strangle her. There it is – I shall strangle her!'

Alan looked squarely at his friend, apparently at a loss; searching for the best form of words. He left the desk, and taking one of the easy chairs placed it so that he was exactly facing his friend.

'Now look, John. There is no doubt that this is one of the oddest things I've ever come across, but I assure you there is some perfectly normal explanation. I'll talk to you as I might not to the average patient. Not that I'm regarding you as a patient,' he put in quickly at a frown from John. 'The point is that, as odd as it may seem to you, you probably had the first series of dreams *after* Alice's death, not before. I know, I know,' he continued quickly, as John made to protest, 'but believe me, it's the most likely explanation. It doesn't mean you're round the bend, or anything like that. You'd be amazed just how common hallucinations of this kind are with people who have had a really serious emotional shock. When is the next dream likely to be?'

'Almost certainly tonight. It would have been last night, I'm sure, but I somehow managed to keep awake all night – anything rather than go through that. That's why I came to see you. I can't explain it to Sue, but I can't sleep in that house tonight. I must be somewhere far away. I was hoping you could put me up, and sort of keep an eye on me. We would have to find some reasonable-sounding excuse for Sue, but I've told her that I've been having awful dreams and that I was probably going to mention them to you.'

Alan looked at his friend's anxious, pleading face.

'Now look, John. You probably do need analysing, and I think we ought to arrange it, but almost certainly the best thing you can do is to sleep at home tonight. Have the dream. You'll wake up to find that all is well and be half-way to being cured.'

'Alan, I'm not sleeping in that house tonight.'

A flicker of impatience crossed Alan's face, but he said nothing for several minutes.

'Can you find any good reason for me staying with *you* tonight?' he asked at last.

John's eyes lit up. 'That's it. Alan, could you really? It's a bit short notice for Jean.'

'Yes,' said Alan, 'and at an awkward time, too: I've been away rather a lot recently. But it can be done without much trouble. What can you tell Sue, though?'

'Oh, heavens, don't worry about that,' said John, his face transformed. 'Now. We won't put you in the guest room. We'll put you on the couch downstairs. Anybody going out of the house from upstairs has to pass through the lounge. The house is very much like yours, come to think of it; sort of open-plan.'

'I'll have to go home to collect some things,' said Alan, moving towards the desk. 'I'll have a word with Jean.'

Alan waited for all movement upstairs to stop, then got up from the couch, put on his dressing-gown, feeling cold in spite of the central heating. He debated whether or not to switch on the main lighting, but decided to move the table-lamp from its stand to the gate-leg table. He opened out one leaf of the table, took a large notebook from his bag and began to make notes about John's case.

He had promised to stay awake and this was one way he intended to pass the night. He finished the notes and looked at his watch: 1.05. He had planned to spend a good part of the rest of the night going through the rough notes of the previous month's executive committee meeting, putting them into some sort of order, but he had drunk a little more than usual during the evening and now felt disinclined. He hunted through John's shelves for something to read. Hesitating between *Don Quixote* and O. Henry, he decided for the noble Spaniard, and after pouring himself a bitter lemon settled into an armchair, nicely placed for the lamp. After three pages he left the Don to his own devices and plunged into the O. Henry.

A long time later, deep into a moving tale concerning the sacrifice of a young woman's tresses for the man she loved, he was startled to look up and find John coming down the stairs, looking very dishevelled, a lock of his thinning hair plastered across his damp forehead.

'You had the dream?' asked Alan, lowering him into the chair.

'Yes, by God,' said John, watching his friend bring a blanket from the couch and tuck it in round him. 'Exactly like last time,' he was almost sobbing. 'Except that I knew that the woman wasn't really Alice, and this time I enjoyed it. I enjoyed killing her! Oh my God!' And now he really did sob, crying as a man does, deep, juddering sobs twisting his body.

Alan left him to it and went and fixed a whisky and soda and another bitter lemon.

'It's the best thing that could have happened. And now the thing to do is to drink this and get back to bed. Those pyjamas are soaked – change them. It's a bit late for a sleeping pill, it would leave you dopey in the morning, but try to get some sleep. Then come over to our place on Sunday, as planned, and we'll take a look at this thing.'

John wiped his eyes with the back of his hand and then with the collar of his pyjamas. He sipped at the whisky and stared in front, his eyes unfocused.

'Just the same,' he said at last, 'I won't feel happy until I see that woman walking around again, unharmed. You can't imagine how vivid these dreams are.' He took another sip at the whisky and put it down. 'Will you finish that so that it's not around in the morning? How does Sue manage to sleep through things the way she does?'

He stood up, draped the blanket over the back of the couch and went slowly up the stairs.

Alan watched him go, then crossed to the table and took up his pen to make a further note. After a moment's thought he changed his mind, took up the drinks and went through to the kitchen, where he poured them down the sink and ran the tap for a few moments. He went back into the lounge, turned out the lamp, groped his way to the couch, took off his dressing-gown and clambered into the crumpled bedding, pulling the dangling blanket more or less over the others. Briefly he wondered how the O. Henry story ended, and then was asleep.

Sue watched with satisfaction as Alan finished a substantial breakfast, and took the opportunity of chiding John on his usual thin slice of toast and honey. John paid no attention and later had to be woken out of a reverie to answer the children's calls as they stormed out of the front door. He heard Sue giving her usual last-minute instructions about crossing the roads and then was dimly aware that she was talking to someone at the door. This went on for some minutes, when suddenly something in their way of speaking alerted him. Jumping from his chair he rushed to the door just as Sue turned to call to him.

'Something's happened down the road. Dr Ellis's car is outside.'

He pushed her to one side and she disappeared out of his line of vision as Alan too pushed past her.

A little way down the road a small group of people were

clustered round a garden gate, looking up the drive towards the open door of one of the houses. A green Zodiac was stationed outside and from a side turning further down the road the familiar black shape of a police car emerged and came purring towards them.

GREEN FINGERS

R. C. Cook

Widow Bowen was getting old. She was seventy-five, perhaps, or eighty. No one in Breth Common really knew. But then, it didn't really matter. She looked the same trim little person that she had always been, even while her husband, Ernest, had been alive, and he had died ten years ago.

The little grey stone cottage on the hill lane up to the common was half hidden by damson trees from the road, and wrapped snugly, as if in a woollen comforter, by the flowering creeper which grew up beside the door. The round hawthorn hedge at the bottom of the garden by the road was neatly trimmed and looked like a long green sponge roll.

At times, the villagers expressed surprise and a little pride in the old lady when they saw how well kept the garden still was. It was a lot of work for an old woman, and a house-proud woman at that. Widow Bowen would just smile when the baker remarked on how strong and green her shallots were growing, or when Nurse Foley called up from the road, with her laughing red face, to say that the broad beans looked a picture. Widow Bowen would say, and her blue eyes would twinkle, 'I think I must have green fingers. Everything grows well here.' And she thought she was being rather modest at that, for she could not remember anything that had not grown for her when she planted it.

She would say the same thing to Mrs Beddoe at the farm when, in summer, she took down a basketful of long runner beans to help pay for the milk she fetched. 'I must have green fingers,' she would say and smile into Mrs Beddoe's sceptical face. Mrs Beddoe didn't quite know what to think. She didn't really want the vegetables that Widow Bowen brought in her basket, and yet, neither did she want to show the old lady how mercenary she was by asking for money instead, so she just looked down at the white bobbed hair and placed the jug of milk carefully into the thin hands.

Often when Widow Bowen knelt polishing the red-tiled step at her front door she would pause and smile to herself because the brass edge on the step and the kettle on the hob in the kitchen gleamed so brightly. There could not have been a brighter house on the common than hers, for Ernest and she had never had children, and she was a spotless housekeeper. But most of all she was pleased with the garden behind her. Not a weed showing itself, and everything so very green and growing. 'Really, I must be very clever,' she thought. She was not superstitious, and wasn't sure at times that there was in fact a God in the sky – often she would look up when it was blue and couldn't see even a trace of him – but she felt that, in some way, she must have a gift. She would trot on her small feet round into the shade at the back of the house and plant another cutting from the rose tree near the lavatory which had a seat scrubbed white as snow.

'I think I could make just anything grow,' she said to herself once, and to prove it she broke a twig off the old apple tree and stuck it into the ground. It was February, and the buds were still hard. Sure enough, in a week, the buds began to show green. She examined the twig each morning, and soon there were slender green shoots bursting out with a flare of leaf at their tips.

She felt it was all so very simple. Indeed, they were only ordinary things that she planted, such as anyone on the common might grow. It wasn't enough for a person with really green fingers. So, when the gardener from the big house in the valley walked by, up the hill, one Sunday afternoon, she stopped him at her gate and asked him in a quiet little voice if he would do her the kindness of bringing her a few bits of the tropical plants from the hothouses. He smiled at her, thinking that she couldn't possibly have anywhere to plant them, but promised, 'It'd be a pleasure, Mrs Bowen,' he said, touching his cap. 'I'll find something for you.' And on the following Sunday he brought a chip basket to her door filled with queer little bits of dark shiny leaves and pieces of cactus.

'Won't you come in and have a cup of tea?' she asked, smiling up at him, and though he was anxious to be off to his sister's house at the corner of the coppice, he took off his cap and bowed his head to go in under the low doorway. He blushed and mumbled, 'Thank you, kindly,' when she brought him sweet milky tea in a china cup with blackberries painted on it. He wet his finger on his tongue and dabbed up all the crumbs of the piece of faintly scented cake she placed by his arm.

'I can make those plants grow,' she said, smoothing her hands on her black apron.

'Are you going to have them in pots indoors, then?' he asked.

'Oh, no,' she laughed, carelessly. 'In the garden. They'll grow all right.'

'I think you'll find it's too cold for 'em out there,' he said. 'I could've brought you some proper outdoor plants if you'd said, only . . .'

'No. These are just what I want. I want to try something really difficult for a change.'

He was puzzled a little, and when he had gone down the path and the gate had clicked behind him she fetched her broom and tidied up the dust his boots had brought in.

'How are they growing?' he asked with a secret sort of smile when he came up on the following Sunday. 'I've brought you a few more.'

'Very nicely,' she said, with a rather straight face, because she could see that he didn't quite believe. 'The grey woolly one is in flower,' she added, looking up at him from under her eyebrows. She watched his eyes open just a little wider. 'Come and see,' she said, and took him along to the corner of the house.

There they were against the wall: dark shiny blue-green leaves, coloured fancy-patterned leaves, and on the grey woolly plant a deep wine-coloured flower. He lifted his cap and scratched his head thoughtfully, trying to work out how he had made a mistake, but he left his new lot of cuttings and took away his old basket and determined to find something she wouldn't be able to grow for next week.

Widow Bowen chuckled to herself as he went through the gate, and knelt down on the path to sort out the plants. 'They shall grow!' she said with her mouth held rather tight, and she puddled them into the soil with a little pot of rain water. When she looked at them next morning they had already begun to perk up and look settled. Fern fronds and spiky leaves reached out towards the wall of the house, and the narrow border had begun to look like a section of tropical jungle. 'I'll show that gardener what he knows about growing things,' she muttered as she scrubbed at the lavatory seat, and it was with a little high-pitched laugh of triumph that she met him at the gate at the weekend.

When he had gone, Widow Bowen wondered if she could have offended him because he made no promise to bring anything more. She did not press him. She thought that perhaps it was as well that she had finished with him. His plants grew so very easily. She even had a sense of having wasted time, and she pressed the roots of the delicate trailing creeper he had brought into the ground with an offhand dig of her thin fingers. She said to Mrs Beddoe the next morning when she went to fetch her jug of milk, 'You know, I really believe I could make a stick of firewood grow.'

The woman looked at her with uncertain eyes and felt that perhaps Widow Bowen was going a little dotty in her old age. It was not altogether surprising after losing her husband and living on her own all the time. The old lady understood the look, but she did not care very deeply. Mrs Beddoe's thoughts did not worry her, and as she sat knitting by her fire in the evening she said, 'Well, and why not? A stick of firewood had to grow at one time or another.' And she decided to try it. No harm could come of it, after all. 'If it doesn't grow, perhaps it will stop me being a conceited old woman for a bit.' But in spite of this she laughed in her throat as she thought of the gardener and his tropical plants. 'Oh! the look on his face!' She laughed until a tear fell on her knitting.

She had been buying bundles of chopped firewood from the shop up the hill for more than a month. Her tree prunings had all been used up, and she was too nervous of the dark coppice to fetch sticks from there, so it was a piece of the shop firewood that she took out into the garden the following morning. She shook her head over it as she carried it round to the back of the house. 'I really am stupid,' she thought. 'It looks as dead as a doornail.' She couldn't decide what sort of wood it was, either. The grain was very straight and soft – nothing like apple or damson wood. As she bent down to press it into the ground she looked round carefully for fear someone might be watching her. 'Then they would think I'm mad!' she said loudly to make herself feel better. She stood back and looked at the stick in the ground, holding her soiled hands away from her sides. It stuck up out of the earth like a long thin bar of yellow soap cut off smartly at the top. For a moment she seriously considered the possibility that she might be going mad, and then she hurried away to put the potatoes on for dinner.

The delicate creeper grew just as if she had planted it with the utmost care, just as though it were in its native climate, and she stopped bothering about her tropical plants. When no one was passing up the lane and she thought she was unobserved she would hurry round to the back of the house, up past the rainwater butt, to look at her piece of firewood. Each time she went she felt more and more silly. After three days had gone by and she couldn't see any change she was tempted to pull it up and have done with the whole business. But then it rained hard for three or four days so that she was hardly able to go out of the house at all. She sat at her window and watched the mist of rain sweeping up the valley. When she got tired of that she would put on the headphones of Ernest's crystal set and sit listening to the radio programme. And she cleaned and polished the house from top to bottom until she could see her wrinkled little face in the shine on the floor tiles.

Only when the rain had stopped and she was able to go out into the garden again did she realise how long she had been cooped up. Little specks of chickweed and groundsel were dotting the spaces between her rows of peas and onions. She put on her or
leather-topped clogs and went to work with the rake. The piece of firewood was completely forgotten. It was only when she took a steaming hot bucket of water and a scrubbing brush up the steps outside the back door to scour the lavatory seat that it came to mind. When she saw it she set down her bucket with a clank. Flaky brown bark had covered up the yellow wood, and the chopped-off top was now a beautifully pointed spear, a shoot, reaching nearly a foot high, with a small arrow head of pale green pine needles at its top. Then she said, 'Well of course, I knew it would,' and picked up her bucket and went into the lavatory to scrub the seat. But when she had finished and dried the woodwork off with a steaming cloth she examined her new plant carefully. It was a little thick round the base, perhaps, but a very pretty little tree for all that. She looked about to see if anyone was

watching, but the house was a perfect screen from the road, and the damson trees in the top corner of the orchard hid her effectively from all the cottages higher up the hill. A sudden feeling of elation filled her so that she picked up her bucket and almost danced down the steps into her small kitchen. Over and over again she sang, 'I've got green fingers,' to a tune that came into her head, and she got out a small pot of honey for tea.

Next morning while she was washing in the kitchen she studied her face in the mirror. 'Your hair wants cutting!' she said suddenly, noticing some stray pieces that had become rather long. Before she coiled her hair into its bob and pinned it she fetched her best scissors from her sewing basket in the window and cut the wisps of hair carefully. 'Really, you still look quite pretty,' she said to the glass and twisted the corners of her mouth into a mocking little smile. For a few seconds she stood daydreaming with the puffs of white hair in her hand. Then, coming to with a start, she went out to the dark little patch of earth at the back and pressed the hair together in a little tuft in the ground.

The tree was growing fast. It was many inches higher, and shoots had begun to press out all round the sides of it. Suddenly she was worried in case it should become a large tree because the small kitchen window needed all the light it could get. 'If it grows too big,' she said firmly, 'I shall have to chop it down.' And with that she went back into the house and put on the kettle for her morning cup of tea.

She began to say less and less to Mrs Beddoe when she went down for her milk. She took money now and refrained from offering the woman vegetables. She knew that if she mentioned her garden now she wouldn't be believed. The tuft of hair was growing tall and bushy, and new sprouts of golden brown were coming up from the bottom. She couldn't possibly tell Mrs Beddoe that. By the middle of summer she was becoming a little uneasy. The tropical creeper was growing all up the end wall of the house and was beginning to push back her own wistaria. She had tried to cut it back, but it only seemed to shoot out more strongly. The bush of hair needed trimming every few days or it hung over the path in great curling locks. And the piece of firewood was now a strong tree over seven feet tall. She was worried, too, by the little accidents she had been having. They depressed her. The first had happened when she clipped back the climbing plant. Being a tiny woman she was unable to reach the higher tentacles it shot out, and she fetched a chair to stand on. As she reached high to cut the last spray the chair tipped sideways, and she fell, twisting her ankle, so that for a few days it was swollen and painful. While she was hobbling about with this she tried to twist off one of the branches of the young tree because it was reaching out in front of the lavatory door. A tuft of pine needles caught her in the eye so that she believed for a few painful moments that it had blinded her. She had hardly recovered from these injuries when she scratched her leg deeply with the point of the shears while she was clipping the bush of hair. As she said to the baker when he called, 'I've been knocking myself about lately.'

But pushing things into the ground had become a habit with her. Any little pieces of wood or vegetable peelings she had she pressed into the ground behind the house. In time, they all began to grow, and the small hidden patch of earth was becoming a flourishing little garden of mixed odds and ends. She wondered at times whether the lack of sun behind the house might not prevent some of her experiments from doing well, but the various growths seemed to prefer the shade. Thinking of the hair that had grown, she pushed into the soil one day a piece of broken finger nail that she had cut off. It grew up like a long slender leaf, milky white and swaying in the wind. At times, when she stood and watched it, there seemed to be something mocking and truculent about it. She had the feeling that it, and the other things too, were returning a challenge that she had thrown down by sticking them into the soil. It increased her uneasiness, but she couldn't stop herself doing it. She swung between moods of triumphant success and timid disgust.

It was about the time when her leg had finally healed that she noticed something sticking out of her little plot of earth that had not been there a few days before. She racked her brain to remember what she could possibly have planted, but she could think of nothing, and she couldn't quite see what it was that was growing. It wasn't green certainly. It seemed to be a small brown knob covered with a thin greyish slime: 'Oh, a toadstool, I expect,' she said and went off up the road to the shop. But on the way back with her groceries and firewood a thought suddenly struck her. The gamekeeper from the big house had brought her a rabbit the week before, and rather than suffer the smell of burning the bones, she had buried them.

'But I never meant those to be planted!' she said aloud as she hurried down the lane. 'Not to grow!' Without stopping to put her shopping basket indoors she hastened round to the back of the house and peered closely again at the new thing. At last she decided that it was in fact one of the rabbit bones, but rather high out of the ground, and looking very sticky and wet. It was ugly, too, and she drew her hand back quickly when she realised that she had just been about to touch it.

The next day she refused to look at it as she went past. Indeed, for a few days she managed to half convince herself that if she ceased to show any more interest in her experiments they would stop growing. 'After all,' she said, 'it's me that has the green fingers – not them!' But at last she could not curb her curiosity, and she went to examine the thing. There was more of it out of the ground by this time. The slimy covering had dried a little, and there were thin red lines running criss-cross all over it. Right down near the ground a fine grey mould had begun to form.

Gradually she accommodated herself to the idea. There were soon three more shoots near the first, all beginning to reach up to the same height. The grey mould had become thick and fluffy, growing nearly to the tops of the stems, which were beginning to spread out so much in the manner of tall toadstools that she began to think her first idea had been the right explanation. And yet their centres remained pink and milky, unlike any toadstool she had ever seen.

When her damsons were ripe Widow Bowen spent all her time picking and packing them off to market. She refused all the offers of the menfolk of the village to help with the ladder work. And so, for a few weeks, her secret garden was forgotten. By the beginning of October many of her plants had died off, and the leaves on the various young trees had turned yellow. Even the bush of hair had begun to slow in its growth, and she was able to gather up handfuls of the trailing fronds and lay them back from the path on to the garden. The four grey plants had spread right out at the top until they met, and were growing one thick bulbous blob on top of them all.

'There's no doubt about it,' she said quietly as she stood looking at it. 'It's them rabbit bones. What would that smarty gardener say if I showed him this?' She couldn't imagine. It was the last thing in the world she would have dreamt of mentioning to anyone. By the time winter came, all signs of pink in the peculiar animal plant had been covered up by the grey fur, and the rough form of the animal had become apparent. Widow Bowen was not always sure in the dull light of the late afternoons whether she imagined it or whether the form did actually twitch as it appeared to do.

At last, in early January, the snow came and hung in sheets on the branches of the pine tree. The whole of her cottage was lit up with the whiteness of the snow outside. Only the top of the rabbit plant was visible, but short ears had begun to sprout, and now, definitely, she noticed that there was some movement in the snow. It was this that disturbed her far more than the growth itself, though she did not know why. For nearly a fortnight she woke each morning to find it had snowed in the night, and she would stand at her bedroom window and look out across the valley with its fields, trees, everything, covered in white. Then she would look down sadly at her paths and know that she must put on stockings over her shoes and go out with tingling fingers to sweep.

One morning the snow was marked with black dots leading down to the hedge. She knew at once what they were, and because she knew she was shocked. She hurried out to the back of the house with a fearful choking in her throat. It was gone. There was a black hole in the snow and four imprints in the damp earth beneath. She stood a long time too dazed to think. When at last she was able to think her thoughts frightened her so much that she ran back into the house and did not venture out again all day. She sat huddled in her chair by the empty fireplace too frightened to move and did not think of eating. She slept there that night.

Next morning the sun shone fiercely and the snow began to melt. Widow Bowen stirred herself and laid the fire. The sunlight shone into her room and everything seemed cheerful once more. She thought carefully about her fears, and the more she thought the more silly they appeared. 'It's gone. I'm well rid of it.' With that she began to clean up the house and sweep the slushy snow away from her door. By afternoon nearly all the snow had gone. 'I've been worried more than enough by all these growing things,' she said firmly. 'I'm the one with the green fingers, and I'm going to have my own way with them.' She fetched out the shears and oiled them and cut back the hair bush. She trimmed the creeper and the frond of white nail back to decent limits with a sharp kitchen knife. 'And now,' she announced loudly to herself, 'I'm going to lay my axe at the butt of that tree. It's darkened my window long enough.'

The axe was heavy and sharp. Milk-white chips of wood jumped out on to the earth as she chopped at the small V-shaped cut she had made in the trunk, and after a few minutes she was very hot and tired. She stood up with the branches all about her head, looking at her little cottage. For the first time in many years she wished that Ernest was still alive. Chopping this small tree down would have been nothing to him. It was less than four inches across at the bottom, but she had made very little progress.

At her second attempt she steadied herself by resting her left hand low down on the trunk, and swung the axe slowly with one hand, letting the weight of the head do the work. The chips were smaller now, and the neat V had become a ragged notch in the white wood. She felt that she was going to expend all her energy without cutting more than halfway through it, and with a burst of determination she began to hack fiercely at it so that the blood came to her bowed head making her feel a little dizzy. The end of the haft caught her bent knee as she swung the axe. With a sickening pain the blade swung up into her hand on the trunk. She fell down in a faint with the blood spurting from the stump of her forefinger. When her vision cleared she knew what had happened. She felt weak and knew that the bleeding must be stopped. There was no pain now, only a dull numbness all up her arm. She crawled shakily to her feet and tottered uncertainly down the steps into her kitchen. She found a piece of white cloth and wrapped it round her bleeding hand. She felt old, very old, and wanted to die.

Soon the blood was soaking through the cloth, and she realised that she needed a doctor or she would indeed die very soon. She stirred herself and went down to the front gate, holding her bandaged hand up in front of her like a dog with a lame paw. Her neighbour's little boy was circling in the lane on his bicycle, and she called weakly to him to ride down the hill and ask the nurse to come quickly in her little car.

When the nurse came, Widow Bowen was leaning on the gate for support with the blood dripping from her bandage. Nurse Foley took one look at the hand and carried the old lady into the back of her car. Then she set off for the town hospital.

It was only when they were driving back in the dark that Widow Bowen truly woke up to what had happened to her. A huge white pad of bandage held her mutilated hand firmly bound.

'You must take things easy for a week or so,' said Nurse Foley, half turning her red face to the back seat. 'You've lost a lot of blood, you know. I asked them if they could keep you in for a few days, but they just haven't got a bed to spare.' Widow Bowen smiled weakly and said she felt very well, considering. But there was something troubling her at the back of her mind. 'Shall I ask Mrs Jones to come in and help you get your tea?' the nurse asked when she had taken the old lady in and lit the lamp for her.

'I think I can manage well enough one-handed,' said Widow Bowen, and her blue eyes twinkled a little again now that she was back home. To prove it she made a cup of tea for herself and the nurse and sat gazing at the big round-faced woman in her sitting-room. The tea made her feel a lot better, and she brought out some scones and put a light to the laid fire in the grate. She felt quite safe with the house round her.

At last the nurse went, promising to call in the morning, and the old woman sat thinking in her chair. Her fingers, her precious green fingers, were irrevocably damaged. Slowly she got up and walked, carrying the lamp, out through the kitchen to the back of the house. Little splashes of blood had dried in a trail across the kitchen floor. She stood in the wavering light of the lamp, looking at the hacked tree with the chips of white wood lying all round it, and felt very sorry that she had tried to cut it down. She could sympathize now that the axe had cut her too. The axe lay at the foot of the tree with a little stain of blood on the blade. Suddenly, in the chippings, she saw her finger, bent and white. Her stomach lurched, and she felt a bit dizzy again. Wondering, she stooped and set her lamp down and picked up the finger and looked at it. It looked so old and wrinkled and white. Many times she had pressed holes into the earth with it for seedlings, and now it was cut off. She held it against her breast crying a little. It looked so forlorn. 'And you'll never plant another thing!' she sobbed sadly to it, as though it were a dead child. The frustrated maternal instincts of years welled up in her small bent body, and she nursed this small part of her close in the warmth of her dress.

After standing there a long while, with the lamp at her feet throwing up the shadows all around her, she said with sudden determination, 'You shan't die! I'll put you in the ground and you shall grow.' In spite of her resolve her heart was beating rapidly as she stepped on to the garden and crouched down in the darkness behind the rose bush at the side of the lavatory. With tears pooling in her eyes she made a hole in the ground and placed her finger in it. For minutes she crouched brooding over this strange child of her body until her old legs ached with cramp, and then she went into the house and up to bed.

Many times in the night she woke crying with the pain in her hand, and when the morning came she was pale and worn out. Nurse Foley suggested that a woman should come in and look after her for a few days, but the old woman refused fiercely. The nurse sighed and said, 'Very well.' She tucked the stray ends of her grey hair into her cap and left. Widow Bowen went round to the back of the house to look at her finger. The dew of the night had taken all the limpness out of it. It pointed straight up at the sky and had a tinge of colour again around the knuckles. A wave of defiant will flowed through her, and then left her feeling weary and apathetic.

She was no longer surprised. It was difficult for her even to think clearly about it. The thing was growing. She only felt that at all costs she must prevent anyone from ever seeing it. In a few days there were the tips of other fingers showing. The old lady nodded her white head tiredly when she saw them. She felt it was out of her control now. In a fortnight a full hand had appeared. Fear began to fill the old widow. She wandered about her cottage in a vague dream. The brass door knob began to discolour and the kettle grew tarnished and blackened. Crumbs of food lay on the floors, and a fine film of dust was thickening on her sideboard. Out in the garden the unplanted earth had a thin carpet of weeds,

and the hedge at the roadside grew woolly. Often she forgot to go
for her milk, and cried peevishly one morning when Mrs Beddoe
brought it up to her. For many days at a time she was too
frightened to go and look at the growing thing in the shadows
behind her house, but eventually she would have to go, and would
stand staring at it with a glaze over her blue eyes. A wrist and an
arm had appeared, with the skin wrinkled lightly like her own, and
by the time the cherries blossomed the crest of a white head had
begun to appear, like the top of a large horse mushroom. She
would spend hours staring at it with a terrible fascination. The
fear that anyone should see it became an obsession with her. She
began to meet the baker at the gate to prevent him walking up to
the house, and she covered the naked head and shoulders over
with brown potato sacks. The eyes of the figure were closed, but
on the face and the bare shoulders were the wrinkles and freckles
that resembled her own in the minutest detail. Night after night
she lay tossing in a half stupor of sleep while horrible dreams
flashed through her frightened mind.

By the time the damsons were ripe the white body was out of
the ground to its knees, bent slightly forward as she herself stood.
Widow Bowen let her damsons rot on the trees. Birds settled in
screaming crowds, pecking at the decaying fruit, and as the
season passed over shrivelled brown drops remained to hang like
tiny bats from all the branches. The cottage was now thick in dirt,
and the forest of weeds in the garden had already begun to die
down. The hawthorn hedge had sprung up unchecked, hiding the
house from the view of the villagers, and, but for her occasional
dishevelled appearance at the gate to wait for the baker, they
would have believed her to be dead. At first they had enquired
whether they might lend a hand in the house or garden, but she
answered them with such hysterical outbursts that they stopped
asking, and hurried past her gate with heads down whenever she
happened to be standing there.

As December passed the snow came again, bearing down the
tall raggedness of the hedge, and settling like a mantle on the
sack-covered shoulders of the growing figure behind the house.
Mornings would come, and the old lady would wake from her
fitful sleep to find the room flooded with white light from the
blanket of snow outside. She dreaded it. Each morning she

expected to see a dark trail leading across the garden from the back of the house as she had done the year before. But each morning the snow stretched, untouched, down to the hedge, startlingly white. Every day she would take a quick frightened look behind the rambling rose tree beside the lavatory to be sure the figure still stood there. At times it would sway slightly, and Widow Bowen would stand, rigid with horror, until it was still again.

The lavatory seat was no longer white. Cobwebs and dusty bits of newspaper littered its once-scrubbed surface. Widow Bowen was almost too frightened to go in there for fear of the figure standing close outside.

The snow still covered the ground in a hard frozen layer when she came out of the lavatory one afternoon and took her usual hurried look behind the rose bush. Her heart stopped beating for a second, and the breath choked in her throat. Two black patches of soil were all that remained to show where it had been. She looked wildly about her. There were no tracks in the snow. It was frozen far too hard. With a terrified scream she stumbled down the steps into her kitchen and slammed the door behind her. She bolted it at top and bottom with dithering fingers, and scurried into the sitting-room to lock the front door.

There in her chair sat the figure, staring at her. She stood with her back against the door, unable to move. The other did not move either. It was her exact double, from the white hair to the twinkling blue eyes, but clothed, almost demurely, in sacks. The old lady stared at the white thin hands spread out on the arms of the chair. The fingers were complete, whole. Widow Bowen looked up into the eyes again, and they looked into hers with a faint mocking smile, as though they could see into the deepest corners of her mind. She was rigid with terror. The blood began to leave her head. A gradual blackness clouded out her sight, and she sank to the floor unconscious.

Nurse Foley came down the hill in her car next morning. The snow had almost melted in the night, and the sun was shining. Catching sight of the old lady, she stopped and put her head out. 'I'm glad to see you trimming your hedge,' she said. 'It had begun to look untidy.'

The old lady smiled, holding the shears in front of her. 'Yes,' she said, 'the whole place is in a terrible mess. I've been dying to get started on it, but the snow held me up, you know.' Her blue eyes twinkled brightly.

'I suppose you've heard the news,' said the nurse, pushing her head further out of the window.

'No, I haven't. What's that, then?'

'Oh, my dear! I've been up there for hours. They found a body in the coppice, you know. Little Chris Bradley found it first – at least, a piece of it. Horrible it is – all chopped to pieces with an axe or something. The police are there now. They think it's probably an old woman, but it's so wickedly smashed about that they can't recognise anything.'

'What a nasty thing!'

'Oh, terrible! Yes. Still, you don't want to bother your head about that. You've had enough trouble. How is your hand getting on?' She looked from one hand to the other, confused between left and right, but there was no missing finger.

'Oh, beautifully,' said the old lady, smiling and nodding her head. 'Everything grows well here. I think I must have green fingers.'

THE TOWER

Marghanita Laski

The road begins to rise in a series of gentle curves, passing through pleasing groves of olives and vines. 5 km. on the left is the fork for Florence. To the right may be seen the Tower of Sacrifice (470 steps) built in 1535 by Niccolo di Ferramano; superstitious fear left the tower intact when, in 1549, the surrounding village was completely destroyed . . .

Triumphantly Caroline lifted her finger from the fine italic type. There was nothing to mar the success of this afternoon. Not only had she taken the car out alone for the first time, driving unerringly on the right-hand side of the road, but what she had achieved was not a simple drive but a cultural excursion. She had taken the Italian guide-book Neville was always urging on her, and hesitantly, haltingly, she had managed to piece out enough of the language to choose a route that took in four well-thought-of frescoes, two universally-admired campaniles, and one wooden crucifix in a village church quite a long way from the main road. It was not, after all, such a bad thing that a British Council meeting had kept Neville in Florence. True, he was certain to know all about the campaniles and the frescoes, but there was just a chance that he hadn't discovered the crucifix, and how gratifying if she could, at last, have something of her own to contribute to his constantly accumulating hoard of culture.

But could she add still more? There was at least another hour of daylight, and it wouldn't take more than thirty-five minutes to get back to the flat in Florence. Perhaps there would just be time to add this tower to her dutiful collection? What was it called? She bent to the guide-book again, carefully tracing the text with her finger to be sure she was translating it correctly, word by word.

But this time her moving finger stopped abruptly at the name of Niccolo di Ferramano. There had risen in her mind a picture –

no, not a picture, a portrait – of a thin white face with deep-set black eyes that stared intently into hers. Why a portrait? she asked, and then she remembered.

It had been about three months ago, just after they were married, when Neville had first brought her to Florence. He himself had already lived there for two years, and during that time had been at least as concerned to accumulate Tuscan culture for himself as to disseminate English culture to the Italians. What could be more natural than that he should wish to share – perhaps even to show off – his discoveries to his young wife?

Caroline had come out to Italy with the idea that when she had worked through one or two galleries and made a few trips – say to Assisi and Siena – she would have done her duty as a British Council wife, and could then settle down to examining the Florentine shops, which everyone had told her were too marvellous for words. But Neville had been contemptuous of her programme. 'You can see the stuff in the galleries at any time,' he had said, 'but I'd like you to start with the pieces that the ordinary tourist doesn't see,' and of course Caroline couldn't possibly let herself be classed as an ordinary tourist. She had been proud to accompany Neville to castles and palaces privately owned to which his work gave him entry, and there to gaze with what she hoped was pleasure on the undiscovered Raphael, the Titian that had hung on the same wall ever since it was painted, the Giotto fresco under which the family that had originally commissioned it still said their prayers.

It had been on one of these pilgrimages that she had seen the face of the young man with the black eyes. They had made a long slow drive over narrow ill-made roads and at last had come to a castle on the top of a hill. The family was, to Neville's disappointment, away, but the housekeeper remembered him and led them to a long gallery lined with five centuries of family portraits.

Though she could not have admitted it even to herself, Caroline had become almost anæsthetised to Italian art. Dutifully she had followed Neville along the gallery, listening politely while in his light well-bred voice he had told her intimate anecdotes of history, and involuntarily she had let her eyes wander round the room, glancing anywhere but at the particular portrait of Neville's immediate dissertation.

It was thus that her eye was caught by a face on the other side of the room, and forgetting what was due to politeness she caught her husband's arm and demanded, 'Neville, who's that girl over there?'

But he was pleased with her. He said, 'Ah, I'm glad you picked that one out. It's generally thought to be the best thing in the collection – a Bronzino, of course,' and they went over to look at it.

The picture was painted in rich pale colours, a green curtain, a blue dress, a young face with calm brown eyes under plaits of honey-gold hair. Caroline read out the name under the picture – *Giovanna di Ferramano, 1531–1549.* That was the year the village was destroyed, she remembered now, sitting in the car by the roadside, but then she had exclaimed, 'Neville, she was only eighteen when she died.'

'They married young in those days,' Neville commented, and Caroline said in surprise, 'Oh, was she married?' It had been the radiantly virginal character of the face that had caught at her inattention.

'Yes, she was married,' Neville answered, and added, 'Look at the portrait beside her. It's Bronzino again. What do you think of it?'

And this was when Caroline had seen the pale young man. There were no clear light colours in this picture. There was only the whiteness of the face, the blackness of the eyes, the hair, the clothes, and the glint of gold letters on the pile of books on which the young man rested his hand. Underneath this picture was written *Portrait of an Unknown Gentleman.*

'Do you mean he's her husband?' Caroline asked. 'Surely they'd know if he was, instead of calling him an Unknown Gentleman?'

'He's Niccolo di Ferramano all right,' said Neville. 'I've seen another portrait of him somewhere, and it's not a face one would forget, but,' he added reluctantly, because he hated to admit ignorance, 'there's apparently some queer scandal about him, and though they don't turn his picture out, they won't even mention his name. Last time I was here, the old Count himself took me through the gallery. I asked him about little Giovanna and her husband.' He laughed uneasily. 'Mind you, my Italian was far from perfect at that time, but it was horribly clear that I shouldn't have asked.' 'But what did he *say?*' Caroline demanded. 'I've tried to remember,' said Neville. 'For some reason it stuck in my mind. He said either "She was lost" or "She was damned", but which word it was I can never be sure. The portrait of Niccolo he just ignored altogether.'

'What was wrong with Niccolo, I wonder?' mused Caroline, and Neville answered, 'I don't know but I can guess. Do you notice the lettering on those books up there, under his hand? It's all in Hebrew or Arabic. Undoubtedly the unmentionable Niccolo dabbled in Black Magic.'

Caroline shivered. 'I don't like him,' she said. 'Let's look at Giovanna again,' and they had moved back to the first portrait, and Neville had said casually, 'Do you know, she's rather like you.'

'I've just got time to look at the tower,' Caroline now said aloud, and she put the guide-book in the pigeon-hole under the dashboard, and drove carefully along the gentle curves until she came to the fork for Florence on the left.

On the top of a little hill to the right stood a tall round tower. There was no other building in sight. In a land where every available piece of ground is cultivated, there was no cultivated ground around this tower. On the left was the fork for Florence: on the right a rough track led up to the top of the hill.

Caroline knew that she wanted to take the fork to the left, to Florence and home and Neville and – said an urgent voice inside her – for safety. This voice so much shocked her that she got out of the car and began to trudge up the dusty track towards the tower.

After all, I may not come this way again, she argued; it seems silly to miss the chance of seeing it when I've already got a reason for being interested. I'm only just going to have a quick look – and she glanced at the setting sun, telling herself that she would indeed have to be quick if she were to get back to Florence before dark.

And now she had climbed the hill and was standing in front of the tower. It was built of narrow red bricks, and only thin slits pierced its surface right up to the top where Caroline could see some kind of narrow platform encircling it. Before her was an arched doorway. I'm just going to have a quick look, she assured herself again, and then she walked in.

She was in an empty room with a low arched ceiling. A narrow stone staircase clung to the wall and circled round the room to disappear through a hole in the ceiling.

'There ought to be a wonderful view at the top,' said Caroline firmly to herself, and she laid her hand on the rusty rail and started to climb, and as she climbed, she counted.

' – thirty-nine, forty, forty-one,' she said, and with the forty-first step she came through the ceiling and saw over her head, far far above, the deep blue evening sky, a small circle of blue framed in a narrowing shaft round which the narrow staircase spiralled. There was no inner wall; only the rusty railing protected the climber on the inside.

' – eighty-three, eighty-four – ' counted Caroline. The sky above her was losing its colour and she wondered why the narrow slit windows in the wall had all been so placed that they spiralled round the staircase too high for anyone climbing it to see through them.

'It's getting dark very quickly,' said Caroline at the hundred-and-fiftieth step. 'I know what the tower is like now. It would be much more sensible to give up and go home.'

At the two-hundred-and-sixty-ninth step, her hand, moving forward on the railing, met only empty space. For an interminable second she shivered, pressing back to the hard brick on the other side. Then hesitantly she groped forwards, upwards, and at last her fingers met the rusty rail again, and again she climbed.

But now the breaks in the rail became more and more frequent. Sometimes she had to climb several steps with her left shoulder pressed tightly to the brick wall before her searching hand could find the tenuous rusty comfort again.

At the three-hundred-and-seventy-fifth step, the rail, as her moving hand clutched it, crumpled away under her fingers. 'I'd better just go by the wall,' she told herself, and now her left hand traced the rough brick as she climbed up and up.

'Four-hundred-and-twenty-two, four-hundred-and-twenty-three,' counted Caroline with part of her brain. 'I really ought to go down now,' said another part, 'I wish – oh, I want to go down now – ' but she could not. 'It would be so silly to give up,' she told herself, desperately trying to rationalize what drove her on. 'Just because one's afraid – ' and then she had to stifle that thought too, and there was nothing left in her brain but the steadily mounting tally of the steps.

' – four-hundred-and-seventy!' said Caroline aloud with explosive relief, and then she stopped abruptly because the steps had stopped too. There was nothing ahead but a piece of broken railing barring her way, and the sky, drained now of all its colour, was still some twenty feet above her head.

'But how idiotic,' she said to the air. 'The whole thing's absolutely pointless,' and then the fingers of her left hand, exploring the wall beside her, met not brick but wood.

She turned to see what it was, and there in the wall, level with the top step, was a small wooden door. 'So it does go somewhere after all,' she said, and she fumbled with the rusty handle. The door pushed open and she stepped through.

She was on a narrow stone platform about a yard wide. It seemed to encircle the tower. The platform sloped downwards away from the tower and its stones were smooth and very shiny – and this was all she noticed before she looked beyond the stones and down.

She was immeasurably, unbelievably high and alone and the ground below was a world away. It was not credible, not possible that she should be so far from the ground. All her being was suddenly absorbed in the single impulse to hurl herself from the sloping platform. 'I cannot go down any other way,' she said, and then she heard what she said and stepped back, frenziedly clutching the soft rotten wood of the doorway with hands sodden with sweat. There is no other way, said the voice in her brain, there is no other way.

'This is vertigo,' said Caroline. 'I've only got to close my eyes and keep still for a minute and it will pass off. It's bound to pass off. I've never had it before but I know what it is and it's vertigo.' She closed her eyes and kept very still and felt the cold sweat running down her body.

'I should be all right now,' she said at last, and carefully she stepped back through the doorway on to the four-hundred-and-seventieth step and pulled the door shut before her. She looked up at the sky, swiftly darkening with night. Then, for the first time, she looked down into the shaft of the tower, down to the narrow unprotected staircase spiralling round and round and round, and disappearing into the dark. She said – she screamed – 'I can't go down.'

She stood still on the top step, staring downwards, and slowly the last light faded from the tower. She could not move. It was not possible that she should dare to go down, step by step down the unprotected stairs into the dark below. It would be much easier to fall, said the voice in her head, to take one step to the left and fall and it would all be over. You cannot climb down.

She began to cry, shuddering wth the pain of her sobs. It could not be true that she had brought herself to this peril, that there could be no safety for her unless she could climb down the menacing stairs. The reality *must* be that she was safe at home with Neville – but this was the reality and here were the stairs; at last she stopped crying and said 'Now I shall go down.'

'One!' she counted and, her right hand tearing at the brick wall, she moved first one and then the other foot down to the second step. 'Two!' she counted, and then she thought of the depth below her and stood still, stupefied with terror. The stone beneath her feet, the brick against her hand were too frail protections for her exposed body. They could not save her from the voice that repeated that it would be easier to fall. Abruptly she sat down on the step.

'Two,' she counted again, and spreading both her hands tightly against the step on each side of her, she swung her body off the second step, down on to the third. 'Three,' she counted, then 'four' then 'five', pressing closer and closer into the wall, away from the empty drop on the other side.

At the twenty-first step she said, 'I think I can do it now.' She slid her right hand up the rough wall and slowly stood upright. Then with the other hand she reached for the railing it was now too dark to see, but it was not there.

For timeless time she stood there, knowing nothing but fear. 'Twenty-one,' she said, 'twenty-one,' over and over again, but she could not step on to the twenty-second stair.

Something brushed her face. She knew it was a bat, not a hand, that touched her but still it was horror beyond conceivable horror, and it was this horror, without any sense of moving from dread to safety, that at last impelled her down the stairs.

'Twenty-three, twenty-four, twenty-five – ' she counted, and around her the air was full of whispering skin-stretched wings. If one of them should touch her again, she must fall. 'Twenty-six, twenty-seven, twenty-eight – ' The skin of her right hand was torn and hot with blood, for she would never lift it from the wall, only press it slowly down and force her rigid legs to move from the knowledge of each step to the peril of the next.

So Caroline came down the dark tower. She could not think. She could know nothing but fear. Only her brain remorselessly recorded the tally. 'Five-hundred-and-one,' it counted, 'five-hundred-and-two-and three-and four – '

THE DOLL

Francis King

In three separate shop-windows he had seen that photograph –
with above it the question 'HAVE YOU EVER SEEN THIS GIRL?' and
below it the admonition 'IF YOU HAVE SPEAK NOW!' But one did
not want to be observed studying a notice like that, did one?
People might suspect one of being in some way involved oneself.
So each time he gave no more than a shying glance, to be followed
by that curious gesture of first lowering his pointed chin down on
to his collar and then pushing it outward, which indicated to those
who knew him that he was feeling self-conscious or embarrassed.

'Morning, Mr Reynolds!'

'Morning Eunice.'

'*Good* morning, Mr Reynolds. Quite a nip in the air, isn't
there?'

'Yes, quite a nip.'

'Now what else for you, Mr Reynolds? We have some nice
chicory in.'

'My gentleman's off chicory.'

But the chatty exchanges which he usually enjoyed so much
now were a burden to him. He wanted to gaze at that photograph
somewhere where no one could watch him doing so.

'Oh, Mr Reynolds!'

That woman who had been recommended for the loose-covers
and who had made them so badly was barring his path.

'Good morning.' He nodded and tried to hurry round her.

'I wanted to explain. About those loose-covers. It was a
question of cutting the cloth on the bias. Sir Malcolm just didn't
seem to understand. You should have heard him on the phone! It
was the bias. And then that finicky floral pattern he chose . . .'

Reynolds, a shopping bag in either hand, shifted from one foot
to another, his eyes not on the moist, pale blue eyes in the

quivering face opposite to him but darting among the passers-by in an agony of restlessness.

'Is it his custom to talk in that kind of tone to a lady? I must say he gave me quite a shock. One doesn't look for a man of his refinement . . .'

Silly bitch!

At last he got away from her; and there, as he entered St Ann's Well Gardens, loomed up another of the mammoth photographs. Hurriedly he glanced in all directions; then he gave himself up, with an almost voluptuous sigh, to a long contemplation.

Oh, it was a shame, a terrible shame, to think of a poor little thing like that lying out somewhere dead. If she *was* dead. They were not sure of that of course, there was only the evidence of what they had called a 'bloodstained article of clothing.' What could that have been? Knickers most like. Her mother had recognized them as hers together with that comic she had been carrying the day she had disappeared. On the beach that elderly woman with the dog had found them – they said the woman kept that shop called Dog's Den.

It was a shame, a real shame to think of anything happening to such a pretty little thing, with that lovely long hair like silk and that little turned-up nose and that gay little smile. Well, if she hadn't been such a dainty little darling no one would have been interested in her. They said in the paper that, though she was twelve, her mental age had been that of a girl of five, but to look at the photograph you'd never think that she wasn't just as bright as a new pin. Oh, that face looked just brimful of intelligence.

She was a doll, a real little doll. But dolls were dead things, whereas the one thing the photograph told one was that here was a kiddy who was really *alive*, full of *joie de vivre*, with that lovely smile of hers and those laughing eyes of hers, and that, oh, so fun-loving expression of hers, as though she were telling one that the world was a marvellous place. Poor kid, poor little kiddy! Because of course it wasn't a marvellous place, not for her any more than for anyone else, with that awful bloodstained 'article of clothing' and who knows what ghastly tortures she must have suffered before it was over.

He put his head on one side, musingly oblivious of the weight of the two shopping-bags full of the groceries for which Mrs

Evans was waiting. He couldn't rightly remember ever having seen her with the other children from that special school and that was odd, because it was the kind of face, so gentle and trusting and well, yes, beautiful that would stick in the memory. He had talked to some of the children on his way back through the gardens after shopping in the mornings but he had never seen anyone like her, of that he was sure. With most of them you could tell that something was wrong as soon as you clapped eyes on them; there was this curious way in which all their features seemed to have been drawn together to the front of their faces and the features themselves were tiny. But everything about that poor little mite's features was perfect. Oh yes, he would certainly have noticed her if she had been playing on the swings with the others. Unless, of course, he hadn't realized that she was one of them and had imagined that she was one of the normal children who also played there. But the normal children were usually much younger – one didn't play on swings when one was twelve; and in any case when the children from that special school arrived the other children would usually drift off. He thought it cruel the way that mothers of the normal children would begin to wheel away their prams, shouting over their shoulders. 'Come along, Fiona – time we moved on!' or 'Rex! *Rex*! Come *on*!' Often he himself brought some sweets with him and the children would remember this – oh, they could be bright enough if they wanted to be – and then two or three would spot him on the bench on which he always sat and they would at once run over, to be followed by a whole jostling, gabbling pack of them. The two women in charge would go on knitting and chatting. Once he had tried to engage them in conversation but he understood at once, from the way in which neither looked up as the larger of them answered, that they didn't want any company except each other's.

'What a pretty little thing!'

Reynolds started at the sound of the croaking voice behind him.

It was the old man with the tottering, grey muzzled labrador bitch on the end of a piece of string. Reynolds always tried to avoid him.

'Shocking,' he said, swallowing on the word.

'And yet they do away with capital punishment. The world's going stark, staring bonkers.'

The labrador bitch was now straddled, back legs wide apart and an expression of patient suffering on her face as her whole body strained and strained again.

'I gave her some paraffin last night,' the old man said. 'I thought it might ease her, like.'

But Reynolds was hurrying off.

'Well, you certainly took your time,' Mrs Evans said. She banged the fish down on the table as though she wished to hurt it. 'It's me that gets the blame if his lordship's lunch is late. "I think that a little Sole Véronique might perhaps tempt my invalid's appetite".' The far from exact imitation of Sir Malcolm's 'posh' voice voided, on this occasion as on many others, the accumulated venom which her small, neat person could no longer contain. ' "And don't forget the mousseline potatoes, now will you, Mrs Evans?" How does he imagine that I'm to cook that kind of meal for him if you don't bring me the fish until nearly twelve o'clock?' As she spoke these last words she picked up the sole and began to sniff at it.

'It's quite fresh,' Reynolds said.

She sniffed at it again, a look of scepticism on her yellow face.

'He's in a fine old mood,' she said. 'One of his best.'

'Why? What's the matter?'

'If he tells anyone it will be you, now won't it?' she said. 'I'm not the one who gets his little confidences.' She began to move him away from the refrigerator, the flat of one hand patting at his ribs. 'Two men called to see him,' she said.

'Two men? What men?'

'Police. They *said*. Didn't look like it to me.'

'Police!'

'Scruffy like, one of them was. Just a boy really. They were with him quite a time. Oh, I knew he was upset from the way he started up again about that noise of the next-door radio. As soon as they had left him. It's not as though the radio's on at night-time. Not late, that is.'

'What would the police want here?'

'Your guess is as good as mine.'

At once, Reynolds did not know why, there had come into his mind that photograph of that poor little thing with her pretty doll-like face and blue, blue eyes and long hair like silk. Perhaps they were making a house-to-house check like the one they made when that woman had been murdered in the off-licence in the Lanes. Two such polite men they had been – 'just a routine check' they had called it. It had been the night when he had been attending the Whist Drive at St Barnabas's, so he had had no difficulty in giving them an alibi. But in an odd way, for all their courtesy and for all the certainty of that alibi, they had made him feel somehow furtive and guilty, so that even as he talked to them he was conscious of his face beginning to redden, of his hands beginning to tremble and of the words emerging from between his lips with the parched, laborious preciseness of someone nervously repeating a lesson learned by rote.

'It might be something to do with the car.'

Mrs Evans shrugged.

'Or perhaps he complained to the police about the radio.'

This time Mrs Evans made no response at all, as she continued to busy herself with removing the skins and pips from some grapes.

'What a footling job!' she muttered to herself at last.

Sir Malcolm did not mention the visit of the police all that day and Reynolds knew better than to ask him.

'Oh, dear, oh dear, oh dear!' he exclaimed as Reynolds carefully eased the luncheon tray across his knees. 'I see that our good Mrs E. has again been digging into that confounded deep-freeze.'

'Sir?'

'These beans look more than a little jaded.'

'There were no fresh beans in the shops this morning, sir.'

'Well, there must have been *something* fresh. What about chicory?'

'But I thought that you said that you didn't like – '

'I've nothing against chicory. Nothing at all. In moderation, that is.' Sir Malcolm suddenly gave Reynolds one of his piercing glances from under the loosely wrinkled, pale-grey skin of his eyelids. 'Are you all right, Reynolds?'

'Perfectly, sir.'

'Your hands are shaking.'

Reynolds had just drawn Sir Malcolm's napkin out of its ring and had unfurled it with a single downward flick.

'My hands, sir?'

'You look as if something had upset you.'

'Oh, no, sir. Not at all.'

Sir Malcolm picked up a single grape on the end of his fork and peered at it from every angle. Then he popped it into his mouth and sucking on it said: 'All right, Reynolds.'

It was only when Reynolds was preparing Sir Malcolm for bed, holding out the tray with a tumbler of water and the two sleeping-pills on it, that the old man at last mentioned the visit.

Having gulped first one pill and then the other, he went through his habitual gesture of stroking the wattles of his throat with a palsied right hand, presumably to coax the pills on their downward passage, before he said: 'Oh, I had an enquiry about you today, Reynolds.'

'An enquiry, sir?'

'Yes, an enquiry.' The old man paused as though maliciously eager to prolong the other's anxiety. 'A police enquiry.'

'A police enquiry, sir?' Reynolds was conscious that his hands holding the tray had again begun to tremble and knew that it would be only a matter of time before Sir Malcolm again commented on the fact.

'No need for alarm. It was about this – er – this squalid case of the vanishing girl. How her parents allowed her to consort with a total stranger – or strangers – is quite beyond my understanding. It would be odd enough if she had been in full possession of her faculties but in the case of a child who was actually simple – *subnormal*, I think was the word used by our two friends – well, such irresponsibility is little short of criminal. Wouldn't you agree?'

'Yes, indeed, sir.'

'Now don't look so worried! I – er – got you off the hook. I can promise you that. Fortunately I had only to look at my diary in order to satisfy them that on the two – or was it three? – days at issue, you were with me in London. It was when I was having those confounded tests at the London Clinic. Remember? Oh, you have nothing to fear, my dear Reynolds! I'd have lied for you, if need be, that goes without saying. After all it's no easy matter to find a good servant in times like these. But in fact no lie was necessary.'

'But why – why did they pick on me?'

'You may well ask. It was because – as they put it – they could not leave a single avenue unexplored. Or was it that they could not leave a single stone unturned? I forget. Anyway – it seems that some busybody had telephoned them to suggest that they might – er – investigate you.'

Reynolds was appalled. 'But who would want to do such a thing?'

'Oh, someone who wished to be *public-spirited*, I expect. I do hate public spirit, don't you?' Sir Malcolm turned to slap at the pillows against which he was propped. 'It seems, you see, that this little girl – this Veronica or Valerie or Vivienne or whatever it was – numbered among her friends a middle-aged gentleman who was known to her parents merely as Ray.'

'Ray!'

'Yes, Ray. Not a name for which I care. I could never call *you* Ray, for example. But the anonymous caller suggested that Ray might have been a – um – diminutive for Reynolds.'

'But that's slander, that's nothing but slander!'

'Now don't get so agitated. As I told you, I at once got you – er – off the hook. The police informed me – something of which I am bound to say I had always been ignorant – that it is often your way to sit in St Ann's Well Gardens and talk to the children from the same school to which this unfortunate little Vera or Violet or whatever it was used to go. No, no' – Sir Malcolm raised a purple-veined hand as Reynolds's mouth was about to open in expostulation – 'I think such an interest in the afflicted to be entirely to your credit. Entirely. And I told our two gentlemen that.'

'Thank you, sir.'

'No, obviously you could not have been this Ray. And so' – Sir Malcolm leant far back on the pillows, smiling – 'it seems most unlikely that you will be summoned for an identification parade!' He drew the sheet up to his pointed chin: 'Do you know,' he asked, 'how this Ray first met the child Victoria?'

'I've no idea, sir.'

'No, of course you wouldn't. Well, believe it or not, he just walked up to her parents on the front, said, "What a pretty little girl you have there!" and offered to take her to the Aquarium. Now just think of that!'

'It's incredible, sir.'

'As you say – incredible.' The creased eyelids fluttered and descended. 'Well, now I must turn in. Now don't worry, Reynolds. I've no intention of losing you. You're far too valuable to me.'

'Thank you, sir.'

Mrs Evans was still in the kitchen, though it was long after the hour when she usually left for home. When Reynolds came in with the tray, she reached for her crocheted brindle beret and began to tug it over her close-cropped grey curls. 'Has our lord and master turned in?'

Reynolds nodded.

'Did he say anything about those visitors?'

'What visitors?'

'Those visitors this morning. Those so-called detectives.'

It suddenly came to Reynolds that perhaps it had been Mrs Evans who had telephoned to the police. He knew that she disliked him.

'Oh, those.'

'Yes. Did he say anything about them?'

Reynolds shook his head.

'Perhaps he'll tell you tomorrow.'

'Maybe.'

'He tells you everything. In the end. Doesn't he?'

Sir Malcolm told Mrs Evans nothing and this infuriated her. When Reynolds did not answer, she went on: 'Yes, you'll know about it soon enough.'

There was something in her tone which was not merely vindictive, as so often in the past, but even grimly menacing. Or had he imagined that? He stared after her, eyes wide and hands trembling as he clutched them together over his stomach as though in some sudden attack of abdominal cramp. Meanwhile she gave a last tug to the beret, and called out, 'Bye for now!' and started out into the darkness.

Reynolds lay in bed, trying to think of the date when he and Sir Malcolm had gone up to London. He had no memory for that kind of thing. No, his memory had never been good; it had always been a worry to him. He could memorize a long shopping-list or all the items sent in a week to the laundry, but whole blocks of events had a way of slipping imperceptibly into oblivion. Once when he had complained of the vagaries of his memory to Mrs Evans she had fixed him with that sardonically appraising gaze of hers and had commented, 'Oh, you can always remember what it suits you to remember.'

'What do you mean by that, Mrs E?' he had demanded, nettled.

'Oh, I don't mean you in particular. I mean you in the general sense. People. Everyone.'

If Sir Malcolm said that they had been in London at the time, then they must have been there. Sir Malcolm never failed to fill in his diary every evening after dinner, however bad his health. But there had been something *queer* – almost as though he was making game of him – in the way he had said that about getting him off the hook and being prepared to lie for him. In fact, Sir Malcolm never told lies; in all his twenty-two years with him Reynolds had never known him to tell a lie – not a lie that mattered. But in this case had there not been some vague hint of conspiracy between them?

Reynolds turned over on to his back and stared up at the shadowy ceiling, his head cradled on his skinny arms. He hoped he wasn't going to have another of his spells of sleeplessness, like the one he had when Mrs Evans had first come to work for them and Sir Malcolm had seemed to take a malicious pleasure in favouring her, although she was the newcomer. He had those pills from the doctor but after the first, which had made him feel giddy and light-headed all the next day, he had never taken another.

He would *know* if he had ever had anything to do with her. Wouldn't he? Surely? That was not the kind of thing one could forget. It was true that he could not remember – well, not properly – the death of his mother or of Iris in the air-raid. But his mother had died when he was only six; and in the case of Iris he himself had been half-buried under all that masonry beside her, so that was not really so surprising. Shock could do things like that to your memory, that was well known.

Such a pretty little thing, like a doll, with those blue eyes of hers (yes, he was sure they must have been blue) and that long, silk-like hair and that sweet, upturned nose. Who would want to hurt her? He certainly wouldn't. She was the kind of little girl he would like to have had for his own – the sort of girl Iris might have been when she was small, the sort of girl she might have had – and if he had met her all he would want to have done would have been to stroke her hair and talk to her and sit her on his knee and buy her some sweeties. It was terrible to think of those blue eyes shut forever and those chubby arms and legs sprawled out on that lonely stretch of beach and sand in the hair and sand on that lovely little mouth of hers . . .

All at once he remembered the doll and his whole body went rigid as though in a sudden spasm. He had forgotten the doll, he hadn't thought about it once for, well, going on forty years. Mimsie – that was the name he gave her because he couldn't bring himself to call her Mummy whatever his father said – had often scolded him about it – 'A big boy like you, going round with a doll! You should be ashamed of yourself.' He was seven at the time. Mummy, his real Mummy, had given him the doll for Christmas and it had this lovely flaxen hair and these blue eyes that opened and shut and this peaches-and-cream complexion. He would carry it around with him and even trail it by one arm through the dank weeds that overgrew the bottom of the garden, so that the dainty, frilly little skirt would get all soggy and the legs would be scratched by the brambles and stung by the nettles, just like his own. 'I'll give it to the dustman the next time they call,' Mimsie threatened. 'You'll see if I don't.' It was then that he buried the doll, before tea on a cold winter's evening, his whole body trembling and the gulping sobs rising in his throat as he first scrabbled away at the mouldering leaves from under the beech-tree and then began to dig, dig, dig ferociously with a trowel while the breath wreathed out from between his clenched teeth. 'Dust to dust, ashes to ashes,' he muttered, because he remembered those words from Mummy's burial; and then he scattered the first earth over that dainty little frilly pale blue skirt and on to the shut eyes and over the rose-bud mouth.

Once it was over he felt an extraordinary exhilaration, so that having raced back to the house, he burst into the cramped sitting-room with so much violence that everything in it shook and Mimsie looked up from painting her finger-nails to tell him to quieten down.

He forgot about the doll; yes, that was odd – he completely forgot about her, she might never have existed. Until one day, when Daddy and Mimsie had gone into Colchester for the day, leaving him behind all alone, he had wandered, disconsolate and bored, down into the undergrowth at the bottom of the narrow strip of garden. Suddenly, with a curious mingling of terror and excitement, he had remembered that she lay somewhere here near his feet and, stopping, he had begun to burrow away with his bare hands, breaking some of his finger-nails and clogging others with dirt and mould. There at last she was, her dainty dress all rotted and in tatters and her eyelashes and her mouth and her delicate nostrils filled with mud. He ran with her up into the house and placed her in the kitchen sink with some soap-flakes in warm water. Gently he began to wash her, running his hands over the smoothness of her arms and legs and body, until bit by bit she came back to life for him.

The dress of course could never be the same; so he wrapped her up in an old vest of his that Mimsie had put in the shoe-box to use on the shoes.

After that she often died for him, was buried and was brought back to life. Daddy and Mimsie never knew anything about it; it was a secret not to be told them. Slowly, however, from the long stays in the earth and the scrubbings at the sink, the hair began to fall out, the silken eyelashes and then even the eyes themselves to disappear and the fingers and toes to crumble. Each such change he would watch with a fatalistic curiosity, pierced at times with a sudden brief pang of grief; until the time came when he knew that the burial would be the last and that he would never again disturb the grave of leaf-mould.

Yet how odd, he thought now, that between each death and resurrection he should completely have forgotten her! Involuntarily the memory of her would erase itself from his mind until, no less involuntarily, it would flash back with stabbing vividness, making him long for the first moment when he would be alone for long enough to dig her up again.

Reynolds sat up in the bed, clutching at his bony knees with hands equally bony. If he could so easily forget about her, might he not have forgotten about the other one too? Perhaps in the case of that poor little kiddy no less than in the case of the doll the sleeping memory would one day – perhaps soon – rouse itself to glide back, snake-like, into his conscious mind. *Could* he have known her? *Could* he have done such a thing?

He jumped out of bed and scrabbled in a drawer for the bottle of sleeping-pills. He put one on his tongue and then, while beginning to savour its bitterness, put another and another. He had to obliterate that fear as soon as possible.

'You're half asleep, man! What's the matter with you?'

'Sorry, sir.' Reynolds fumbled to insert in the razor the blade he had forgotten.

'Aren't you feeling well?'

'Perfectly well, thank you, sir.'

'You look pale. And I shouldn't be surprised if you weren't about to get a stye in that right eye of yours. Well, I hope you're not sickening for anything. That would be a fine kettle of fish.'

A middle-aged woman sat on a swing and screamed each time that it rose higher and higher. She had on a shapeless, belted raincoat and a plastic sou'wester. Reynolds watched, his body hunched forward on the bench, with the two laden shopping bags resting against his shins.

Perhaps the woman was not really middle-aged; many of them had a prematurely grown-up look, some who were only sixteen or seventeen one could mistake for thirty or forty.

. . . On that afternoon he might have been sitting here like this and she might have slowly, dreamily detached herself from that group of them playing some prolonged, meaningless game in the bushes, and wandered over in his direction. He might have smiled at her and felt in his pocket for a sweet and then held it out. That was what he usually did with them – it was like coaxing a nervous dog to come nearer and nearer to one. She might have sidled up and put out her hand and then he might have smiled at her, reassuringly, and she might have smiled back. 'What's your name, dear?' 'Vivienne.' 'That's a pretty name.' Then one of the two women in charge might have called to her, looking up over her clicking needles, and Vivienne would have wandered off, with a whispered thank-you.

But he would see her again. He was strolling along the pier (was, now, not might be) and there she was walking between two grown-ups, each of whom held one of her hands. It was a Saturday (Sunday?) and that was when those children were allowed out with their parents. The two grown-ups and the doll-like child paused to look down at the fishermen below and he paused behind them. They turned and, courage coming to him in some miraculous fashion, he found himself saying 'What a pretty little girl you have there!' Of course she did not recognize him and he was not going to let on that he had met her before.

'Yes,' said the mother, running a plump hand through that silk-soft hair. 'But we mustn't tell her that or we'll make her vain, won't we?' The mother wore glasses so thick that her eyes bulged like hard-boiled eggs behind them. Her voice was cooing and falsely genteel.

It was all so easy: they seemed to *want* him to take Vivienne off their hands.

'Wouldn't you like to see the Aquarium with your Uncle Ray?' he asked after some minutes of desultory conversation.

'Yes, you'd love that, wouldn't you, pet?'

'That's right,' chimed in the father, sucking on his pipe. 'You run along with your Uncle Ray.'

Reynolds retched for a long time uselessly in the ammonia-smelling lavatory in one corner of the gardens. Then he pressed his ice-cold forehead against the ice-cold tiles. Yes, that was how it had been! That was it! He remembered how he had taken the car from the garage, slipping the key off Sir Malcolm's ring when he had shuffled from the bedroom to the lavatory, and how he had driven the poor, dear little thing out to that lonely stretch of beach, with the plastic sheet and the Thermos and the beach-ball in the back. He had not meant to do anything, of course he hadn't. But the screams, a magnified echo of the gulls circling above their sprawling bodies, and the sight of the blood and the scratch she had given him on the inside of his thigh – well, how could anyone be expected to keep his head with all that going on?

Poor dolly, poor broken little dolly! He had bundled her into the car – oh, gently, gently, of course – and had thrown the plastic sheet over her and had driven back through a narrow cleft in the Downs with the sky a blue as pale and serene as the blue of those darling eyes. He would have to bury her somewhere secret under a tree; and then later, when no one knew that he had gone up there again, he would go back and find her once more. Yes, that was what he would do. That was it.

The leaves had a curious sweetish smell on them, like the mouldering leaves at the bottom of the narrow garden. The eyes were shut in the same way and the long, silk-soft hair lay in the same way on its bed of earth. The frilly skirt stuck out stiffly; there was a patch of blood on it, like a scab. 'I'll come back for you,' he whispered. 'I'll come back.' He put his lips to the porcelain forehead, his hands in the hair. 'I'll come back, my darling.'

'Well, surely *I* should know!' he cried out in exasperation at them. But they shook their heads and yet again exchanged those glances, at once amused, annoyed and pitying, with which they had greeted each fresh protestation of his guilt.

'Where does he live?' one of them asked.

'We ought to telephone to someone to fetch him.'

'Maybe an ambulance would be the best plan.'

'Look, old chap, we know that it just *can't* be you. For all kinds of reasons. So stop pulling our legs, eh?'

'Where does he live?'

'Who *is* the old boy?'

'Look, old chap, you'd better cut along and forget all about it.'

'Where does he *live*? Just get him off my hands.'

So it took a long time of patient and persistent arguing to persuade them that he could show them the place on the Downs where he had buried her. He could see it so well, out there before him, even while he was gazing into their red, stupid faces and shouting at them. 'Let me show you! Just let me show you!' He could see the stile, over which he had had such difficulty in carrying her in the dark, and the moonlit path, a vast silvery-skinned snake slithering away from him, and then the three trees, with the interlaced branches that made a curious pattering noise against each other as the wind blew through them. The plastic sheet felt oddly warm, as thought it were no more than a living skin to what lay beneath it. But of course that must have been his imagination, because when he unwrapped her she was as cold as the doll.

Unerringly he found the way for them through the bright February sunshine, a scurrying figure with bowed shoulders and a curiously tripping gait among the burly men with shovels and spades and the camera-man and the other man with the tripod and the lamps.

They still didn't believe him, he could see that. This was just part of leaving no avenue unexplored, of leaving no stone unturned.

'There!' he pointed.

Again they exchanged those glances, at once amused, annoyed and pitying.

'All right, boys. Get to work!'

They dug, not knowing what they would find. But he knew, oh he knew all right. There she would be, with her dainty little frock all damp and rotted about her, and the mud in her beautiful-silk-soft blonde hair and in her nostrils and over her mouth. But one only had to wash her a little, wash her gently, gently, and the pink porcelain flesh would brighten again under the frilly skirt and the eyes would click open and the pretty little, winsome little smile would appear.

How had he *known*? they asked him over and over again; and when he screamed, 'Because I put her there, you fools!' they shrugged shoulders or looked angry or asked him if he was right off his rocker. How had he *known*? they next asked that middle-aged bus-conductor with a limp, father of three children and a member of the Baptist Church, when eventually they had caught him. But the bus-conductor could not give them the answer they sought. No, he had never seen Reynolds in his life; Reynolds had never followed him, as far as he knew, on that fateful winter evening; no, of course they were not accomplices – he always had those turns of his alone.

'But how did you know?' Sir Malcolm would often ask Reynolds in the months and years that followed.

But Reynolds could not tell him; he himself did not know how he had known.

DEAD CALL

William F. Nolan

Len had been dead for a month when the phone rang.

Midnight. Cold in the house and me dragged up from sleep to answer the call. Helen gone for the weekend. Me, alone in the house. And the phone ringing . . .

'Hello.'

'Hello, Frank.'

'Who is this?'

'You know *me*. It's Len . . . old Len Stiles.'

Cold. Deep and intense. The receiver dead-cold metal in my hand.

'Leonard Stiles died four weeks ago.'

'Four weeks, three days, two hours and twenty-seven minutes ago – to be exact.'

'I want to know who you are!'

A chuckle. The same dry chuckle I'd heard so many times. 'C'mon, ole buddy – after twenty years. Hell, you *know* me.'

'This is a damned poor joke!'

'No joke, Frank. You're there, alive. And I'm here, dead. And you know something ole buddy? I'm really *glad* I did it.'

'Did . . . what?'

'Killed myself. Because . . . death is just what I hoped it would be: beautiful . . . grey . . . quiet. No pressures.'

'Len Stiles's death was an accident . . . a concrete freeway barrier . . . His car – '

'I *aimed* my car for that barrier. Pedal to the floor. Doing almost a hundred when I hit . . . No accident, Frank.' The voice cold . . . Cold. 'I *wanted* to be dead . . . and no regrets.'

I tried to laugh, make light of this – matching his chuckle with my own. 'Dead men don't use telephones.'

'I'm not really using a phone, not in a physical sense. It's just that I chose to contact you this way. You might say it's a matter of "psychic electricity". As a detached spirit, I'm able to align my cosmic vibrations to match the vibrations of this power line. Simple, really.'

'Sure. A snap. Nothing to it.'

'Naturally you're sceptical. I expected you to be. But . . . listen carefully to me, Frank.'

And I listened – with the phone gripped in my hand in that cold night house – as the voice told me things that *only* Len could know . . . intimate details of shared experiences extending back through two decades. And when he'd finished I was certain of one thing:

He *was* Len Stiles.

'But how . . . I still don't . . .'

'Think of this phone as a "medium" – a line of force through which I can bridge the gap between us.' The dry chuckle again. 'Hell, you gotta admit it beats holding hands around a table in the dark – yet the principle is the same.'

I'd been standing by my desk, transfixed by the voice. Now I moved behind the desk, sat down, trying to absorb this dark miracle. My muscles were wire-taut, my fingers cramped about the metal receiver. I dragged in a slow breath, the night dampness of the room pressing at me. 'All right . . . I don't believe in ghosts, don't pretend to understand any of this, but . . . I'll accept it. I *must* accept it.'

'I'm glad, Frank – because it's important that we talk.' A long moment of hesitation. Then the voice, lower now, softer. 'I *know* how lousy things have been, ole buddy.'

'What do you mean?'

'I just know how things are going for you. And . . . I want to help. As your friend, I want you to know that I understand.'

'Well . . . I'm really not – '

'You've been feeling bad, haven't you? Kind of "*down*" . . . right?'

'Yeah. A little, I guess.'

'And I don't blame you. You've got reasons. Lots of reasons . . . For one, there's your money problem.'

'I'm expecting a raise. Cooney promised me one – within the next few weeks.'

'You won't get it, Frank. I *know*. He's lying to you. Right now, at this moment, he's looking for a man to replace you at the company. Cooney's planning to fire you.'

'He never liked me. We never got along from the day I walked into that office.'

'And your wife . . . All the arguments you've been having with her lately . . . It's a pattern, Frank. Your marriage is all over. Helen's going to ask you for a divorce. She's in love with another man.'

'Who, dammit? What's his name?'

'You don't know him. Wouldn't change things if you did. There's nothing you can do about it now. Helen just . . . doesn't love you any more. These things happen to people.'

'We've been drifting apart for the last year . . . But I didn't know why. I had no idea that she – '

'And then there's Jan. She's back on it, Frank. Only it's worse now. A lot worse.'

I knew what he meant – and the coldness raked along my body. Jan was nineteen, my oldest daughter, and she'd been into drugs for the past three years. But she'd promised to quit.

'What do you know about Jan? Tell me!'

'She's into the heavy stuff, Frank. She's hooked bad. It's too late for her.'

'What the hell are you saying?'

'I'm saying she's lost to you . . . She's rejected you, and there's no reaching her. She *hates* you . . . Blames you for everything.'

'I won't *accept* that kind of blame. I did my best for her.'

'It wasn't enough, Frank. We both know that. You'll never see Jan again.'

The blackness was welling within me, a choking wave through my body.

'Listen to me, old buddy . . . Things are going to get worse, not better. I know. I went through my own kind of hell when I was alive.'

'I'll . . . start over. Leave the city. Go East, work with my brother in New York.'

'Your brother doesn't want you in his life. You'd be an intruder . . . an alien. He never writes you, does he?'

'No, but that doesn't mean – '

'Not even a card last Christmas. No letters or calls. He doesn't *want* you with him, Frank, believe me.'

And then he began to tell me other things. He began to talk about middle age, and how it was too late now to make any kind of new beginning. He spoke of disease . . . loneliness . . . of rejection and despair. And the blackness was complete.

'There's only one real solution to things, Frank – just *one*. That gun you keep in your desk upstairs. Use it Frank. Use the gun.'

'I couldn't do that.'

'But why not? What other choice have you got? The solution is *there*. Go upstairs and use the gun. I'll be waiting for you afterwards. You won't be alone. It'll be like the old days . . . We'll be together . . . Death is beautiful . . . Use the gun, Frank . . . The gun . . . Use the gun . . . The gun . . . The gun . . .'

I've been dead for a month now, and Len was right. It's fine here. No pressures. No worries. Grey and quiet and beautiful . . .

I know how lousy things have been going for you. And they won't get any better.

Isn't that your phone ringing?

Better answer it.

It's important that we talk.